J. J. Connington and The Murder Room

>>> This title is part of The Murder Room, our series dedicated to making available out-of-print or hard-to-find titles by classic crime writers.

Crime fiction has always held up a mirror to society. The Victorians were fascinated by sensational murder and the emerging science of detection; now we are obsessed with the forensic detail of violent death. And no other genre has so captivated and enthralled readers.

Vast troves of classic crime writing have for a long time been unavailable to all but the most dedicated frequenters of second-hand bookshops. The advent of digital publishing means that we are now able to bring you the backlists of a huge range of titles by classic and contemporary crime writers, some of which have been out of print for decades.

From the genteel amateur private eyes of the Golden Age and the femmes fatales of pulp fiction, to the morally ambiguous hard-boiled detectives of mid twentieth-century America and their descendants who walk our twenty-first century streets, The Murder Room has it all. >>>

The Murder Room
Where Criminal Minds Meet

themurderroom.com

T0352171

J. J. Connington (1880–1947)

Alfred Walter Stewart, who wrote under the pen name J. J. Connington, was born in Glasgow, the youngest of three sons of Reverend Dr Stewart. He graduated from Glasgow University and pursued an academic career as a chemistry professor, working for the Admiralty during the First World War. Known for his ingenious and carefully worked-out puzzles and in-depth character development, he was admired by a host of his better-known contemporaries, including Dorothy L. Sayers and John Dickson Carr, who both paid tribute to his influence on their work. He married Jessie Lily Courts in 1916 and they had one daughter.

By J. J. Connington

Sir Clinton Driffield Mysteries
Murder in the Maze (1927)
Tragedy at Ravensthorpe
  (1927)
The Case with Nine Solutions
  (1928)
Mystery at Lynden Sands
  (1928)
Nemesis at Raynham Parva
  (1929)
  (a.k.a. *Grim Vengenace*)
The Boathouse Riddle (1931)
The Sweepstake Murders
  (1931)
The Castleford Conundrum
  (1932)
The Ha-Ha Case (1934)
  (a.k.a. *The Brandon Case*)
In Whose Dim Shadow (1935)
  (a.k.a. *The Tau Cross Mystery*)
A Minor Operation (1937)

Murder Will Speak (1938)
Truth Comes Limping (1938)
The Twenty-One Clues (1941)
No Past is Dead (1942)
Jack-in-the-Box (1944)
Common Sense Is All You
  Need (1947)

Supt Ross Mysteries
The Eye in the Museum (1929)
The Two Tickets Puzzle (1930)

Novels
Death at Swaythling Court
  (1926)
The Dangerfield Talisman
  (1926)
Tom Tiddler's Island (1933)
  (a.k.a. *Gold Brick Island*)
The Counsellor (1939)
The Four Defences (1940)

The Dangerfield Talisman

J. J. Connington

An Orion book

Copyright © The Professor A. W. Stewart Deceased Trust 1926, 2014

The right of J. J. Connington to be identified as the author of this work has been asserted in accordance with the Copyright, Designs and Patents Act 1988.

This edition published by
The Orion Publishing Group Ltd
Orion House
5 Upper St Martin's Lane
London WC2H 9EA

An Hachette UK company
A CIP catalogue record for this book is available from the British Library

ISBN 978 1 4719 0633 6

www.orionbooks.co.uk

Introduction
by
Curtis Evans

During the Golden Age of the detective novel, in the 1920s and 1930s, J. J. Connington stood with fellow crime writers R. Austin Freeman, Cecil John Charles Street and Freeman Wills Crofts as the foremost practitioner in British mystery fiction of the science of pure detection. I use the word 'science' advisedly, for the man behind J. J. Connington, Alfred Walter Stewart, was an esteemed Scottish-born scientist. A 'small, unassuming, moustached polymath', Stewart was 'a strikingly effective lecturer with an excellent sense of humor, fertile imagination and fantastically retentive memory', qualities that also served him well in his fiction. He held the Chair of Chemistry at Queens University, Belfast for twenty-five years, from 1919 until his retirement in 1944.

During roughly this period, the busy Professor Stewart found time to author a remarkable apocalyptic science fiction tale, *Nordenholt's Million* (1923), a mainstream novel, *Almighty Gold* (1924), a collection of essays, *Alias J. J. Connington* (1947), and, between 1926 and 1947, twenty-four mysteries (all but one tales of detection), many of them sterling examples of the Golden Age puzzle-oriented detective novel at its considerable best. 'For those who ask first of all in a detective story for exact and mathematical accuracy in the construction of the plot', avowed a contemporary *London Daily Mail* reviewer, 'there is no author to equal the distinguished scientist who writes under the name of J. J. Connington.'[1]

Alfred Stewart's background as a man of science is reflected in his fiction, not only in the impressive puzzle plot mechanics he devised for his mysteries but in his choices of themes and depictions of characters. Along with Stanley Nordenholt of *Nordenholt's Million*, a novel about a plutocrat's pitiless efforts to preserve a ruthlessly remolded remnant of human life after a global environmental calamity, Stewart's most notable character is Chief Constable Sir Clinton Driffield, the detective in seventeen of the twenty-four Connington crime novels. Driffield is one of crime fiction's most highhanded investigators, occasionally taking on the functions of judge and jury as well as chief of police.

Absent from Stewart's fiction is the hail-fellow-well-met quality found in John Street's works or the religious ethos suffusing those of Freeman Wills Crofts, not to mention the effervescent novel-of-manners style of the British Golden Age Crime Queens Dorothy L. Sayers, Margery Allingham and Ngaio Marsh. Instead we see an often disdainful cynicism about the human animal and a marked admiration for detached supermen with superior intellects. For this reason, reading a Connington novel can be a challenging experience for modern readers inculcated in gentler social beliefs. Yet Alfred Stewart produced a classic apocalyptic science fiction tale in *Nordenholt's Million* (justly dubbed 'exciting and terrifying reading' by the *Spectator*) as well as superb detective novels boasting well-wrought puzzles, bracing characterization and an occasional leavening of dry humor. Not long after Stewart's death in 1947, the Connington novels fell entirely out of print. The recent embrace of Stewart's fiction by Orion's Murder Room imprint is a welcome event indeed, correcting as it does over sixty years of underserved neglect of an accomplished genre writer.

Born in Glasgow on 5 September 1880, Alfred Stewart had significant exposure to religion in his earlier life. His father was William Stewart, longtime Professor of Divinity and Biblical Criticism at Glasgow University, and he married Lily Coats, a daughter of the Reverend Jervis Coats and member of one of

Scotland's preeminent Baptist families. Religious sensibility is entirely absent from the Connington corpus, however. A confirmed secularist, Stewart once referred to one of his wife's brothers, the Reverend William Holms Coats (1881–1954), principal of the Scottish Baptist College, as his 'mental and spiritual antithesis', bemusedly adding: 'It's quite an education to see what one would look like if one were turned into one's mirror-image.'

Stewart's J. J. Connington pseudonym was derived from a nineteenth-century Oxford Professor of Latin and translator of Horace, indicating that Stewart's literary interests lay not in pietistic writing but rather in the pre-Christian classics ('I prefer the *Odyssey* to *Paradise Lost*,' the author once avowed). Possessing an inquisitive and expansive mind, Stewart was in fact an uncommonly well-read individual, freely ranging over a variety of literary genres. His deep immersion in French literature and supernatural horror fiction, for example, is documented in his lively correspondence with the noted horologist Rupert Thomas Gould.[2]

It thus is not surprising that in the 1920s the intellectually restless Stewart, having achieved a distinguished middle age as a highly regarded man of science, decided to apply his creative energy to a new endeavor, the writing of fiction. After several years he settled, like other gifted men and women of his generation, on the wildly popular mystery genre. Stewart was modest about his accomplishments in this particular field of light fiction, telling Rupert Gould later in life that 'I write these things [what Stewart called tec yarns] because they amuse me in parts when I am putting them together and because they are the only writings of mine that the public will look at. Also, in a minor degree, because I like to think some people get pleasure out of them.' No doubt Stewart's single most impressive literary accomplishment is *Nordenholt's Million*, yet in their time the two dozen J. J. Connington mysteries did indeed give readers in Great Britain, the United States and other countries much diversionary reading pleasure. Today these works constitute an estimable addition to British crime fiction.

After his 'prentice pastiche mystery, *Death at Swaythling Court* (1926), a rural English country-house tale set in the highly traditional village of Fernhurst Parva, Stewart published another, superior country-house affair, *The Dangerfield Talisman* (1926), a novel about the baffling theft of a precious family heirloom, an ancient, jewel-encrusted armlet. This clever, murderless tale, which likely is the one that the author told Rupert Gould he wrote in under six weeks, was praised in *The Bookman* as 'continuously exciting and interesting' and in the *New York Times Book Review* as 'ingeniously fitted together and, what is more, written with a deal of real literary charm'. Despite its virtues, however, *The Dangerfield Talisman* is not fully characteristic of mature Connington detective fiction. The author needed a memorable series sleuth, more representative of his own forceful personality.

It was the next year, 1927, that saw J. J. Connington make his break to the front of the murdermongerer's pack with a third country-house mystery, *Murder in the Maze*, wherein debuted as the author's great series detective the assertive and acerbic Sir Clinton Driffield, along with Sir Clinton's neighbor and 'Watson', the more genial (if much less astute) Squire Wendover. In this much-praised novel, Stewart's detective duo confronts some truly diabolical doings, including slayings by means of curare-tipped darts in the double-centered hedge maze at a country estate, Whistlefield. No less a fan of the genre than T. S. Eliot praised *Murder in the Maze* for its construction ('we are provided early in the story with all the clues which guide the detective') and its liveliness ('The very idea of murder in a box-hedge labyrinth does the author great credit, and he makes full use of its possibilities'). The delighted Eliot concluded that

Murder in the Maze was 'a really first-rate detective story'. For his part, the critic H. C. Harwood declared in *The Outlook* that with the publication of *Murder in the Maze* Connington demanded and deserved 'comparison with the masters'. 'Buy, borrow, or – anyhow – get hold of it', he amusingly advised. Two decades later, in his 1946 critical essay 'The Grandest Game in the World', the great locked-room detective novelist John Dickson Carr echoed Eliot's assessment of the novel's virtuoso setting, writing: 'These 1920s [. . .] thronged with sheer brains. What would be one of the best possible settings for violent death? J. J. Connington found the answer, with *Murder in the Maze*.' Certainly in retrospect *Murder in the Maze* stands as one of the finest English country-house mysteries of the 1920s, cleverly yet fairly clued, imaginatively detailed and often grimly suspenseful. As the great American true-crime writer Edmund Lester Pearson noted in his review of *Murder in the Maze* in *The Outlook*, this Connington novel had everything that one could desire in a detective story: 'A shrubbery maze, a hot day, and somebody potting at you with an air gun loaded with darts covered with a deadly South-American arrow-poison – *there* is a situation to wheedle two dollars out of anybody's pocket.'[3]

Staying with what had worked so well for him to date, Stewart the same year produced yet another country-house mystery, *Tragedy at Ravensthorpe*, an ingenious tale of murders and thefts at the ancestral home of the Chacewaters, old family friends of Sir Clinton Driffield. There is much clever matter in *Ravensthorpe*. Especially fascinating is the author's inspired integration of faerie folklore into his plot. Stewart, who had a lifelong – though skeptical – interest in paranormal phenomena, probably was inspired in this instance by the recent hubbub over the Cottingly Faeries photographs that in the early 1920s had famously duped, among other individuals, Arthur Conan Doyle.[4] As with *Murder in the Maze*, critics raved about this new Connington mystery. In the *Spectator*, for example, a reviewer hailed *Tragedy at Ravensthorpe* in the strongest terms, declaring of the novel: 'This is more than a good detective tale. Alike in plot, characterization, and literary style, it is a work of art.'

In 1928 there appeared two additional Sir Clinton Driffield detective novels, *Mystery at Lynden Sands* and *The Case with Nine Solutions*. Once again there was great praise for the latest Conningtons. H. C. Harwood, the critic who had so much admired *Murder in the Maze*, opined of *Mystery at Lynden Sands* that it 'may just fail of being the detective story of the century', while in the United States author and book reviewer Frederic F. Van de Water expressed nearly as high an opinion of *The Case with Nine Solutions*. 'This book is a thoroughbred of a distinguished lineage that runs back to "The Gold Bug" of [Edgar Allan] Poe,' he avowed. 'It represents the highest type of detective fiction.' In both of these Connington novels, Stewart moved away from his customary country-house milieu, setting *Lynden Sands* at a fashionable beach resort and *Nine Solutions* at a scientific research institute. *Nine Solutions* is of particular interest today, I think, for its relatively frank sexual subject matter and its modern urban setting among science professionals, which rather resembles the locales found in P. D. James' classic detective novels *A Mind to Murder* (1963) and *Shroud for a Nightingale* (1971).

By the end of the 1920s, J. J. Connington's critical reputation had achieved enviable heights indeed. At this time Stewart became one of the charter members of the Detection Club, an assemblage of the finest writers of British detective fiction that included, among other distinguished individuals, Agatha Christie, Dorothy L. Sayers and G. K. Chesterton. Certainly Victor Gollancz, the British publisher of the J. J. Connington mysteries, did not stint praise for the author, informing readers that 'J. J. Connington is now established as, in the opinion of many, the greatest living master of the story of pure detection. He is one of those who, discarding all the superfluities, has made of deductive fiction a genuine minor art, with its own laws and its own conventions.'

Such warm praise for J. J. Connington makes it all the more surprising that at this juncture the esteemed author tinkered with his successful formula by dispensing with his original series detective. In the fifth Clinton Driffield detective novel, *Nemesis at Raynham Parva* (1929), Alfred Walter Stewart, rather like Arthur Conan Doyle before him, seemed with a dramatic dénouement to have devised his popular series detective's permanent exit from the fictional stage (read it and see for yourself). The next two Connington detective novels, *The Eye in the Museum* (1929) and *The Two Tickets Puzzle* (1930), have a different series detective, Superintendent Ross, a rather dull dog of a policeman. While both these mysteries are competently done – the railway material in *The Two Tickets Puzzle* is particularly effective and should have appeal today – the presence of Sir Clinton Driffield (no superfluity he!) is missed.

Probably Stewart detected that the public minded the absence of the brilliant and biting Sir Clinton, for the Chief Constable – accompanied, naturally, by his friend Squire Wendover – triumphantly returned in 1931 in *The Boathouse Riddle*, another well-constructed criminous country-house affair. Later in the year came *The Sweepstake Murders*, which boasts the perennially popular tontine multiple-murder plot, in this case a rapid succession of puzzling suspicious deaths afflicting the members of a sweepstake syndicate that has just won nearly £250,000.[5] Adding piquancy to this plot is the fact that Wendover is one of the imperiled syndicate members. Altogether the novel is, as the late Jacques Barzun and his colleague Wendell Hertig Taylor put it in *A Catalogue of Crime* (1971, 1989), their magisterial survey of detective fiction, 'one of Connington's best conceptions'.

Stewart's productivity as a fiction writer slowed in the 1930s, so that, barring the year 1938, at most only one new Connington appeared annually. However, in 1932 Stewart produced one of the best Connington mysteries, *The Castleford Conundrum*. A classic country-house detective novel, Castleford introduces to readers Stewart's most delightfully unpleasant set of greedy relations and one of his most deserving murderees, Winifred Castleford. Stewart also fashions a wonderfully rich puzzle plot, full of meaty material clues for the reader's delectation. *Castleford* presented critics with no conundrum over its quality. 'In *The Castleford Conundrum* Mr Connington goes to work like an accomplished chess player. The moves in the games his detectives are called on to play are a delight to watch,' raved the reviewer for the *Sunday Times*, adding that 'the clues would have rejoiced Mr. Holmes' heart.' For its part, the *Spectator* concurred in the *Sunday Times*' assessment of the novel's masterfully constructed plot: 'Few detective stories show such sound reasoning as that by which the Chief Constable brings the crime home to the culprit.' Additionally, E. C. Bentley, much admired himself as the author of the landmark detective novel *Trent's Last Case*, took time to praise Connington's purely literary virtues, noting: 'Mr Connington has never written better, or drawn characters more full of life.'

With *Tom Tiddler's Island* in 1933 Stewart produced a different sort of Connington, a criminal-gang mystery in the rather more breathless style of such hugely popular English thriller writers as Sapper, Sax Rohmer, John Buchan and Edgar Wallace (in violation of the strict detective fiction rules of Ronald Knox, there is even a secret passage in the novel). Detailing the startling discoveries made by a newlywed couple honeymooning on a remote Scottish island, *Tom Tiddler's Island* is an atmospheric and entertaining tale, though it is not as mentally stimulating for armchair sleuths as Stewart's true detective novels. The title, incidentally, refers to an ancient British children's game, 'Tom Tiddler's Ground', in which one child tries to hold a height against other children.

After his fictional Scottish excursion into thrillerdom, Stewart returned the next year to his English country-house roots with *The Ha-Ha Case* (1934), his last masterwork in this classicmystery setting (for elucidation of non-British readers, a ha-ha is a sunken wall, placed so as to delineate property boundaries while not obstructing views). Although *The Ha-Ha Case* is not set in Scotland, Stewart drew inspiration for the novel from a notorious Scottish true crime, the 1893 Ardlamont murder case. From the facts of the Ardlamont affair Stewart drew several of the key characters in *The Ha-Ha Case*, as well as the circumstances of the novel's murder (a shooting 'accident' while hunting), though he added complications that take the tale in a new direction.[6]

In newspaper reviews both Dorothy L. Sayers and 'Francis Iles' (crime novelist Anthony Berkeley Cox) highly praised this latest mystery by 'The Clever Mr Connington', as he was now dubbed on book jackets by his new English publisher, Hodder & Stoughton. Sayers particularly noted the effective characterisation in *The Ha-Ha Case*: 'There is no need to say that Mr Connington has given us a sound and interesting plot, very carefully and ingeniously worked out. In addition, there are the three portraits of the three brothers, cleverly and rather subtly characterised, of the [governess], and of Inspector Hinton, whose admirable qualities are counteracted by that besetting sin of the man who has made his own way: a jealousy of delegating responsibility.' The reviewer for the *Times Literary Supplement* detected signs that the sardonic Sir Clinton Driffield had begun mellowing with age: 'Those who have never really liked Sir Clinton's perhaps excessively soldierly manner will be surprised to find that he makes his discovery not only by the pure light of intelligence, but partly as a reward for amiability and tact, qualities in which the Inspector [Hinton] was strikingly deficient.' This is true enough, although the classic Sir Clinton emerges a number of times in the novel, as in his subtly sarcastic recurrent backhanded praise of Inspector Hinton: 'He writes a first class report.'

Clinton Driffield returned the next year in the detective novel *In Whose Dim Shadow* (1935), a tale set in a recently erected English suburb, the denizens of which seem to have committed an impressive number of indiscretions, including sexual ones. The intriguing title of the British edition of the novel is drawn from a poem by the British historian Thomas Babington Macaulay: 'Those trees in whose dim shadow/The ghastly priest doth reign/The priest who slew the slayer/And shall himself be slain.' Stewart's puzzle plot in *In Whose Dim Shadow* is well clued and compelling, the kicker of a closing paragraph is a classic of its kind and, additionally, the author paints some excellent character portraits. I fully concur with the *Sunday Times*' assessment of the tale: 'Quiet domestic murder, full of the neatest detective points [. . .] These are not the detective's stock figures, but fully realised human beings.'[7]

Uncharacteristically for Stewart, nearly twenty months elapsed between the publication of *In Whose Dim Shadow* and his next book, *A Minor Operation* (1937). The reason for the author's delay in production was the onset in 1935–36 of the afflictions of cataracts and heart disease (Stewart ultimately succumbed to heart disease in 1947). Despite these grave health complications, Stewart in late 1936 was able to complete *A Minor Operation*, a first-rate Clinton Driffield story of murder and a most baffling disappearance. A *Times Literary Supplement* reviewer found that *A Minor Operation* treated the reader 'to exactly the right mixture of mystification and clue' and that, in addition to its impressive construction, the novel boasted 'character-drawing above the average' for a detective novel.

Alfred Stewart's final eight mysteries, which appeared between 1938 and 1947, the year of the author's death, are, on the whole, a somewhat weaker group of tales than the sixteen that appeared between 1926 and 1937, yet they are not without interest. In 1938 Stewart for the last time managed to publish two detective novels, *Truth Comes Limping* and *For Murder Will Speak* (also published as *Murder Will Speak*). The latter tale is much the superior of the two, having an interesting suburban setting and a bevy of female characters found to have motives when a contemptible philandering businessman meets with foul play. Sexual neurosis plays a major role in *For Murder Will Speak*, the ever-thorough Stewart obviously having made a study of the subject when writing the novel. The somewhat squeamish reviewer for *Scribner's Magazine* considered the subject matter of *For Murder Will Speak* 'rather unsavory at times', yet this individual conceded that the novel nevertheless made 'first-class reading for those who enjoy a good puzzle intricately worked out'. 'Judge Lynch' in the *Saturday Review* apparently had no such moral reservations about the latest Clinton Driffield murder case, avowing simply of the novel: 'They don't come any better'.

Over the next couple of years Stewart again sent Sir Clinton Driffield temporarily packing, replacing him with a new series detective, a brash radio personality named Mark Brand, in *The Counsellor* (1939) and *The Four Defences* (1940). The better of these two novels is *The Four Defences*, which Stewart based on another notorious British true-crime case, the Alfred Rouse blazing-car murder. (Rouse is believed to have fabricated his death by murdering an unknown man, placing the dead man's body in his car and setting the car on fire, in the hope that the murdered man's body would be taken for his.) Though admittedly a thinly characterised academic exercise in ratiocination, Stewart's *Four Defences* surely is also one of the most complexly plotted Golden Age detective novels and should delight devotees of classical detection. Taking the Rouse blazing-car affair as his theme, Stewart composes from it a stunning set of diabolically ingenious criminal variations. 'This is in the cold-blooded category which [. . .] excites a crossword puzzle kind of interest,' the reviewer for the *Times Literary Supplement* acutely noted of the novel. 'Nothing in the Rouse case would prepare you for these complications upon complications [. . .] What they prove is that Mr Connington has the power of penetrating into the puzzle-corner of the brain. He leaves it dazedly wondering whether in the records of actual crime there can be any dark deed to equal this in its planned convolutions.'

Sir Clinton Driffield returned to action in the remaining four detective novels in the Connington oeuvre, *The Twenty-One Clues* (1941), *No Past is Dead* (1942), *Jack-in-the-Box* (1944) and *Commonsense is All You Need* (1947), all of which were written as Stewart's heart disease steadily worsened and reflect to some extent his diminishing physical and mental energy. Although *The Twenty-One Clues* was inspired by the notorious Hall-Mills double murder case – probably the most publicised murder case in the United States in the 1920s – and the American critic and novelist Anthony Boucher commended *Jack-in-the-Box*, I believe the best of these later mysteries is *No Past Is Dead*, which Stewart partly based on a bizarre French true-crime affair, the 1891 Achet-Lepine murder case.[8] Besides providing an interesting background for the tale, the ailing author managed some virtuoso plot twists, of the sort most associated today with that ingenious Golden Age Queen of Crime, Agatha Christie.

What Stewart with characteristic bluntness referred to as 'my complete crack-up' forced his retirement from Queen's University in 1944. 'I am afraid,' Stewart wrote a friend, the chemist and forensic scientist F. Gerald Tryhorn, in August 1946, eleven months before his death, 'that I shall never be much use again. Very stupidly, I tried for a session to combine a full course of lecturing with angina pectoris; and ended up by establishing that the two are immiscible.' He added that since retiring in 1944, he had been physically 'limited to my house, since even a fifty-yard crawl brings on the usual cramps'. Stewart completed his essay collection and a final novel before he died at his study desk in his Belfast home on 1 July 1947, at the age of sixty-six. When death came to the author he was busy at work, writing.

More than six decades after Alfred Walter Stewart's death, his J. J. Connington fiction is again available to a wider audience of classic-mystery fans, rather than strictly limited to a select company of rare-book collectors with deep pockets. This is fitting for an individual who was one of the finest writers of British genre fiction between the two world wars. 'Heaven forfend that you should imagine I take myself for anything out of the common in the tec yarn stuff,' Stewart once self-deprecatingly declared in a letter to Rupert Gould. Yet, as contemporary critics recognised, as a writer of detective and science fiction Stewart indeed was something out of the common. Now more modern readers can find this out for themselves. They have much good sleuthing in store.

1. For more on Street, Crofts and particularly Stewart, see Curtis Evans, *Masters of the 'Humdrum' Mystery: Cecil John Charles Street, Freeman Wills Crofts, Alfred Walter Stewart and the British Detective Novel, 1920–1961* (Jefferson, NC: McFarland, 2012). On the academic career of Alfred Walter Stewart, see his entry in *Oxford Dictionary of National Biography* (London and New York: Oxford University Press, 2004), vol. 52, 627–628.
2. The Gould-Stewart correspondence is discussed in considerable detail in *Masters of the 'Humdrum' Mystery*. For more on the life of the fascinating Rupert Thomas Gould, see Jonathan Betts, *Time Restored: The Harrison Timekeepers and R. T. Gould, the*

Man Who Knew (Almost) Everything (London and New York: Oxford University Press, 2006) and *Longitude,* the 2000 British film adaptation of Dava Sobel's book *Longitude:The True Story of a Lone Genius Who Solved the Greatest Scientific Problem of His Time* (London: Harper Collins, 1995), which details Gould's restoration of the marine chronometers built by in the eighteenth century by the clockmaker John Harrison.

3. Potential purchasers of *Murder in the Maze* should keep in mind that $2 in 1927 is worth over $26 today.

4. In a 1920 article in *The Strand Magazine,* Arthur Conan Doyle endorsed as real prank photographs of purported fairies taken by two English girls in the garden of a house in the village of Cottingley. In the aftermath of the Great War Doyle had become a fervent believer in Spiritualism and other paranormal phenomena. Especially embarrassing to Doyle's admirers today, he also published *The Coming of the Faeries* (1922), wherein he argued that these mystical creatures genuinely existed. 'When the spirits came in, the common sense oozed out,' Stewart once wrote bluntly to his friend Rupert Gould of the creator of Sherlock Holmes. Like Gould, however, Stewart had an intense interest in the subject of the Loch Ness Monster, believing that he, his wife and daughter had sighted a large marine creature of some sort in Loch Ness in 1935. A year earlier Gould had authored *The Loch Ness Monster and Others,* and it was this book that led Stewart, after he made his 'Nessie' sighting, to initiate correspondence with Gould.

5. A tontine is a financial arrangement wherein shareowners in a common fund receive annuities that increase in value with the death of each participant, with the entire amount of the fund going to the last survivor. The impetus that the tontine provided to the deadly creative imaginations of Golden Age mystery writers should be sufficiently obvious.

6. At Ardlamont, a large country estate in Argyll, Cecil Hambrough died from a gunshot wound while hunting. Cecil's tutor, Alfred John Monson, and another man, both of whom were out hunting with Cecil, claimed that Cecil had accidentally shot himself, but Monson was arrested and tried for Cecil's murder. The verdict delivered was 'not proven', but Monson was then – and is today – considered almost certain to have been guilty of the murder. On the Ardlamont case, see William Roughead, *Classic Crimes* (1951; repr., New York: New York Review Books Classics, 2000), 378–464.

7. For the genesis of the title, see Macaulay's 'The Battle of the Lake

Regillus', from his narrative poem collection *Lays of Ancient Rome*. In this poem Macaulay alludes to the ancient cult of Diana Nemorensis, which elevated its priests through trial by combat. Study of the practices of the Diana Nemorensis cult influenced Sir James George Frazer's cultural interpretation of religion in his most renowned work, *The Golden Bough: A Study in Magic and Religion*. As with *Tom Tiddler's Island* and *The Ha-Ha Case* the title *In Whose Dim Shadow* proved too esoteric for Connington's American publishers, Little, Brown and Co., who altered it to the more prosaic *The Tau Cross Mystery*.

8. Stewart analysed the Achet-Lepine case in detail in 'The Mystery of Chantelle', one of the best essays in his 1947 collection *Alias J. J. Connington*.

CHAPTER I

"LUCKY again, partner," commented Westenhanger, breaking into Eileen Cressage's thoughts as he took up the scoring-block. "That's game and rubber, Douglas. Your mind must be wandering."

Douglas Fairmile had glanced down the room to where a fair-haired girl was sitting with a rather red-faced man. Douglas's brows contracted slightly. That fellow Morchard had attempted to monopolise Cynthia this evening; but surely anyone could see that the girl was bored. A persistent creature, Morchard—rather too persistent at times, Douglas felt. Then, at the sound of Westenhanger's voice, his attention came back to the bridge-table.

"Game and rubber?" he repeated. "Sorry, partner. My fault entirely. You see, I'm getting rusty in auction nowadays. It's nearly gone out at my club; nobody plays it any more. We're all on to this new game that's just come in."

"New game? What new game?" demanded Westenhanger, arranging the cards for his shuffle. "Have the Cardsharpers rediscovered Old Maid or the simple joys of Happy Families? Out with it, Douglas."

Douglas Fairmile made a gesture as though apologising for Westenhanger.

"Tut! Tut! He's jealous, poor fellow. My fault for mentioning the Romarin Club. A sore subject with Conway, and no wonder. You know, we have an entrance examination for candidates: test 'em in following suit and remembering what's trump. And somehow Conway didn't get in. Or else he was afraid to enter. A sad business, anyhow; don't let's dwell on it. So he calls us the Cardsharpers out of spite."

Mrs. Caistor Scorton began to deal. Douglas passed the box of cigarettes to Eileen; and, when she refused, took one himself. Westenhanger looked at him with feigned anxiety.

"I notice a certain tendency to wander in your talk, of late. This inconsecutiveness of mind is growing on you, Douglas. Do you ever find yourself, in the morning, putting on your jacket first and your waistcoat afterwards? Pull yourself together. Squails Up-to-date, or something like that, was what you were trying to tell us about before you began to ramble."

"Oh! Suspension Bridge, that's it. Suspension Bridge. Never heard of it? Well, well. These soulless mechanics! You take the two of spades out of the pack, put in a joker instead; and then play according to auction rules. You've no notion of the superior feeling it gives you when you go No Trump with five aces in your hand. Confidence, that's the word! A splendid game."

"Splendid!" Westenhanger conceded, sarcastically. "Invite me to take a hand in the inaugural game, will you? It'll be an historic occasion, no doubt; and I might get my name into the newspapers."

Douglas looked hurt.

"He doesn't believe me, Eileen; he thinks I'm . . . Oh, sorry!"

He picked up his cards, and the game continued. For the third time in succession, Eileen Cressage laid down her hand with an inaudible sigh of relief. Being dummy, she could think about other things than the table before her. She had never been a keen bridge-player; her card-memory was too weak for anything beyond the most obvious tactics. And on this evening especially, her interest in the game was of the slightest. She played mechanically; and she had quite failed to note how, time and again, a skilful intervention by her partner had extricated her from a risky declaration.

As Westenhanger gathered up their first trick, her mind went back to her ever-present money difficulties. Some bills had reached her by the last post. Somehow, bills always dropped in at that time; and she had begun to dread the very sight of an unsealed envelope among her correspondence. If these wretched things had come in the morning, the affairs of the day might have helped to put them out of her mind; but when they arrived after dinner, they seemed to rivet her attention through the whole night.

The problems of a girl trying to keep up a decent appearance on a tiny income seemed to be approaching an insoluble state. Her quarter's income was nearly exhausted; and yet something would have to be done. It was no use approaching her trustees in the hope of anticipating her income for the next three months. She had tried that before; and all she had got was a lecture on the folly of over-spending. It appeared that the thing was impossible under the will. Besides, the trustees were simply lawyers, without a spark of personal interest ·in her affairs or herself. So far as they were concerned, Eileen Cressage was a name on a deed-box or a docket. No help there, obviously.

And yet something would have to be done. She could pay some of her creditors and leave the rest of the affairs standing; but which people ought she to attend to first? Her mind was busy with a sort of jig-saw puzzle with the bills as a picture and the available money as the pieces; but with half the fragments missing, it was a hopeless business. One fact was evident: some of these bills would have to be settled, and settled soon.

With an effort she put the whole affair at the back of her mind and tried to divert her attention. But her first glance across the room brought the thing back to her from a different angle. There was her host, old Rollo Dangerfield, sitting in a despondent attitude beside the window. What had he to be low-spirited about? If she herself owned the Dangerfield Talisman, her troubles would be conjured away. The thing was worth £50,000 on the last occasion when it had been valued; and the price of diamonds had gone up a good deal since then.

Her eyes passed to where Mrs. Brent and the American collector sat. Neither of them had money worries. At sixty, Mrs. Brent seemed to get a good deal out of life; and the steam yacht in the bay at the foot of the garden was a fair proof that a few hundred pounds one way or the other was not likely to trouble her.

A rustle of the cards brought Eileen's attention to the bridge-table. She leaned back a little in her chair and glanced, with an envy which was quite devoid of malice, at the three players intent on their game.

Mrs. Caistor Scorton's husband had been one of those hard-faced men who had made fortunes in the War. When he died she had got the money; and her enemies said that the hard face had been bequeathed also, in a codicil to his will. She certainly had a very keen appreciation of the value of a Treasury note.

Then there was Douglas Fairmile, with a big private income. His only worry at present was whether Cynthia Pennard would marry him or not. No great need for anxiety there, Eileen reflected. Cynthia wasn't throwing herself at his head, certainly; but it was one of those affairs which are bound to come right in the end. If only her own affairs would look as bright!

Finally, her partner, Conway Westenhanger, very obviously hadn't a care in the world. Those mechanical inventions of his were known to be small gold mines; he wasn't in love with anyone; and he got on well with people. What more could a man want?

Half unconsciously she compared the two men. Douglas was once described to her as "one of those delightful people who can always be cheery without getting on your nerves with it." He had the gift of playing the fool in season without looking like a fool while he was doing it. One laughed with him, always, and never at him. Conway Westenhanger was a more complex person, but just as attractive in his own way. She liked his mouth; its clean-cut lines seemed to have something sympathetic in their curves; and the thinker's sharply-marked vertical lines between the eyebrows rather added to the attractiveness of his face.

Mrs. Brent broke the silence, addressing her host:

"Rollo! would you mind if we have that window opened farther! The heat's almost unbearable to-night."

Old Dangerfield came out of his brown study with a start, made a gesture of acquiescence, and threw open the window to its full extent. Through the embrasure a faint breath of air wandered in from the outer twilight, laden with the smell of parched soil and the heavy perfume of flowers; but it brought no coolness with it.

"I suppose this doesn't affect you, Mr. Wraxall?" Mrs. Brent turned to the American beside her. "You're a New Yorker, aren't you? Heat waves won't trouble you as much as they do me. You're acclimatised, no doubt."

"It's warm to-night. It's certainly not what one calls cool. But I'll admit that I've known it hotter over there. And this air of yours hasn't got that used-up feeling about it that city air has. It's fresh, even if it's hot. You'd know it was garden air and not street air, even if the flowers weren't there. But you're wrong about my being acclimatised. I don't use New York much in the summer."

4

"Of course, you've got a country big enough to let you choose your climate for almost any day in the year, haven't you? Well, there's something to be said for an island. If this heat gets worse I shall simply take the *Kestrel* away for a night or two until the hot spell is over. Another couple of days of this would be unbearable. Luckily the Dangerfields understand me; they won't be offended if I disappear without warning. One would think twice about doing that with most people, but Friocksheim is a real Liberty Hall."

"They've been very kind in asking me down," the American explained. "I didn't know them; but I got an introduction; and when I explained I was interested in some of their things, they invited me to stay for a few days."

He glanced through the window and across the moonlit bay which stretched beyond the lawns.

"The *Kestrel*? Little white yacht with copper funnels lying in the bay? Is that the one? I saw her as I drove up here this evening."

"Yes, that's the *Kestrel*. You liked her looks?"

"Very pretty. Graceful lines, she has. My own yacht's rather larger; but she's not so neat, not so neat. I wanted lots of room on board."

"The very thing I didn't want on the *Kestrel*. I use her as a kind of retreat, Mr. Wraxall, the place for a rest-cure. I've never had a guest on board; there isn't even a spare cabin. Sometimes I want to get clean away from everybody; and that was the best way I could think of for managing it. Callers don't drop in when one's fifty miles from port."

The American looked at her with interest kindling in his eyes.

"You feel that way, too? That's interesting. That's very interesting. I take it you're not a philanthropist, then?"

Mrs. Brent shifted her position slightly and looked up at her neighbour's clean-shaven face. It was of the long rather than the square American type, the face of a man with a certain imagination.

"If you mean contributing to charitable funds and that sort of thing, I'm certainly not philanthropic," she answered. "I don't think I've spent a penny in that way during the last ten years. People come bothering me with tales of sad cases; at least they used to do that. But once you get the name of being kind-hearted, you're simply pestered to death by demands, mostly from frauds. I've shed that reputation long ago. I don't say I don't give something here and there. Everybody does. But unless I see a thing with my own eyes I refuse to part with a farthing. My eyesight is still fairly good for my age; and I'm quite able to see a thing for myself without needing some fussy creature to point it out to me."

She broke off suddenly and showed her fine teeth in a faint smile.

"You've touched there on a thing that always irritates me. I've got rather a bad reputation over it. They call me a skinflint. There's an American phrase for that, isn't there?"

"You mean a tight-wad, perhaps. Yes, that would be it, a tight-wad."

He dismissed the subject, seeming to think of something else.

"A minute or two back you were saying you wanted to get away from humanity now and again. I sympathise with you there. I can understand the feeling. I open the newspaper in the morning and it says a new fibre has made finer lingerie possible. I don't use lingerie. Further on, there's something else about floor stains. That lacks the personal appeal. So does the one about candies. My digestion's too poor for candies. Then I come across 'Buy Jones's Razors.' I don't buy Jones's razors. Perhaps my man buys them. I don't know. But you see how it is. Everywhere one goes these things hit the retina. There's no escape from this modern way of pushing things. My own company does it. I get tired of it. I want to forget Jones's razors, and Smith's Confected Candies, and . . . and . . . dollars, and cents, and the whole twentieth century. I want to blot it all out of my mind. I want to get among old things, things that were made long before dollars were thought of. That's restful. That's the kind of thing I like. Something that looks as if your Queen Elizabeth might have used it, or one of your Henries. If it's got a history attached to it, I like it all the more."

Mrs. Brent's face showed a blend of sympathy and amusement.

"So *that's* how you became a collector?"

Wraxall smiled also.

"Well, Mrs. Brent, that's part of the truth. That certainly is a factor. But there's more to it than that. You may laugh at me if you like. You may certainly laugh. But I love these old things for themselves. It gives me a real pleasure to handle them, just to turn them over and over and look at them. And to wonder about the people who wore them. These things mean more to me than all the history-books. Much more."

Mrs. Brent's white-framed face became more sympathetic. She recognised a kindred spirit in the American, although his line of escape from the modern world was not the same as her own.

"Don't forget to see the Dangerfield Talisman before you go, Mr. Wraxall. They'll be glad to show it to you and to tell you the legend. There are some photographs of it, too. You might be able to take one of them back for your collection."

Mr. Wraxall brushed the suggestion aside.

"Photographs would be no use to me. They haven't the appeal. No."

He paused for a moment; then, studying her face, he continued:

"I thought of taking the thing itself back with me in the fall, if it could be arranged."

"The Dangerfield Talisman?" Mrs. Brent almost lost her manners in her astonishment. "You thought of taking that back with you! Why, the thing's absurd. They'd sooner part with Friocksheim than with the Talisman; and they've held Friocksheim since before the Conquest."

"I wouldn't stick at a few thousand pounds one way or the other. I'd set my heart on getting that Talisman. I've come four thousand miles for it, specially. That shows I'm interested. I'm keenly interested. I'm not a bargainer. They've only to name their price and I'll pay it."

"But my dear man, this isn't a case where money comes in at all, don't you see? The thing's unbuyable, you may take my word for it."

The American scanned her face carefully.

"I see you mean it," he commented, "but I came here specially to procure that Talisman. I couldn't be content to take your word for it. Maybe you're right. Perhaps you know best. But I'll have to go to headquarters with my offer and make sure. I'm not doubting what you say.

7

Not at all. I hadn't a notion there was any difficulty in the road. None at all. But you'll understand that, without doubting what you say in the very least, I've got to make sure?"

Mrs. Brent had recovered from her astonishment.

"Oh, certainly, go ahead. I shan't feel offended, if that's what you mean. But I warn you that it's quite useless—out of the question."

The American made a non-committal gesture. Mrs. Brent thought it best to change the subject.

"This heat seems to be getting worse, if anything. I must really get a fan. I'm old-fashioned enough to have one."

She rose and left the room. Wraxall transferred his interest to his host, who was still gazing absently out over the gardens. Mrs. Brent's evident amazement at his suggestion had given the American something to think about. Things were not going to be so simple as he had imagined. He glanced across at Rollo Dangerfield's profile, trying to estimate the chances of overcoming his objections if he really proved obdurate.

"Why, he might be an old Norseman come to life," Wraxall said to himself. "Put one of those winged helmets on his head, and with that profile and that big white moustache he could sit to any painter for the portrait of a Viking. He's not likely to be anybody's money when it comes to bargaining. Stubborn. Obstinate. It's going to be none so easy after all."

He studied his host covertly until he was interrupted by Mrs. Brent's return. She slipped into her chair and began to fan herself with an air of relief.

"This is the kind of night when one appreciates the Dangerfield methods," she said, after a time. "They know how I hate climbing stairs; and they gave me a room on the ground floor. It's the only one; all the rest are above. I blessed them just now as I passed the staircase and remembered that I might have had to climb it. I've got to the age when one economises on the unnecessary as far as possible; and I count stair climbing as a luxury on that standard."

A great moth swept suddenly in through the open window, veered and swerved blindly over Rollo Dangerfield's head, and then blundered out once more into the darkness. Mrs. Brent followed its flight; and her eyes caught the sky beyond the embrasure.

8

"Rollo!" she raised her voice to attract his attention. "Is there any sign of that thunderstorm breaking? I wish it would come, and perhaps the air would clear a little after it."

Old Dangerfield leaned forward a little and scanned the visible horizon.

"I'm afraid it's no good. The clouds are lighter than they were an hour ago; and I shouldn't expect it to break to-night now."

Mrs. Brent fanned herself resignedly.

"I'm not altogether sorry. That cure is almost as bad as the disease for me, Mr. Wraxall. A thunderstorm shakes my nerves to pieces always—I don't know why. I'm not afraid of being struck, or anything of that kind; but the noise of thunder seems to get down somewhere into my subconsciousness and set me all on edge. After a real bad storm I'm hardly normal. I feel I might do anything wild; try to fly downstairs, steal my best friend's spoons, or something equally idiotic."

The American looked at her with a faint twinkle in his eye.

"Now that's curious, Mrs. Brent, that's very curious indeed. For, you see, thunderstorms take me quite the other way. I like them. I'd sit up all night to watch a good thunderstorm. Give me a chair, and a good wide window, with not too much iron near it, and I'd be content to watch the flashes so long as they like to come."

He turned to the nearest window as he spoke, and then seemed to study it for a moment or two.

"That kind of window wouldn't be much use as a stall for the performance. It's too deep-set. Are the walls of this house really a couple of yards thick, the way they seem to be at the window-sill there?"

"Several feet thick in this part of Friocksheim. This is the old part of the house, you know—some of it dates from the time when the place was a castle, and they had to make walls thick and windows small. And of course that's quite a recent thing. Here and there about the building you'll find remnants of a much older Friocksheim. There's a gateway you must get the Dangerfields to show you. It's old enough to satisfy you, I should think."

"I'd like to see it. It would be very interesting to me. And there must be some things worth visiting in the neighbourhood too. Perhaps you could tell me what I ought to go and see."

"There's a battered sort of monument on the road to Frogsholme village, about a mile and a half from here. I believe I remember hearing that it had something to do with Runic, whatever that is. And there are one or two other things you might care to look at."

For a time she gave him the benefit of her rather scrappy knowledge of the local antiquities, while he jotted down notes in his pocket-book. At last, when he had exhausted her store, he looked at his watch and made a gesture of apology.

"It's late, Mrs. Brent. I really hadn't meant to keep you so long. But what you've been telling me is interesting, and I've got a thirst for knowledge about that kind of thing. You've helped me considerably. That information will be of great assistance to me."

"Why not begin with the nearest? Mr. Dangerfield will be delighted to show you the Talisman to-night, I'm sure, if you wish it. And be sure to get him to tell you the legend of the Pool. It may save you trouble, you know. You'll see that your idea about the Talisman is quite hopeless."

"That's an idea. That's a good idea, Mrs. Brent. I always like to know, right away, what sort of proposition I'm up against. I've not given up hope yet, you understand? I'm quite set on taking that Talisman home with me somehow, if it can be managed. And I think it can, one way or another."

Conway Westenhanger's voice came across the room. The bridge-table was breaking up.

"I make it twenty-seven pounds twelve. You might check the figures, Douglas. I'm more at home in the calculus than in simple arithmetic; and it's quite likely I've made a slip."

"Right," said Douglas. "It isn't your honesty I'm in doubt about, merely your capacity. The great brains are always a bit one-sided—top-heavy, if you take my meaning. Let's see. Eight and six . . ."

He rapidly checked the addition.

"Correct! Well, you scrape through with a caution this time; but don't do it again."

Mrs. Caistor Scorton produced a roll of notes and counted out twenty-seven pounds ten on the table between Eileen and herself.

"One moment. I have a florin somewhere."

"Don't trouble about it," Eileen hastened to reassure her. "You needn't hunt for it. Let it stand."

Mrs. Caistor Scorton continued her search and at last discovered the missing coin.

"I don't like letting things stand over. Settle for cash, that's always been my principle in bridge. I can't be worried with remembering odd shillings from day to day."

Eileen Cressage picked up her winnings gratefully. She was not disturbed by Mrs. Caistor Scorton's manner. She was too overwhelmed by relief. Here was an absolute windfall which would go some distance towards solving the problem of her debts. Twenty-seven pounds! And she had given only half her attention to the game. If she had put her mind to it they might have won a good deal more. She had not even asked what stakes they were playing for; she had been too worried to think about that. A couple more nights like this and she would be able to pay off all her creditors.

"Sorry I shan't be able to give you your revenge to-morrow, Douglas," she heard Conway Westenhanger say, as he rose from the table. "I've got to run up to town for a couple of days. My patent-agent seems to have got on the track of an infringement of one of my affairs, and he wants to go into the business. That means Chancery Lane, Patent Office Library, and all the rest of it. Whew! It will be hot!"

Douglas's good-natured face corrugated in a grin of commiseration; but already he was moving across the room to where Cynthia Pennard was sitting. Morchard watched his coming with a discontented eye.

Mrs. Brent, glad to be relieved from the American's inquisition on local monuments, went across to Rollo Dangerfield's chair and gazed out of the window.

"No, that storm won't break to-night, I'm afraid. It's moved further on. But it's on my nerves already, I wish it would break and get the thing over. This heat wave might pass, then."

She drew back from the embrasure and bent over old Dangerfield.

"Rollo! I think Mr. Wraxall would like to have a look at the Talisman to-night, if you aren't too tired."

Rollo Dangerfield heaved himself up out of his chair, his six-foot height overtopping Mrs. Brent's slight figure as he rose.

"Certainly, if Mr. Wraxall wishes it. We can go along now, if he cares about it."

Eileen Cressage had caught the rapid interchange of talk.

"Oh! Are you going to tell him the legend? May I come? I'd like to hear it."

"What legend? About the Talisman? I haven't heard it either," said Westenhanger. "Do you mind my coming along with the rest?"

Rollo Dangerfield's smile had a touch of wistfulness, in which it seemed curiously alien from the general cast of his features.

"Anyone who is interested will be welcome," he said, with a touch of an old-fashioned courtesy which seemed to be much in character in his case. And, crossing the room, he opened the door for the party to pass out under his guidance.

CHAPTER II

THE group of Rollo Dangerfield's followers diminished
as it passed along the corridor. At the main entrance,
Douglas and Cynthia slipped aside and went off by themselves down the broad steps into the gardens. Further on,
beyond the great staircase, Mrs. Brent bade her companions
good night and turned into her room. Only five of his
guests were left to follow the old man to the end of the
corridor, where he threw open an unlocked door.

"This is what we call the Corinthian's Room," he
explained as he ushered them into it. "It was my grandfather's favourite spot in the house, and it got its name from
him. He was one of the Regency bucks—no worse than
the rest of them, perhaps, but a hard liver and a hard
gambler in his day. An eccentric, too, like most of them.
I can show you one of his eccentricities in a moment, if
you care to see it."

The room was about forty feet square, with a huge stone
fireplace. A great cupboard of oak occupied part of one
wall. Another wall was hung with an aged tapestry
representing Diana pursuing a stag. The floor was of
marble slabs, mainly white; but in the centre, black squares
of marble had been introduced so as to make a gigantic
chess-board pattern. Opposite the fireplace was a narrow
and shallow niche filled with a glass case.

Rollo Dangerfield switched on the electric lights and led
the visitors towards the recess. As they came near it,
they saw within the case a bell of faintly tinted glass, under
which lay, on a velvet bed, an ancient ornament.

"That is the Dangerfield Talisman," said old Rollo,
pointing to the case. "You can see what it is; one of
those golden armlets which were worn in the olden times.
It's too heavy for our modern tastes, I'm afraid. You
would hardly care to carry that, Miss Cressage."

He turned to Eileen with a faint smile.

"It's very heavy for an ornament—something over a

13

pound, I believe," he went on, as his guests drew nearer to look closely at the jewel. "Of course, the value of the gold is nothing to speak of, perhaps under a hundred pounds. The stones are of more interest in some people's eyes. There are eight of them in all—you can see the others reflected in the mirror at the back, if you look closely."

Mrs. Caistor Scorton examined the Talisman with an appraising eye.

"I agree with you. It's too heavy in the design."

Eileen Cressage bent forward and seemed to compare the size of the ornament with her own white arm.

"If a girl wore that," she said, "she must have been splendid. It's not a bit clumsy. She must have been slim, if anything, with small hands, or she couldn't have got it over them."

"Let's try it on Miss Cressage," said Morchard, suddenly, and he moved forward as he spoke. The case had a plain sheet of glass immediately in front of the jewel, through which it could be examined, whilst at either side was a glass door kept secured by a tiny handle. As Morchard put out his hand, Rollo Dangerfield stopped him with a gesture.

"I'm sorry," he said, "but it's one of our family customs never to take the Talisman out of its case—never even to lift the shade from it." .

He smiled, faintly apologetic, but evidently unbending in defence of his traditions.

"These ideas grow up somehow, in ways that are difficult to trace back to their births; but as time goes on, they gain a sort of sanctity from tradition, and speaking for myself, I should be sorry if I were the first of us to break this particular custom. There are so few of the old things left in this twentieth-century world, and perhaps you young people won't grudge me this one, if I keep it."

The touch of wistfulness had come back into his voice, robbing his refusal of the faintest trace of offence. Eileen, afraid that some of the others might embarrass the old man by pressing him to let them handle the jewel, hastened to put in a word before Morchard could open his mouth.

"I'd love to try it on; but what Mr. Dangerfield says is quite right. And now, I'd like to hear its story—the legend, I mean."

Rollo Dangerfield silently invited them to seat themselves. Then, leaning against the case containing the

Talisman, he turned to face his audience and began to speak. At first he seemed nervous of his effect; but as the tale went on, his voice changed into a monotone, as though he were reciting some well-remembered ritual.

"You must bear in mind that this is a very old tale, far older than any written document that we have. True enough, it fits the geography of Friocksheim; but for all we know, the legend may be far older than Friocksheim and may deal with some pool which none of us has ever seen. You know that we Dangerfields came into England from the North, away back in the troubled days before the Conquest. Friocksheim, I'm told, is a corruption of Fricca's Heim, Frea's Heim, the dwelling of Frea, the wife of Odin. There is no doubt about us as a race."

He lifted his old head proudly, and the Viking resemblance stood out undeniably in his features. Then, with a smile that showed the strong white teeth, he added:

"I needn't emphasise the final stage in the corruption of the name as you find it in the village: our Friocksheim has changed to Frogsholme, on the lips of these godless aborigines."

He paused for a moment and shifted his position slightly, so that he could see the Talisman as it lay under his arm.

"You must understand, then," he went on, "that this legend comes down to us from days when Valhalla still opened its gates to the heroes; and the spirits of winds, and woods, and streams, moved among men in their visible forms. It may be mere allegory; possibly it is the trans- mutation of some quite normal happening, a love tale magnified and distorted in the telling.

"One summer's night, the legend runs, Ulric, the Lord of Friocksheim, went out into the moonlight, seeking coolness after the heat of his castle walls. And, so wandering, he came by the Pool and sat beside the water, watching the rising of the mist from the surface of the mere. As he sat thus, lost in thought, the moonlight sparkled upon some- thing before him, and, bending forward, he grasped the Talisman. So he sat, with the armlet in his hand; and as he watched, the mists of the lake grew denser and drew closer; and there stepped at last from among their folds a maiden."

Old Rollo bent towards the Talisman, so that his face was partly hidden from his audience.

"Very little has come down to us—only a few words in

a tale. Yet even these halting words conjure up for me a wonder; a being, young, and proud, and fair, a form and grace surpassing all the beauty of women, a flash of the divinity passing across the screen of the flesh."

He let his voice drop into silence for a moment before he continued:

"The legend tells that she was betrothed to the Spirit of the Pool, the Frog King. But Ulric won her. She gave him the Talisman which she had come back to seek; and, when he desired her, he had but to dip it in the Pool and she came to him—for so long as that moon still shone. And she charged him, when she was with him, to keep the Talisman and to hand it down; for it would be the Luck of Friocksheim. And so, night after night, the Lord of Friocksheim went down to the Pool and washed the Talisman in its waters and wandered with his love in the wood beside the mere—until the moon came no more over the trees. But the next night, when he dipped the Talisman in the waters, there came swimming to him a loathsome little shape which laughed and jeered at him, saying: 'The Frog King has her for his bride.'"

Old Rollo turned back towards his audience again.

"So the Dangerfield Talisman is only a reminder of an old lie. Even at its best, it's a memorial of lying and deceit—and punishment."

His voice sounded bitter for a moment, but he went back at once to his ordinary tone:

"There it is: the Dangerfield Luck. I don't say I believe the legend; I won't say I doubt it. However the thing came to us, it's our oldest possession and experts tell me that the workmanship is extraordinarily old. And now, I think I can show you something less romantic, though it's not without its interest."

He moved forward and pushed aside some rugs with his foot, so that the black and white marble squares in the centre of the floor were cleared.

"I told you, I think, that this was the room mainly used by my grandfather, the Corinthian. It was, in fact, the very last room he ever entered. Possibly some of you remember something about the Regency times, the gambling, the prize-fighting, the duelling that went on. Eccentricity was often the pass-key to notoriety in those days; some of the bucks cultivated it wilfully. I believe that my grandfather was genuinely eccentric in this particular affair. He was a fanatic for chess playing and this was his chess-board. You see the marble squares on the floor."

He stooped down and lifted a metal plug from the centre of a square.

"Each of these squares has a plug like this at its centre. They're really put in to keep dirt out of the holes when no game is being played. When they wanted to set the pieces, all the plugs were taken out; and then the board was ready."

He stepped across the room and threw open the oaken cupboard on the wall.

"These are the chess-men. You see they are on a scale to match the board, each of them about a foot and a half high. Mr. Westenhanger, would you mind lifting one of them out—a pawn will do. They're too heavy for me, nowadays."

Westenhanger came forward and gripped one of the iron pieces.

"Lift it up off the shelf before you pull it forward," said old Dangerfield. "There's a spike on the foot of each piece, fitting into a hole in the shelf—the spike that goes into the hole in the chess-board, so that the piece can't be accidentally knocked over. They're top-heavy things. The Staunton pattern wasn't invented in those days."

It took more effort than Westenhanger had expected to lift the thing from its place and carry it over to the chess-board. He dropped it into position on one of the squares, the iron rod slipping easily into the hole and fixing the piece firmly.

"Rather like a railway chess-board, isn't it?" he said, as he went back to his seat, "but a good deal of trouble to play a game with pieces of that weight, I should think."

Old Rollo's eyes twinkled.

"I doubt if they'd have played much if they'd been left to their own exertions. As a matter of fact, each player had a lackey to shift his pieces for him while he sat comfortably in his chair."

He came forward and sat down as he spoke.

"This chess-board looks innocent enough; but it brought the death of my grandfather. You know what it was like in those days: men would quarrel about the tint of a snuff-box and fight a fatal duel over the fit of a cravat. My grandfather was as much of a fire-eater as his friends. Some miserable squabble took place in this room while they were actually playing on that board; probably a mere drunken difference of opinion about some absurd trifle or other. They went out with pistols in the dawn; and the other man was the luckier of the two. Perhaps he deserved to be. No one knows now what they fought about. My grandfather was shot in the head—killed instantly."

Rollo Dangerfield rose, and drawing from his pocket a bunch of keys, he opened a small safe buried in the wall of the room beside the fire-place. From one of the divisions of the safe he extracted a worn-looking paper and a peculiar disc-like object.

"Here are two other relics. We preserve most things; and as this was the last document my grandfather put on paper, we've kept it in safety. You may as well see it."

He handed the paper to Wraxall, who studied it intently before passing it to his neighbour. At the top of the sheet were two lines of handwriting:

NOX NOCTI INDICAT SCIENTIAM.

MATT. VI. 21; LUKE XII. 34.

Below this was a rough diagram of a chess-board with certain pieces placed as in an end-game or a problem.

Wraxall turned the paper over in search of something further; but the back of the sheet was blank.

The American passed the manuscript to Mrs. Caistor Scorton and held out his hand for the second object which

Rollo Dangerfield had taken from the safe. It was a circular disc cut from a sheet of leather. Originally the sheet may have been the same thickness as a boot-sole, or rather thinner; but a century of atmospheric changes had warped and contorted its form. Evidently when new it had been about two and a half inches in diameter. Through the centre of the leather there passed a piece of twine secured on one side of the disc by a knot and looped on the other side into a fixed ringlet of a size which would just admit a hand. Wraxall turned the object over and over, but it suggested nothing to him. After a final inspection, he passed it also to his neighbour, and then turned inquiringly to Rollo Dangerfield.

, "It suggests nothing to you?" old Dangerfield demanded perfunctorily. He took back both objects after they had been examined by everyone, and held up the paper so that they could see it. "This first line, in Latin, is simply part of the second verse of the Nineteenth Psalm: *Night unto night sheweth knowledge.* The two references to the Gospels give you the verse: *Where your treasure is, there will your heart be also.* I am afraid we can't discover anything from that part of the document. The rest of it seems easier to account for, if I tell you a little more about the paper."

He put the sheet on his knee and leaned back in his chair as though tired.

"You see the rough sketch of the chess-board," he went on after a moment or two. "That gives the position in which the pieces were found on this board here after his death. Possibly it represents the end-position in that game during which the quarrel arose between him and his opponent. He must have attached some importance to it himself, for he came into this room just before going off to his duel, jotted the thing down, and left orders that it was to be given to his son if anything happened. That, I must admit, seems to suggest that he was not quite in a normal frame of mind when he put the thing on paper; for at that date my father was a boy of four or five years old. We Dangerfields are a very late-marrying family, for some reason or other. Obviously a child of that age could have no interest in chess-endings. Put that together with the three texts; and I believe the normal mind would say that my grandfather's brain was still bemused with his night's wine—he drank an enormous quantity of port, they say—and that in a muddled-headed way he scribbled down his

19

end-game, added one or two of his favourite texts, and then, with some idea that the texts might be of service to his son, he left directions for the paper to be handed on."

He glanced amusedly round the circle to see if they shared his view.

"Unfortunately," he continued, "that explanation falls short of completeness on one matter. This little leather disc was also to be handed to my father. Was it a toy that he had made for the boy? Perhaps he had promised it to the child, and even at that dangerous moment he remembered his promise? I like to think that there was something of the kind in his mind. But if there had been any promise of the sort, my father had forgotten it. When they questioned him he knew nothing about it. Quite possibly it was a promised toy. You know what the memory of a four-year-old is like and how difficult it is to catch hold of something which he has once allowed to slip. Nothing came of it."

His fingers played almost affectionately with the wrinkled scrap of leather.

"My grandfather's death left my father an orphan; for his mother had died a year or two earlier. The paper was preserved and handed to my father, when he came of age, by the lawyer of our family who had impounded it shortly after its discovery. It meant nothing to anyone. Whatever meaning it carried had been lost. All that it meant to my father was the last link with his Corinthian ancestor; and I believed that he preserved it on that account. At any rate, it found its way into the Dangerfield archives, and there it is likely to remain."

"And you, yourself, haven't any idea about it, Mr. Dangerfield?" asked Eileen. "Surely he must have had something in his mind when he wrote it. Tell us what you think of it, if you can."

"I can give you a guess," said old Dangerfield, "but it's a guess and nothing more. My own view is that the quarrel had arisen over some question of their play; and my grandfather wanted a permanent record left, so as to be able to prove his point in cold blood later on. In addition to being a gambler and one of the most remarkable spendthrifts of his day, he was an obstinate man. We know that to our cost. The Dangerfield jewels used to be a very fine collection; but after his death it was found that most of the good things had vanished—converted into cash and gambled away in backing that obstinate opinion of his. After a couple of generations we're still suffering from the inroads he made into the estate."

"Is anything more known about him?" asked Westenhanger.

"Not very much that's creditable, I'm afraid. Oh, yes! I believe that he made himself rather ridiculous by an improvement of the hobby-horse."

"He must have been a rum bird!" commented Westenhanger.

Rollo Dangerfield hastened to explain.

"Not a rocking-horse. I mean that two-wheeled thing like a safety bicycle that some of the Corinthians used to amuse themselves with. One sat in the saddle and pushed the thing along with one's feet on the ground—like running in a chair, rather. It had a vogue at one time. I'm told that he brought out a new pattern with treadles—something like the present child's scooter in principle. At any rate, it was rather frowned on, and he was glad to let it drop. But you see that he was evidently akin to you on one side at least."

"Now there's just one other thing I'd like to hear about, if you can tell us, Mr. Dangerfield." Eileen Cressage looked rather doubtfully at the old man as she spoke. "Perhaps I'm indiscreet; and if I am, please say so at once. People talk about the Dangerfield Secret. They say it's something like the one in that Scots family up in the north —you know, the thing the heir is told when he's twenty-one. Is there really a Dangerfield secret?"

Old Rollo Dangerfield's face hardened perceptibly for a moment; and he looked at the girl with an inscrutable expression. Then, evidently reading in her face a fear that she had offended him, he relaxed his attitude slightly and tried to put her at her ease again. Nevertheless, the tone of his voice was sufficient to show that he disliked the subject.

"There is something which people call the Dangerfield Secret. Helga doesn't know it. She'll be told when she's twenty-five. My nephew Eric knows it, since he's the next male heir. I can say no more about it."

Westenhanger relieved the slight strain that followed by getting up and stepping across to the Talisman's case.

"I suppose you put this in the safe each night, Mr. Dangerfield? It would hardly do to leave it exposed like this for anyone to pick up. It must be worth a small fortune."

Old Dangerfield looked across the room.

"It was valued in my grandfather's time, and they put it down as being worth some £50,000 then. The diamonds were said to be very fine; and you can see the size of the stones for yourself."

"I don't think I'd trust it in a small safe like that, if it were mine," said Westenhanger, glancing at the little iron door from which Rollo Dangerfield had taken the document. "Any man with a pocket crow-bar could open that thing and get away with the Talisman."

The old man laughed shortly.

"Don't trouble about the safe. The Talisman is never put into that. The fact is, you have come up against another of the Dangerfield superstitions. The Talisman is never moved from its place by day or night. It stands where you see it, always."

The American sat up suddenly.

"You leave it there, sir? You take no precautions against crooks? You don't mean to tell me anyone could step in here, lift that bell, and clear off with the goods?"

He paused, as if struck by a thought. Then he continued in another tone.

"I take it that you're fully covered by insurance?"

Rollo Dangerfield's face took on a faintly sardonic expression. He seemed to enjoy surprising the American.

"Not at all. The Talisman has never been insured. Why should we insure it? It always comes back. We have electric alarms on all the outer doors and the windows, of course; but they are merely put on because my wife is nervous. The Talisman can look after itself, I assure you."

Wraxall looked at his host in amazement.

"Do you really mean that?"

He thought for a moment, and then a fresh idea seemed to strike him.

"Now I see! You've got some mediæval man-trap or spring-gun attached to the thing, something that grips your burglar if he comes after your property?"

Rollo Dangerfield's laugh was quite free from sarcasm; he evidently enjoyed the jest which he alone could see.

"No, Mr. Wraxall, nary a spring-gun, as I believe some of your compatriots might say. Not so much as a man-trap. You could lift the thing from its bed at any hour of the day or night without the slightest risk. My nephew Eric has rooms in the tower above us; but even if he heard you, I doubt if he would trouble to interrupt you. We know our Talisman. It always comes home."

The American was plainly astounded.

"It seems to me, Mr. Dangerfield, that you're presuming a good deal on your safety in the past. Crooks nowadays aren't likely to be frightened off by talk. No, it would take more than a Castle Spectre to keep some of our smashers out of here if they only knew what you've told us."

Rollo Dangerfield's white eyebrows contracted slightly. It was evident to them all that he was displeased at being doubted. He leaned forward and spoke directly to the American.

"Now this is authentic, Mr. Wraxall. You can look up the accounts in the local papers of the time, if you care to go to the trouble. I shall be very pleased to give you the dates, if necessary. At least twice within the last half-century an attempt has been made to rob us of the Talisman. Once a drunken tramp made his way in here during the night and took the armlet. He was afraid to get rid of it anywhere near here; and three days later he was arrested for some other crime; the Talisman was found on him and returned to us. The second case was a genuine burglary. One of the keepers saw the man leave the house and gave chase. The fellow dropped dead—heart failure, it was said to be—and the Talisman was found in his hand."

The American said nothing; but quite obviously he was not convinced. Old Dangerfield seemed to be nettled.

"I am not trying to convince you, Mr. Wraxall. I suppose that would be quite impossible. But I tell you this frankly: If the Talisman disappeared to-night, the last thing I should think of doing would be to call in the police. The Talisman guards itself. Within seven days at the outside, it would be back there under the bell."

Eileen Cressage had been listening eagerly to the old man's words; but at this last statement, her surprise broke out.

"You wouldn't call in the police, Mr. Dangerfield? You'd really trust to the Talisman finding its way home? It seems amazing."

"You may take me at my word, Miss Cressage. I mean exactly what I say in this matter. If the Talisman disappeared, either by day or by night, I should not trouble to call in police assistance. Why should I, when I know what I do know? Of course I mean what I say. Did you ever see anything like the Talisman guarded with so little care? If I did not believe implicitly that it would come back, wouldn't I have it trenched round with all manner of protections? Of course! Let it go! What does that matter, since it is certain to be over there again before long."

Conway Westenhanger turned from the Talisman's niche, but as he crossed the tessellated floor his eye was caught by something which he had not noticed before. He stopped for an instant and glanced keenly at the corners of one or two squares.

"Something there that's got plugged with dirt," he reflected. "Holes a bit bigger than a large pin's head, they seem to be. Nothing important, evidently, since they're choked up in that fashion."

24

CHAPTER III

FREDDIE STICKNEY owed his presence in the Friocksheim house-party to qualities other than those which make a welcome guest. He was a mean little man, with a skin which invariably proved itself impenetrable to ordinary social pin-pricks; and this thickness of hide enabled him to thrust himself into positions wherein an average individual would have felt too keenly that he was an intruder. He had invited himself, knowing Rollo Dangerfield's dislike for hurting people's feelings and counting on that quality to avoid a refusal; and, having arrived, he proposed to stay for just as long as it suited him to do so. Not that he had any special interest in the Dangerfields. He had angled for three other invitations before turning to Friocksheim as a last resource. However, he was quite prepared to make the most of it, now that he had fixed the thing up. "Even the best of us," he reflected philosophically, "even the best of us have to put up with the second-best at times." And in this kindly spirit he had come down from town.

Freddie's lack of popularity was due to certain peculiarities in his mind. An acquaintance of his, hard put to it to account for the matter, had explained it thus: "Freddie's got a certain acuteness. Give him a fact and he'll worry at it and draw inferences from it. And the funny thing is that every inference he draws tends to discredit somebody or something. And yet he doesn't do it out of malice. It's just Freddie's way. He's got that kind of mind—can't help making people uncomfortable."

On the afternoon of the day after Rollo Dangerfield had shown the Talisman to his guests, Freddie was lounging on a seat in the garden when one of these inference-bearing facts crossed his mind.

"Why," he said to himself, "now that Westenhanger's gone to town, we shall be thirteen at table to-night. That's very thoughtless of the Dangerfields. Out of thirteen people there's certain to be at least one person who's superstitious. That'll be most uncomfortable for everybody: I think I'd better mention it before we sit down."

As it chanced he had not to wait so long before announcing his discovery. Before he had finished a mental analysis of the probable distribution of superstition among his fellow-guests, Mrs. Dangerfield came into view, armed with gloves and scissors. Freddie rose and joined her.

"Going to cut some flowers?" he inquired. "May I help?"

Mrs. Dangerfield refused his assistance; but Freddie was not to be shaken off.

"Friend of mine once suffered badly. Tore his finger with a thorn, then let some dirt into it. Careless fellow he was, poor chap. It suppurated, swelled up, they had to take the finger off at last."

Mrs. Dangerfield deliberately put on her gardening gloves.

"I don't think I shall run much risk in these, Mr. Stickney."

"No? Perhaps not. Still, one never can tell, you know. A single prick from a rose-thorn would be enough."

Mrs. Dangerfield laughed.

"You must be a terribly thoughtful person to live with."

Freddie considered this for a moment.

"No. Just a knack I have of seeing a thing and knowing how it happens. That reminds me—we shall be thirteen at table to-night. Don't mind myself, of course—and I'm sure you don't mind either—but some of the people might, you know. It's awkward."

"I shouldn't trouble about it, Mr. Stickney. As a matter of fact, I remembered it yesterday and rang up Mrs. Tuxford. She and the doctor will dine with us to-night. So no one's feelings will be ruffled. And of course we never have a full party at lunch. Is your mind relieved?"

Mrs. Dangerfield did not like Freddie Stickney.

"But what about breakfast to-morrow?" pursued the indefatigable inquirer. "They might happen to turn up all at the same time."

"Mrs. Brent always breakfasts in her own room," said Mrs. Dangerfield, who was tired of the subject. "I'm sorry. I have some orders to give to this gardener."

Dismissed in this summary fashion Freddie Stickney

26

wandered about the grounds until it was time to got into the house and dress. He was feeling rather bored. Friocksheim might be cheaper than the Continent, but undeniably it was slow. Nothing happened at Friocksheim. These people seemed to have no interest in scandal. He began to·wish that something would turn up to liven things a little. He had had some hopes of Morchard at first. The mottle-faced fellow seemed to be keen on the girls; and anything might turn up. But none of the girls seemed interested in Morchard. Nor did they seem fascinated by Freddie himself. A slow place, decidedly slow. He was thoughtful while he dressed. If the Dangerfield circle was going to turn out so boring he might be forced to leave earlier than he had intended; but that would mean paying hotel bills somewhere, and Freddie's frugal mind could hardly. bring itself to consider that prospect except as a last resort.

After dinner the party split up. Douglas Fairmile, complaining bitterly of the heat and clamouring for fresh air, easily persuaded Cynthia to follow him out into the gardens. Old Dangerfield impressed Freddie Stickney to make up a bridge four with Nina Lindale and the doctor's wife. As they sat down Mrs. Tuxford put in a plea for small stakes.

"What do you call 'small stakes'?" demanded Freddie. "As low as ten bob a hundred? They're playing their usual points at the other table, I think."

He glanced over his shoulder as he spoke, and noted that Mrs. Caistor Scorton and Morchard were playing against Eric Dangerfield and Eileen.

The doctor's wife, a shy-looking girl, seemed taken aback by Freddie's ideas.

"I simply can't afford to play for anything higher than a shilling a hundred," she said, ignoring Freddie's ill-suppressed astonishment at the figure. "I'm sorry, but there it is."

Rollo Dangerfield winced under Freddie's tactlessness. He knew that the doctor's practice was a very small one; and he admired the girl for having the grit to keep the stakes down.

"Quite right," he interjected, swiftly, before Freddie could say anything further, "I agree with you, Mrs. Tuxford. A shilling a hundred suits well enough if one's keen on the game for its own sake. I'd much rather play with people who want to win a rubber than with other people who only want to win a sovereign."

"I'm quite pleased to play for a shilling a hundred," said Nina Lindale.

Freddie could take a hint as well as most people. His eyes opened a little wider but nothing else showed whether he was pleased or displeased. As the game began, the doctor came across the room and glanced at his wife's hand.

Mrs. Brent, feeling the thunderous closeness of the night, had made her way to a chair beside one of the deep windows; and leaning back in it she tried to persuade herself that she felt a breath of cooler air. Wraxall and Mrs. Dangerfield followed her, and they were joined almost immediately by the doctor. Helga Dangerfield circled round the two tables, halting for a moment or two to scan the cards. Then, saying she had some letters to write, she left the room.

"The storm must be coming to-night," Mrs. Brent asserted, as a faint puff of sultry air momentarily stirred the curtain beside her. "It's been banking up all day; and I'm sure it can't keep off much longer. I can feel all my nerves atwitch."

Wraxall bent forward in his chair and scanned the heavy clouds.

"I'm not up in your weather-signs," he said, "but it does seem to me that there's a shake-up coming. I should certainly judge we'd have rain soon. I should say we're in for a regular water-spout if those clouds burst overhead. It will be wet."

The doctor was examining Mrs. Brent's face with an interest more friendly than professional.

"Nerves?" he asked kindly.

She nodded.

"A dose of bromide? Quieten them, and give you a chance to get to sleep. I can take my car down and make it up for you in ten minutes, if you'd like it."

Mrs. Brent thanked him with a smile; but she nodded dissent to his suggestion.

"No," she answered, "I don't believe in running away from things. I loathe thunder; but I'm not so feeble as all that. I'd much rather take it as it comes."

The doctor was about to say something when she stopped him with a gesture and bent forward to the window, listening intensely.

"What bird was that?" she asked.

"I heard nothing," said the doctor.

"Listen!" she motioned for silence, and they sat with ears strained. "There! Didn't you hear it?"

"No, nothing," said the American.

"There it is again!" Mrs. Brent held up her hand for a moment. "It's stopped now. Didn't you hear it, Anne?"

Mrs. Dangerfield shook her head.

"You always forget that the rest of us aren't gifted with super-normal hearing, you know."

"Well, I heard it quite distinctly. It's down yonder in the trees near the Pool, I think."

"Nobody else heard it, at any rate," said the doctor. "You must have remarkably sharp ears, Mrs. Brent. Now I begin to see why you dislike thunder so much. It must be a perfect torture to a person with your acute hearing. I withdraw my suggestion about a sedative. Nothing short of morphia would keep you asleep in a storm, I'm afraid."

"Well, I haven't come to that yet," Mrs. Brent retorted. "And I prefer to keep what nerves I have, rather than wreck them further with drugs. One can always stand a thing if one makes up one's mind to it."

"One thing I won't stand," said Mrs. Dangerfield, "and that's the heat in this room. Let's go outside and see if we can't find a cooler spot to sit."

The doctor rose and followed her as she crossed the room; but Mrs. Brent seemed to reject the idea. She remained in her chair and Wraxall, after rising, sat down again. For a time Mrs. Brent remained silent, gazing out at the inky sky; but at last she turned to the American.

"Well, Mr. Wraxall," she demanded in a low voice which could not reach the bridge players. "Are you still confident of getting what you want?"

The American's face betrayed nothing of his thoughts.

"I couldn't say. No, it's too early yet to say. I'll admit that it's a stiffer thing than I expected. It's certainly stiffer than I supposed. But I haven't tried to get it yet. I think I'll wait till I have tried, before I say what I think. But I thank you for what you told me. I take that kindly of you. If you'd said nothing I'd have made a mistake, likely enough. I hadn't quite a grip of the situation; I'll say that frankly."

Mrs. Brent scanned his imperturbable features for a moment and then changed the subject.

"Rather a contrast between those two bridge-tables over there. Mrs. Tuxford plays well; but she kept the stakes down. The play at the other table seems to me little better than gambling. I've heard 'Redouble' twice in the last round or two; and Miss Cressage isn't half as good at bridge as Mrs. Tuxford."

Wraxall looked at her with a faint admiration showing on his face.

"You don't miss much, Mrs. Brent. That's a fact. I've been watching them play, but it hadn't struck me. You're quite right. But I suppose they can stand it."

"I suppose so. No business of mine," retorted Mrs. Brent, shortly.

She turned slightly round in her chair, however, and studied the faces of the players at Eileen's table. Things were going very badly for the girl. She was the worst of the four, and in addition, her nerve was going, and her play was growing more and more reckless. That night she had sat down with the pleasant feeling that in an hour or two she would have won something more towards the payment of these bills which still hung over her. But somehow, this evening, things were different. Instead of Conway Westenhanger, she had Eric Dangerfield as a partner; and without quite realising what the change meant she had found that the games did not run so smoothly as they had done on the night before. Once or twice she had miscalculated, and her partner had left her to fend for herself. A run of bad cards had eaten still further into her nerve.

And then, suddenly, she had realised how much she had already lost; and she had begun to play more wildly in the hope of recouping herself. The gains of the previous evening were gone by now, and she was steadily running up a score against herself. She began to feel the heat of the night; and her play became more erratic.

Mrs. Brent studied her face for a round or two without comment. Then she turned to the American with an expression which might almost have been an ill-concealed sneer.

"If either of us was a philanthropist, Mr. Wraxall, I think we could find a field for our talents by persuading that girl to stop before she makes matters worse. She's making a fool of herself."

"I judge so from her looks. I don't play bridge. It seems to me to lack the complete psychological satisfaction that poker gives. And it hasn't the swiftness of faro. It's too slow and not brainy enough. I regard it as a dud game."

Mrs. Brent turned her back to the bridge-table.

"Well, if we worried ourselves about other people's troubles we should have a full life of it," she said. "As I told you the other night, I'm not a professing philanthropist."

The American made no direct reply.

"You've got a headache?" he asked.

"Frightful. It's the storm, I think."

"I judged so from your eyes. If you'll excuse me, I'll go off and leave you. You won't be anxious to talk when you feel that way."

Mrs. Brent gloomily acquiesced. Wraxall rose from his chair and left the room. As soon as he had gone she turned again slightly and resumed her study of Eileen Cressage's face. The girl was evidently slipping into desperation; and her play had degenerated into mere gambling on long chances. Once or twice she won heavily; but the run of luck was persistently against her. Mrs. Brent shifted her attention to Eric Dangerfield's face; and from it she could learn that he was growing uneasy. Once or twice he endeavoured to take the play out of his partner's hands; but he had nothing like the skill of Conway Westenhanger. More often than not, his attempts at rescue ended in worse disaster. Occasionally he glanced at the score and knitted his brows; but his play continued steady. He had not lost his nerve, like the girl.

After a final disastrous round, the bridge-party completed the rubber and came to a close. Mrs. Brent saw Eileen Cressage lean over and watch Morchard as he added up the long array of figures; and the girl's perturbation at the sight of the scoring-block was written plainly in her face. Morchard was slow in arithmetic; and as he laboriously totted up column after column, the distress deepened and the girl went whiter. At last he jotted down the total and worked out the cash equivalent.

"That's—let's see—two hundred and six pounds eighteen, isn't it?" he said, putting down the scoring-block and pencil.

"What did you say? I didn't quite catch," said Eileen.

Two hundred pounds! She knew they had been losing steadily; but this was far beyond her worst anticipations. She couldn't possibly pay that, even it she were given a year to do it. What had persuaded her to play at all? She felt her throat dry and mechanically moistened her lips.

"Two hundred and six pounds eighteen, I make it," repeated Morchard. "Nòt bad, partner."

Mrs. Caistor Scorton glanced keenly at the girl's face.

"Well!" she said, shortly, pushing her chair back slightly as though to show that the time had come to settle.

Eileen pulled herself together with an effort.

"I'm afraid I haven't enough money to pay just now," she said. "I suppose you won't mind letting it stand over for a little?"

Mrs. Caistor Scorton brought her eyes back to Eileen's face. Her thin lips were compressed for a moment; and when she spoke, her voice was hard:

"I always settle my own bridge debts immediately; and I expect other people to do the same."

Eileen flushed. After all, she had had fair warning. Mrs. Caistor Scorton had said the same thing the night before, when she had been the loser.

"I'm sorry, but I haven't as much money as that on hand."

Mrs. Caistor Scorton reflected for a moment.

"Well, you can give me a cheque, if you like," she conceded. "But, frankly, I prefer to keep these things on a cash basis always. It's a fad of mine; and I don't like to break my rule."

The ungraciousness of the tone was evident; but Eileen cared little for that. All she wanted was to escape the humiliation of a public explanation. A cheque would furnish a way out of present difficulties. She could hand it over; and then, later on, she could explain the state of affairs to her creditor without an embarrassing audience.

"Wait a moment and I'll get my cheque-book," she said, rising from her chair. As she turned, she noticed Morchard's eyes fixed upon her and there seemed to be something speculative in his gaze. In his glance she read that he understood the state of affairs perfectly; but she saw no sign of sympathy in his face. Instead, there seemed to be calculation.

She climbed the great staircase, traversed the long

corridor which ran at the back of the main building, and turned down the passage leading to her own room in the rear of the house. In a moment or two she had found her cheque-book, scribbled a cheque, and was back in the drawing-room. So eager was she to avoid an argument in public that she hardly gave a thought to the possible results of her action.

"£206 18s.—is that right?' she asked, passing the slip of paper across to Mrs. Caistor Scorton.

Mrs. Scorton picked up the cheque, glanced at its face to make sure that it was in order, and then put it away. Eric Dangerfield watched her, with an uncomfortable expression, then he turned to his other opponent:

"Give you a cheque, if you don't mind, Morchard," he said. "I'll let you have it to-night or to-morrow—now, if you're anxious."

Morchard was still studying Eileen's face.

"Oh, any time will do," he said, absently. "There's no hurry."

The second bridge-table completed a rubber and the players rose from their seats. Mrs. Brent, in her turn, left her chair and approached the group.

"I think it's growing closer every minute," she said. "Would anyone care to walk in the gardens for a while? I'm going out."

Morchard seized on the suggestion.

"That's a good idea. Care to come down to the Pool, Miss Cressage? It's sure to be cooler there, beside the water."

The girl assented listlessly. Her mind was still busy with the disaster of the evening. What a fool she had been! But calling herself names would hardly help now. She would have to find some way out of the affair; and the raising of £200 was beyond her resources completely. Perhaps Mrs. Caistor Scorton wasn't so bad as she seemed. Possibly she might turn out to be rather a decent person; these surface-hard people often were like that. Of course the money would have to be found eventually; but if time were given, something might be done.

The group moved out on to the terrace in front of the house. Freddie Stickney attached himself to Nina Lindale, and they went off together down into the gardens. Eric Dangerfield, looking worried, approached his uncle and they followed the other two. Morchard and Eileen descended the steps and turned off into one of the side-alleys. Mrs. Brent turned to the remaining two:

"Mr. Morchard's quite right, I think," she said. "If there's any coolness to be had to-night, it will be down at the Pool. Shall we go?"

She looked up at the inky sky with some distrust. Mrs. Caistor Scorton turned back towards the door.

"It looks very like a downpour," she reflected. "I don't think I'll join you. I have to write a note to my bankers and one or two other things, and I may as well do that now."

"Oh, very well," said Mrs. Brent, placidly. "Perhaps you're right. Will you risk it, Mrs. Tuxford?"

They moved off in the track of the two Dangerfields, leaving Mrs. Scorton to return to the house.

"I think we might walk a shade faster," Mrs. Brent suggested in a moment or two. She seemed anxious about something. "I hate moving about at all on a night like this; but I'd really give a good deal for a breath of fresh air. It's like an oven up there at the house; but down beside the water it ought to be cooler. Really, if this spell doesn't break soon I shall simply take French leave and go off in the *Kestrel*."

She pointed towards the bay, where one or two of the yacht's lights flickered upon the water. Mrs. Tuxford nodded understandingly.

"I know how you feel—nerves all ragged. And you've got a headache, too. Don't bother to talk. Let's walk along quietly and see if the air about the Pool will do you any good."

By winding paths they came at last to the edge of the belt of trees which encircled the sheet of water. Just before they emerged from the shadows, Mrs. Brent pulled up and glanced round the Pool. On the further bank, some forty yards off, she caught a glimpse of Eileen Cressage's dress lit up by the moonlight, and a flash of Morchard's shirt-front as he turned a little.

"I think we'll stop," said Mrs. Brent to her companion. "It's cool enough here under the trees."

She fell into a listening attitude:

"Did you hear that bird-call?"

Mrs. Tuxford strained her ears, but heard nothing. Mrs. Brent excused herself with a gesture.

"I always forget that my hearing is sharp. Can't you

even hear those people talking over there? Sound carries far across water."

Again Mrs. Tuxford listened intently.

"Nothing but a murmur," she said.

Mrs. Brent held up a finger.

"There! That bird-call . . . lovely. Do you mind if I listen to it?"

Mrs. Tuxford nodded acquiescence and watched her companion listening intently to something which she herself could not catch. Her eyes wandered to the two figures across the Pool; but they were standing half in the shadows and she could make very little of them.

Just at that moment, as it happened, Morchard was engaged upon a psychological problem very much after his own heart. He had played bridge that evening with a steadily growing satisfaction. To him, Eileen Cressage's face had been an open book; and he had read without difficulty the thoughts which passed through her mind.

"That girl's in difficulties," he had ruminated, as the game progressed. "I know the signs. She'll not be able to pay. I know the Scorton; she'll want her money. Little Cressage hasn't a blue cent. I like these dark-haired, pale-skinned girls, especially when they're rather shy, like her."

The incident of the cheque had been clear as glass.

"The Scorton won't collect much on that, or I'm mistaken. It'll come back with 'Refer to Drawer' on it, sure enough. And the girl knows it, too. She's just staved off trouble for a few hours. That is, unless someone else foots the bill. Two hundred's only a flea-bite."

He had wandered down to the Pool beside Eileen without saying very much. That would give her time to think over things and to realise what a hole she had got herself into. Card debts were things one simply had to pay. At one point only he had broken the silence, and then it was to relate an anecdote of Mrs. Caistor Scorton, an anecdote which brought out to the full the hardness of that lady's character where money was concerned. When they reached the shore, he glanced round to see that no one was within ear-shot. The figures of Mrs. Brent and her companion, hidden in the belt of trees, escaped his eye.

"Sorry you had bad luck to-night, Miss Cressage. Cards were rather against you people."

J. J. CONNINGTON

Eileen Cressage's voice was not quite under control.
She tried to steady it and speak lightly.

"I suppose one must expect that now and again."

"Oh, yes. Your turn last night; ours to-night. Yours
again to-morrow night, very likely. We'll give you a
chance of your revenge then."

Eileen thought of her worthless cheque and shivered a
little. No matter how things went, there would be no
bridge for her next night.

"I don't think I shall play to-morrow," she said,
hesitatingly. "I'm rather tired of bridge."

"Oh! Sorry to hear that. Quite looked forward to
it."

"No; I shan't play any more." She found her lip
quivering and stiffened it with an effort. Morchard had
caught the movement in her moon-lit face. "Shall we go
back to the house?"

"Wait a moment, Miss Cressage, I've something to say."

She turned back towards him and he studied her features
for a moment; then he continued, as though he had just
made a discovery:

"Now I guess what's wrong. I knew something was
up. You're hard up? Isn't that it?"

Eileen's face was sufficient answer. Morchard's voice
became sympathetic.

"Really hard up? That's beastly."

Then, watching her keenly, he appeared to make a fresh
discovery:

"That cheque you handed over to-night, no good, eh?
Overdrawn your account? Well, well."

He drew closer to the girl.

"Look here, Eileen, this is an awkward affair. You've
got yourself into a bad hole. I know the Scorton. She'll
send that cheque off to-night to her bank—no first thing
to-morrow morning. I could see it in her eye. She
suspects it's a dud. And by to-morrow night she'll know
it hasn't been met. And then she'll make a row. She'll
make the devil of a row. I know her."

He paused, letting this sink in.

"You'll need to get out of it somehow."

The girl's defences were down completely. This brute
with his mottled face and close-set eyes had seen the whole
affair. If he knew, everybody else might know also. He
had told her nothing she had not guessed for herself; but

36

the mere putting of it into definite words made it seem a worse business than ever. She made an unconscious gesture as though trying to ward off the catastrophe. Morchard grew more sympathetic.

"Now, listen, Eileen. There's an easy way out. Two hundred's nothing to me; I can easily spare it. I'll lend it to you. You can pay it back any time you like; I shan't miss it. That's all right now. All your worries over! Come to my room to-night and I'll give you a cheque. You can go up to town to-morrow, first thing, and pay it into your bank in time to meet that cheque you gave the Scorton."

Before the girl could reply Mrs. Brent's voice sounded across the water:

"Miss Cressage!"

Eileen started at the call; and, turning, she saw Mrs. Brent and Mrs. Tuxford coming from among the trees.

"Thank goodness, they're too far off to have heard what we were saying," she reflected, measuring the distance with her eye.

Then she called in reply; and she was further relieved to find it difficult to make them hear what she said.

"Have you ever seen a glow-worm?" Mrs. Brent's voice came faintly over the Pool. "Come round and look at this one I've found."

Eileen turned away from Morchard and made her way round the water's edge to where the two women were standing. Morchard followed her sullenly, his anger at the interruption being evident, though he was doing his best to conceal it.

But when Mrs. Brent led them back into the spinney and tried to point out the glow-worm, it had vanished.

"That's a pity," she said, glancing side-long at Morchard as she spoke. "I really thought I had it and could pick it up again easily enough."

She poked about for a moment or two among the grass at the edge of the little wood.

"No, I'm afraid it's escaped. Creatures do get away, unless one keeps an eye on them. And it was such a pretty little thing, too."

This time her face was in the moonlight, and there was no mistaking the mockery in her expression as she turned to Morchard.

"Well, my headache's a little better. Shall we go back

to the house? These wood-paths won't let us walk four abreast, I'm afraid. Mr. Morchard, you and Mrs. Tuxford had better go first."

She stood aside to let them pass. Then, before following them, she whispered a few words to Eileen. The girl nodded and they went up the path in the track of Morchard and his companion. As they came into the gardens, Mrs. Brent noticed Wraxall and old Dangerfield in one of the alleys. The American was talking earnestly, while his host listened to him with his usual polite aloofness. Again Mrs. Brent's face betrayed a flash of mockery; but she made no remark to the girl at her side, and together they passed on towards the house.

She had been quite correct in her reading of the situation. Wraxall, despite her friendly warning, had made up his mind to approach their host with a direct offer for the Dangerfield Talisman. He had shown considerable tact in his manner of introducing the subject, for Mrs. Brent's hints had not been lost upon him. But, just as she had predicted, he met with an uncompromising refusal.

"Part with our Talisman, Mr. Wraxall? It's out of the question!"

The American tried to work round the flank of the defence.

"One moment, Mr. Dangerfield, before you make up your mind definitely. Perhaps I could say something to alter your views. I'm a collector. I'm not the keeper of a public museum. I want your Talisman for its own sake. I want it for itself and for myself. I shouldn't put it in a show-case with a ticket on it. No one would know that you had transferred it. The matter would be entirely between ourselves—completely private."

Rollo Dangerfield halted for a moment in his stride.

"And how would you propose to account for its disappearance from Friocksheim, then? Anyone looking at our empty cabinet would know that it had gone."

Wraxall had his solution ready.

"A replica, of course. That could be made in a few days, by these modern electro-plating methods; and paste stones could be put in, instead of the real ones. It would serve well enough. It wouldn't be spotted, Mr. Dangerfield, if you kept it out of people's hands. You'd never talk; I wouldn't talk; no one would ever know."

Rollo Dangerfield turned in the moonlight.

"That's a very ingenious idea, Mr. Wraxall. But the Talisman is not for sale."

The American apparently had not quite given up his project.

"Well, think it over," he begged. "No one would ever know. It would only be a case of borrowing the Talisman for a day or two, to get the replica made. Then you put the replica into the cabinet; I get the Talisman, and nobody's any the wiser. Think it over again."

Rollo Dangerfield seemed deep in thought. He made no reply, and they walked on once more. On the horizon a faint flicker of sheet-lightning illumined the sky, heralding the coming storm. As they turned back towards Friocksheim, the moon slipped behind the edge of the thunder-cloud.

CHAPTER IV

DOUGLAS FAIRMILE, coming down to breakfast next morning, found Nina and Cynthia already at table.

"Good morning, Douglas," Cynthia greeted him. "You don't seem quite your usual bright self to-day. A trifle heavy-eyed and even duller-looking than usual. Did the thunder keep you awake?"

"Rather! My sensitive temperament, you know. High strung and all that. The least things puts me off my sleep."

Cynthia looked him over with mock sympathy.

"Ah! Neurasthenic, no doubt. It's hard lines on these healthy-looking people, Nina; their nerves are all fiddlestrings, really, but they get no sympathy because they look so frightfully robust. Observe, however, the leaden eye, the trembling hand. He'll be biting a bit out of his tea-cup if we don't manage to soothe him."

"I'd just love to have you for a nurse if I went sick," Douglas affirmed. "And the toast, please, since you happen to be so handy to it. Thanks. I suppose the storm passed quite unnoticed at your end of the house?"

"No, indeed," Nina said, nervously. "It gave me the fright of my life. I had to creep away to Cynthia's room for comfort. I hate thunder, especially when it comes near."

"It was near enough last night. One of the trees in the garden was struck. You can see it from the door."

"That must have been the peal that drove me out of my wits, then. I knew it was close at hand."

"Well, it's cleared the air, that's one good thing," said Douglas, glancing through the window at the big white clouds sailing in the blue. "All the stuffiness has gone now. This is going to be a day for careful enjoyment, too good to waste on mere reckless frivolity."

He looked sternly at Cynthia.

"I do love Friocksheim," said Nina, irrelevantly. "It's

a place where one can do just as one likes and no one bothers about things."

"What about borrowing the *Kestrel* and going up the coast until the afternoon?" suggested Cynthia. "Mrs. Brent would let us have it if we asked her."

Douglas glanced again through the window.

"Hullo! She's gone!"

"What a nuisance!" Cynthia looked over the empty waters of the bay. "Mrs. Brent said something last night about going off in the yacht, but I didn't think she meant it. She's evidently taken the *Kestrel* herself, though. That notion's knocked on the head."

The door opened to admit Freddie Stickney. Even as he came in, they could see that he was preparing a sensation for them. His prying little eyes ran over the group, estimating the character of his audience.

"Heard the latest?" he demanded, importantly.

"Spare us the usual preliminaries, Freddie," Douglas implored. "Don't drag out the agony. Flop right in at the deep end. If it's an earthquake in Frogsholme or any other little thing like that, why, just give us the simple tale in the fewest words."

Freddie Stickney seemed to feel that his sensation was big enough to let him follow Douglas's advice. He came to the point without more ado.

"The Talisman's been stolen," he announced, with a certain undercurrent of malicious enjoyment in his voice. "That's a nasty knock for the Dangerfields."

For a moment his three hearers failed to take in his news.

"The Talisman?" exclaimed Nina. "You don't mean to say somebody's taken it?"

Freddy confirmed his statement with a smile.

"Are you sure about this, Freddie, or is it just some rot you're making up?" demanded Douglas.

"Quite sure about it. I've been to look at the cabinet where it's kept, to make certain; and it's gone. No sign of it."

Cynthia looked distressed.

"That's a bad business, isn't it? Poor Mr. Dangerfield! The Talisman's the thing he values most in the world, I should think. He'll be fearfully cut up."

"Oh, he'll be all that," agreed Freddie, unsympathetically. "But it's a beastly nuisance. Friocksheim will be swarming with police and detectives—probably unofficial 'tecs as well. The Dangerfields will do anything to get the thing back again, you can bet. It'll be most unpleasant for all of us. They'll expect us to turn out our suit-cases to see that none of us has taken it."

"Well, what's the harm in that?" inquired Cynthia. "They can do what they like, so far as I'm concerned. The main thing is to get the thing back again. I suppose they'll get it back in a day or two?"

Douglas looked doubtful.

"Depends who's taken it, Cynthia. There's no saying. But perhaps it hasn't been stolen at all," he ended hopefully. "It may just have been taken away to be cleaned or something like that."

"Wrong, there," said Freddie, with a self-satisfied air. "It's been stolen. I managed to worm that out of the butler."

"Oh, did you?" Douglas's expression showed what he thought of Freddie's methods.

"Yes. At least, I got enough from him to put two and two together. There's been a theft of some sort, whether it was burglary or stealing from inside the house."

"What a horrible business!" Nina was evidently upset by the affair. "It'll be a terrible shock for the Dangerfields, won't it? I do hope they get it back again almost at once. I wish it hadn't happened. I do wish it hadn't happened!"

Freddie stared at her in a patronising way.

"I shouldn't worry over it. It's really the Dangerfields' own fault for taking no precautions. Fancy leaving the thing standing about in that open cabinet, ready for anyone to lift! One can't have much sympathy with them, after all."

"I think I can spare a little," Cynthia commented, icily.

Freddie had a further tit-bit which he had held in reserve.

"Oh, I don't think so," he said. "Why, they never took the trouble to insure the thing. That's inexcusable carelessness. Really, they seem to deserve all they've got."

Douglas leaned forward in surprise.

"Do you mean to say, Freddie, that the thing wasn't insured?"

"So I believe," asserted Freddie. "I got it out of the butler before he realised what he was saying."

Douglas passed this explanation without comment.

"Why, the thing's impossible! The stones in the Talisman are worth more than £50,000. Nobody would dream of keeping a thing like that uninsured!"

"Well, you'll find I'm right," said Freddie, weightily. "And that's why we shall be flooded out with police and detectives. Obviously they've simply got to get it back. Nobody cares to lose £50,000."

Nina was plainly taken aback by the figure.

"I should think not. I'd no idea it was worth so much. What a loss for poor Mr. Dangerfield."

"Well, he'll have to stand it, if the thing isn't recovered," said Freddie, philosophically.

"It makes me frightfully nervous," admitted Nina. "Just think, Cynthia, that burglar may have been prowling about near us in the night. It gives me the creeps!"

"Oh, that's all over now," Cynthia soothed her. "You're too nervous, Nina. If it had been a burglar, he's not in the least likely to come back again. You can sleep quite quietly so far as that goes."

Freddie hastened to play the part of consoler.

"I don't think you need worry. There's nothing much else in the house. The Dangerfields haven't a big stock of jewellery. The Talisman was about the only thing worth taking in the whole place."

"Well, I'm ever so sorry about it," Nina reaffirmed. "It makes everything different to-day. Friocksheim won't be the same, with this hanging over it. How could one enjoy oneself when this has happened?"

"Oh, one does what one can," Freddie reassured her. "Worrying won't help."

"That's right, Freddie," commented Douglas, contemptuously. "Have your principles, and act according! The stern, unbending Roman touch, eh?"

"Where's Mrs. Caistor Scorton?" inquired Freddie.

He was evidently anxious to find a fresh auditor for this news.

"She was just finishing her breakfast when I came down," volunteered Nina. "I think she's gone out."

Freddie was plainly disappointed by this information.

"She must have been down a good deal earlier than usual," he grumbled. "Where's Wraxall?"

"Not down yet," said Douglas. "I expect the storm kept him awake like the rest of us, and he's been putting in some extra sleep. He'll be down later on."

He glanced at the two girls, and all three rose.

"Well, ta-ta, Freddie. We're leaving you in the best of company, so you'll excuse us if we go."

Freddie's expression showed that he saw the irony without appreciating it.

"See you later," he snapped, going on with his breakfast as the others filed out of the room.

On that day Wraxall awoke later than usual and dressed with a certain leisureliness. He had been about during the small hours of the morning; and even after he went to bed, some time had elapsed before he managed to fall asleep. On reaching the breakfast-room at last, he was not altogether pleased to find Freddie Stickney the only other occupant.

"Thunder keep you awake too?" demanded Freddie, as Wraxall took his seat. "Cleared the air, anyway. That's one blessing."

"I sat up and watched the storm," said the American, shortly.

"Frightful racket, wasn't it?" Freddie inquired.

Wraxall nodded vaguely and attacked his breakfast.

"Heard the great news?" persisted Freddie, not to be baulked.

Wraxall, who preferred to breakfast peacefully, looked across the table with an expression of the very faintest interest.

"News?" he asked. "No. I haven't seen a paper yet My doctor tells me it's better to read later on. He advises me to concentrate at breakfast-time. I share his views. I believe he's right."

Freddie ignored the hint.

"Oh, it's not in the papers. It's a Friocksheim tit-bit, exclusive. The Dangerfield Talisman's been stolen!"

If he expected to read anything in the American's face, he was disappointed. Wraxall's lean countenance betrayed no emotion of any sort, not even surprise. He continued to masticate stolidly for a few moments, as though excluding all extraneous ideas. Freddie felt that a good item of news had been wasted.

"How do you know it's been stolen?" inquired Wraxall, at length.

"Well, it's gone, at any rate."

Wraxall glanced across the table.

"That's hardly the same thing, Mr. Stickney. If I drop a dollar in the street without noticing it, the dollar's gone; but it isn't necessarily stolen. When I send a clock to be cleaned, it's gone too; but the clock-maker isn't a thief for all that. Let's be accurate, if *you* please."

This was hardly the reception Freddie had anticipated.

"Well, it's gone, at any rate," he repeated. "And if it's gone, somebody must have taken it. It didn't walk off by itself. And if anybody took it, that's theft, isn't it?"

Wraxall appeared to consider this proposition with some care before replying.

"No," he replied, after a pause. "No, I'd hardly care to go so far as that. Hardly. Mr. Rollo Dangerfield may have taken it—that wouldn't be theft, since it belongs to him. Somebody may have borrowed it—borrowing isn't theft. No, it seems to me you're rather apt to jump to conclusions, Mr. Stickney. I can't follow you to that length."

Freddie Stickney flushed slightly. This confounded Yank was evidently presuming to pull his leg. Freddie contented himself with a reiteration of his former remark:

"Well, it's gone, at any rate."

As he said it, his eyes swept the American's face, and for an instant he seemed to catch a glimpse of something going on behind the mask. Wraxall was evidently perturbed and his eyes showed that he was thinking hard, though his face gave no clue to the subject which occupied him.

Freddie relapsed for a time into sulky silence, and Wraxall was able to continue his meal undisturbed. From time to time, Freddie's beady eyes ranged round to the American's face; but its set expression betrayed nothing to him. Freddie began to contrast the reception which Wraxall had given to his news with the outburst of sympathy for the Dangerfields which had come from Douglas and the girls.

"Something very fishy about this fellow," he thought to himself. "One would almost think it wasn't news to him at all. And why is he so anxious to make out that it isn't a case of theft? That's very rum."

Freddie chewed the cud of this idea for a minute or two; but at last, feeling the lack of conversation to be too great a strain, he tried another opening.

"Very few at breakfast to-day."

The American glanced round the empty table, but made no audible comment.

"Three of the party went off first thing this morning," Freddie continued. "Mrs. Brent's away in the *Kestrel*. Didn't wait to say good-bye to me."

At last a gleam of interest crossed the American's face. "Mrs. Brent's gone? Now, I'm sorry to hear that, Mr. Stickney. I shall miss her. She's a most understanding person. I'm sorry. But perhaps she's only gone for the day?"

Freddie Stickney had to admit ignorance.

"She didn't leave any message about when she'd be back. And Eileen Cressage went off by the first train. But she'll be back to-night, most likely. So will young Dangerfield. He's gone, too."

Wraxall nodded, but said nothing. Freddie was emboldened to proceed.

"Funny—their going just when the Talisman's disappeared—isn't it? The Dangerfield Luck gone and all of them clear out at once. Like rats leaving a sinking ship, what? It seems rum, doesn't it?"

The American's brief spell of interest in Freddie's conversation came abruptly to an end. This time there was no doubt about it. Freddie's latest news item must have started a fresh train of thought in Wraxall's mind, and he was devoting his whole attention to following it out. Freddie attempted to break in once or twice, but received no encouragement beyond absent-minded nods which might have meant anything; so at last he rose and left the room.

46

CHAPTER V

AFTER Freddie Stickney had closed the door behind him, Wraxall frankly abandoned any pretence of being interested in his food. He pushed back his chair slightly and seemed to concentrate his whole mind for a time upon some intricate problem.

"I'd better see the old man as soon as I can," he said half aloud, at one point in his train of thought. "The first thing to do is to see how the land lies. It's a tight position."

But a final solution of his problem evidently evaded him; and when he got up and went in search of his host, it was clear that he still remained in doubt about something.

"I'll get it over, at least," he said to himself.

In spite of his age, Rollo Dangerfield was an early riser, compared with some of his guests. He had breakfasted an hour before, and Wraxall found him in the morning-room, engrossed in a newspaper. As his guest came in, Rollo put the sheet aside and looked up.

"Terrible storm last night, Mr. Wraxall. I hope it didn't keep you awake through half the night."

"I like storms," the American assured him. "I sat up a good part of the night to watch that one. It would have been a pity to miss it. I enjoyed it—immensely. The effects were very fine at times, Mr. Dangerfield, very fine indeed. A magnificent spectacle."

Rollo Dangerfield seemed relieved that his guest had suffered no inconvenience.

"I wish everybody could say the same," he said. "Poor Mrs. Brent didn't share your enthusiasm, I'm afraid. She's peculiarly sensitive to electrical conditions—always has been so. Her nerves seem to go all to pieces in a storm, and I think that one last night affected her badly. She went off in the *Kestrel* this morning before any of us were up, and I expect she'll stay away until she gets back to normal again."

47

The American paused a moment or two before replying. "I'm sorry to hear that. She didn't strike me as a nervous type. I should have said she was very well balanced, if you'd asked my opinion."

"Each of us has his own special weakness," said the old man phlegmatically. "Some people can't stand cats, for some reason. I dislike house spiders intensely myself, though I can't give you any grounds for my aversion. In Mrs. Brent's case, it seems to be thunder and lightning. A storm shakes her completely."

Wraxall let the subject drop. Old Dangerfield puzzled him at this moment. Of course the English had the knack of concealing their feelings; but he had expected something different in Rollo this morning, if the story about the Talisman were true. He resolved on a direct attack.

"I met young Stickney at breakfast. He said something about the Talisman."

Old Dangerfield let his newspaper slip from his hand as though he were tired of holding it.

"Freddie? Oh, Freddie can be trusted to know all about everything. He's often right, too, quite often. Yes, the Talisman's gone."

The old man's voice was completely indifferent; he might have been discussing some matter of no especial concern, for all the interest that showed in his tone. The American was taken aback. These English, he reflected, don't give much away. Here was a man who had lost overnight the thing that he evidently valued as the first among his possessions; and yet he showed less emotion than he might have done if a cat had gone astray. Wraxall's opinion of Rollo Dangerfield went up considerably. There was a dignity behind this indifference which impressed him deeply. No fuss, no excitement to be seen. The thing was gone; but the old man could hold himself in. His guests wouldn't be disturbed by him. Everything would go on as usual at Friocksheim. Rollo Dangerfield evidently carried the courtesy of a host to the extreme.

"That's a big loss," said Wraxall, slowly. "But I expect you're counting on getting it back. It would be difficult to dispose of. It would certainly be hard to sell. Still . . . aren't you sorry you didn't close with my offer last night?"

Rollo Dangerfield turned an inscrutable face to his guest.

"Sorry I didn't sell the Talisman while I had it? No, it never was for sale. The matter didn't arise."

48

The American persisted.

"I suppose the police have some clue?"

The old man shrugged his shoulders slightly.

"The police have nothing to do with it. How could they have a clue?"

Wraxall was frankly astonished.

"You haven't called them in? Why, I should have thought the very first thing to do would be to get them to work while the scent was fresh?"

A faint shade of irritation showed in Rollo Dangerfield's eyes, the first sign of emotion the American had seen. But when he spoke, his voice was as indifferent as before.

"Why should we call in the police? The Talisman will find its way home without their help. Would you bring the police among your guests, stir up trouble, make everyone uncomfortable with suspicions and cross-questioning? No, Mr. Wraxall, we shan't need the police at Friocksheim. I told you so, before the Talisman disappeared, and you obviously didn't believe me. But you see now that you were mistaken; I meant what I said."

The American was shrewd enough to see what had given offence. Old Dangerfield resented the slight on his veracity much more than the loss of the Talisman. He made amends frankly.

"Quite right, Mr. Dangerfield. Honestly, I thought you were just leading us on, that night. I took it that you were pulling my leg. It seemed to me that perhaps it was one of your English jokes, just put out to see if the stranger would swallow it. We often do that ourselves, over there. But I see you mean it, right enough, now."

Rollo Dangerfield reassured him with a faint smile.

"I see your point of view. I ought to have thought of it in that light."

Wraxall considered for a moment or two before speaking again.

"I think I see what's in your mind," he said, going back to the earlier subject. "You've reason to suspect somebody in particular—one of the maids, perhaps—and you don't want a fuss?"

"I don't suspect any of the maids—or any of the servants," Rollo Dangerfield replied instantly. "That's quite out of the question. I can tell you why. We have a number of old habits at Friocksheim, and fortunately one of them has enabled us to clear our servants of any suspicion in this affair."

He took out his case and lit a cigar before continuing.

"The servants' quarters are all in the west wing of the house, and there is only one door communicating between their section and the other part of the building. That door has a special lock, of which only the butler has a key, and it is his duty at half-past eleven every night to see that that door is secured. After that, no servant can get into this part of the house without his knowledge."

"And the butler himself?" demanded the American.

"The butler's great-grandfather was born on the estate and for four generations we have known absolutely everything about the family. This man has been in our service since he was a boy, and a more absolutely honest man you couldn't find anywhere. You may put him completely out of your calculations, Mr. Wraxall. I say that definitely, because the man can't speak for himself. Not a trace of suspicion could attach to him. Now are you satisfied?"

Wraxall nodded his acquiescence. Then he asked a further question.

"How did you hear that the Talisman had gone?"

"The butler told me this morning. His first business is to go round the house after he has unlocked the communicating door. When he went into the Corinthian's Room he noticed that the Talisman case was open, and the jewel was gone. He came at once and told me."

"And you suspect nobody, then?"

Rollo Dangerfield raised himself slightly in his chair and looked round directly at Wraxall's face. For the first time, the American saw a keenness in the old man's blue eyes, though their expression was inscrutable.

"No, I suspect nobody. I have no evidence, and I do not wish to collect any. The Talisman will be back in its place within a week; and that is the only important thing in the case. For all I know, the whole affair may be a practical joke. Some of these young folks may have taken it into their heads to test the Dangerfield legend."

His eyes scanned the American's features; but Wraxall betrayed nothing under the scrutiny. Rollo Dangerfield pulled at his cigar before continuing.

"I can imagine one of these youngsters playing a practical joke like that. Take away the Talisman and see what old Dangerfield will say! It's quite possible that somebody"

—he glanced again at the American—"may even now be wishing he had left the thing alone and may be looking for a chance to replace it under the bell. It's an awkward thing to have in one's possession—even innocently. Well, they can easily put it back again, if they wish to do so. Nobody's watching the Corinthian's Room."

A faintly sardonic expression crossed his face.

"Don't distress yourself unduly about the Talisman, Mr. Wraxall. It will come home quite safely in the end; you may take my word for that."

With a gesture as though asking permission, he picked up his newspaper again. Wraxall accepted the tacit dismissal and wandered out into the sunlit gardens. The interview had given him a good deal to think about, apparently. He avoided the other guests and spent a considerable time in going over old Dangerfield's words, so far as he could remember them.

"I wonder," he said to himself at last. "I wonder if the old man suspects anything. One or two of these remarks might have been directed to my address, though he was clever enough to give them an inoffensive turn. If he really suspects me, it looks like being a pretty kettle of fish. It certainly looks like that."

He thought it tactful to absent himself for the rest of the day, taking his car and visiting some of the local antiquities which he wished to see. It was dinner-time before he met his fellow-guests once more.

Eileen Cressage had returned, and Westenhanger came into the room immediately after her. As they sat down, Freddie Stickney's eyes travelled round the table, obviously counting the number, and a certain disappointment appeared in his face when he found only twelve persons present. Eric Dangerfield and Mrs. Brent were still away.

"You and Mr. Westenhanger came up by the same train, didn't you, Miss Cressage?" asked Mrs. Dangerfield.

Westenhanger caught the question which Eileen had missed.

"Yes. I happened to run across Miss Cressage just as she was coming out of Starbecks the jewellers. We had just time to get to the station."

Freddie Stickney's sharp ears caught the careless remark.

"Starbecks?" he said, lifting his voice to make it carry down the table. "That's a convenient firm. They'll give you a reasonable advance on any little bit of jewellery you don't happen to need for a time. Sort of superior brand of West End Uncle, aren't they? I've dealt with them once or twice myself and always found them generous."

Freddie was quite shameless in money matters. But his deliberately pitched sentences reached Eileen Cressage's ears; and Freddie, keenly on the look-out, noticed that the girl flushed uncomfortably.

"That shot went home," he reflected, complacently. "One can always get the information one wants if one goes about it tactfully. She's been doing a bit of quiet pawning this afternoon. That's interesting. I wonder what she put away in store. She never wore any jewellery here."

He ruminated on this problem for a time, keeping his sharp eyes on the girl's face; but nothing further of interest fell into his net during the meal.

As they passed into the drawing-room after dinner, Mrs. Caistor Scorton picked up a telegram addressed to her which was lying in the hall. At the sight of it, Morchard's face lighted up with interest and he examined her closely while she read it. He edged himself up to Eileen and put a question in a low voice:

"The Scorton's got her telegram about your cheque. Is it all right?"

"Quite all right, thank you," said the girl, coldly.

She moved away from him immediately, and as she sat down, Conway Westenhanger came up.

"Have a game at bridge, Miss Cressage? They're making up a table and I've reserved a place for you."

"No, thanks. I'd rather not play."

Mrs. Caistor Scorton passed close to them and Eileen made a gesture to catch her attention.

"You found my cheque all right, Mrs. Scorton?"

Westenhanger, to his surprise, detected more than a tinge of irony in the question. Mrs. Caistor Scorton seemed taken aback for a moment; but she recovered herself almost at once:

"Oh, quite all right, quite all right," she confirmed shortly, and passed on to the bridge-table.

Eileen Cressage knitted her brows slightly as she looked after her. At any rate, she had got out of that difficulty. Morchard had been quite right. The woman had obviously sent the cheque off to her bank and asked them to wire if it had been met. That apparently inevitable scandal had passed over safely. She glanced across at Morchard and an angrier flash came into her eyes. She knew what sort of a person he was, too.

Freddie Stickney drifted over and sat down between her and Westenhanger.

"Heard the news, you two? The Talisman's out of print, it seems. No copies available for the public. Somebody's taken a fancy to it and simply lifted it. That's a fine end to all the Dangerfield talk, isn't it?"

With a certain ill-suppressed maliciousness, he gave them all the information he had collected during the day.

"Just as well you were away last night, Westenhanger," he wound up. "You're clear of suspicion. But all the rest of us are in it up to the neck. Servants exonerated without a stain on their character. Strong suspicion attaches to every guest. That's how the land lies."

"Oh, indeed, Freddie," said Westenhanger. "Then, if we must suspect somebody, we may as well begin with yourself. What about it? Anything you say will be used against you at the trial, without regard for age or sex. Where's my note-book?"

"It's all very well for you," protested Freddie. "You're out of it all. But what about the rest of us? It's a nasty idea to feel that the person sitting next to you in this room may be a thief."

Westenhanger looked him up and down for a moment before replying.

"If I were you, Freddie, I don't think I'd begin flinging words like 'thief' about quite so early in the day. These things are apt to be resented by some people. Isn't there any other possible explanation?"

Freddie pondered for a while in silence, then he made a half-hearted suggestion:

"It might be a practical joke."

Westenhanger considered the idea and rejected it almost immediately.

"I shouldn't like to have the taste of the man who played a joke of that sort. Who's your humorist? Douglas is the funny man of the company, but Douglas wouldn't play a trick of that sort on anyone. That's certain. Morchard hasn't that kind of mind. The American has a sense of humour, but not that sort, I'm sure. You don't attribute it to one of the girls, do you? No? Well, then, that leaves us with . . . let's see . . . with Mr. Frederick

Stickney as the only possible culprit. I don't think much of your taste in humour, Freddie, and that's a fact."

"All the same," said Eileen Cressage, "I'd prefer it to be a case of practical joking rather than the other thing. Perhaps it will all come right and we shall find the Talisman back again in a few days, just as Mr. Dangerfield said."

Freddie had recovered from Westenhanger's attack.

"Well, I'm going to find out who did it," he declared. "As things stand, we're all under a cloud. I'm going to get the whole lot into the billiard-room later on, if I can, away from the Dangerfields; and I shall put it to them straight that each person ought to account for his doings during the night. Nobody could object to that."

He glanced at the girl for support and was surprised to see her flush and turn away as though to conceal her face.

"I don't think you'll be altogether popular if you start that kind of thing, Mr. Stickney," she said.

Freddie's bright little eyes fastened themselves on her face; and his well-trained mind automatically set to work to draw inferences from what he saw. As his friend had said, Freddie's inferences always tended to discredit somebody or something. He had sense enough, however, to leave his conclusions unspoken.

"It's a silly idea, Freddie," said Westenhanger, abruptly.

He also had noticed the girl's flush; but the only inference he had cared to draw was that Freddie was making her uncomfortable.

"I can't agree with you." Freddie was emboldened by the girl's embarrassment. "I think everyone would be only too glad to exonerate themselves from suspicion. We oughtn't to be left under a cloud if we can clear ourselves straight off. Decidedly not. I shall insist on it; and I'll point out what it will look like if anyone refuses."

He got up and walked away from them without waiting for a reply.

Westenhanger looked across at Eileen and was puzzled by the distress which he still found in her face.

"That little beast will make trouble unless he gets his way. Miss Cressage, I think I'll have to attend his proposed inquest myself. It seems to be the occasion where an impartial and disinterested person might be useful."

Eileen glanced at his face for a moment. He was relieved to find that she met his eye squarely and showed no signs of flinching.

"I think that would be a good plan, Mr. Westenhanger."

"Well, I suppose we shall have to go through with it, if he gets his way. And he's pretty sure to arrange it, you know. That suggestion that it will look black if anyone refuses is pretty sure to rake in most of them, and the rest can't stand out after that, even if they wished to."

CHAPTER VI

"Now," said Freddie Stickney, "I think we can begin."

He had been as good as his word. Each guest had been approached by him apart from the rest; and the appropriate hint, insinuation, or appeal, had been skilfully employed. They had all come, willingly or not, and Freddie had them at his mercy. His beady little eyes, bright as those of a mouse, glanced from face to face in an attempt to read the expressions. Already, he judged, most of them were uncomfortable; and the production of discomfort was Freddie's strong card. He cleared his throat gently in preparation for his opening statement of the case as he saw it; but just at that moment the door clicked and Westenhanger stepped into the room.

"Look here, Westenhanger, you can't come in just now," protested Freddie, who augured little good from the engineer's presence. "This is a private affair."

Westenhanger stared at him with admirably acted surprise.

"Are you getting up a charade to amuse the Dangerfield family, or something like that? I don't think much of the notion, but I'm quite game to join if all the rest of you are in it. Go ahead; don't let me interrupt."

He selected a chair near Eileen Cressage and sat down. Freddie bit his lip in vexation. Westenhanger's entrance had taken him aback; he had not bargained for the presence of anyone except those who came under suspicion. For a moment he thought of arguing the point and contesting Westenhanger's right to be there at all; but a glance at the engineer's face showed him the uselessness of any such attempt. Quite obviously Westenhanger meant to sit through the business.

"Get on with it, Freddie," directed Douglas Fairmile, impatiently. "You can't expect us to sit here all night merely to look at you, can you?"

Freddie cleared his throat again, and launched into his

exposition; but the two interruptions had flustered him a little and he failed to make his points tell as heavily as he had hoped.

"You all know the Dangerfield Talisman's disappeared. The burglar alarms were all found correctly set in the morning, so obviously nobody could have got into the house from the outside. That limits the thing down to the people in the house. I think that's plain."

"Quite plain," commented Westenhanger. "Self-evident, in fact. Proceed, Freddie."

"The inmates of the house can be divided into three . . ."

"Just like ancient Gaul, eh?" Douglas explained.

Freddie scowled at the interruption and repeated his phrases.

"The inmates can be divided into three groups. First, there's the Dangerfields themselves; second, the servants; third, the guests—ourselves. The Dangerfields don't come into the matter. There's no reason why any of them should take away the Talisman. Then it's a fact that none of the servants can be suspected. At least, so the Dangerfields say, and they ought to know. That leaves ourselves. One of us must have taken it."

He glanced round the group in the hope that, even at this early stage in the inquiry, someone might betray himself. Morchard was leaning back in his chair, lazily following the movement of a smoke-ring which he had blown by accident. Mrs. Caistor Scorton was obviously bored. Nina and Cynthia were trying to repress smiles—evidently the results of some whispered aside by Douglas which Freddie had failed to catch. As for Wraxall, even an expert poker player could have made nothing of his inscrutable mask. Eileen Cressage looked white and tired; and there was something in her face that encouraged Freddie to think that here he had found the weak point in the circle. Quite evidently she dreaded something to come, but she seemed to be hoping that the danger might yet be averted. Westenhanger, of course, showed nothing since he was the solitary individual whose innocence was beyond doubt.

"Now there are two possible explanations of the Talisman's disappearance," Freddie continued. "One is, that it's due to a practical joke. We all know how the Dangerfields boast about taking no precautions with the Talisman. Somebody here may have wanted to give them a lesson about that. That's a possibility. But if that's the explanation, I think we have something to say. Joke or no joke, the thing's gone, and until it turns up again, every one of us is under suspicion of theft. Every one of us!"

He glanced round the faces once more, but still no one betrayed any definite sign of guilt. Eileen Cressage's expression puzzled him. She looked up and caught his eyes for a moment, but it was he who turned away first, so manifest was the dislike in her glance. Quite evidently the girl had something to conceal, and Freddie grew more determined to bring it to light, whatever it was.

"Just a moment, Mr. Stickney!" the American interrupted as Freddie was about to continue. "Let's be accurate, if *you* please. You said 'Every one of us.' That's not correct. Mr. Westenhanger can't be included. He couldn't have had any hand in the affair, on your own showing."

The engineer acknowledged the American's statement with a quick smile. Wraxall, evidently, was a kindred spirit, bent on spoiling Freddie's little effects.

"Very well," snapped Freddie. "Then it's one of us here, excluding Westenhanger."

Rather to Westenhanger's surprise, Morchard joined the critics.

"Wrong again," he declared, weightily. "Mrs. Brent was in the house that night; and she isn't here. I agree with Mr. Wraxall. Let's be accurate."

"Well, well," snarled Freddie, "have it as you like. The main point is that everyone here, bar one, is under suspicion. And whether it's a practical joke or not, it looks like plain theft. And that's a very unpleasant business, very unpleasant to us all—to myself at any rate. It's very unfair. And if this thing isn't cleared up as soon as possible it'll leave a permanent stain on our characters. You know how people talk."

"I hear you, Freddie," interjected Douglas, and Freddie was annoyed to see Nina Lindale's lips twitch in a repressed smile.

"It's no laughing matter," he said, indignantly. "Far from it. Somebody in Friocksheim took the Talisman, that's certain. Now all I suggest is that we should each voluntarily account for our time during the period when the thing was stolen. That's no hardship to anyone.

I'm quite glad to do it myself; and I'm sure everyone else in my position will be just as glad. If anyone here took the Talisman, let him say so now and we won't need to go any further."

He fixed his eye on Douglas Fairmile as he spoke, more by accident than design.

"Meaning me?" inquired Douglas. "Try again, doggie. You're barking up the wrong tree. I never touched the thing in my life."

Freddie ignored the interruption.

"Nobody admits they did it as a joke?" he demanded. "Then it's much worse. It's theft, pure and simple. We owe it to ourselves to clear the thing up. At any rate, that's my view, and I think it will be the view of everybody in my position to-night."

To Freddie's surprise Morchard came to his assistance.

"There's something in that," he admitted. "I doubt if it'll lead to anything; but since the thing's been allowed to go so far, I don't see any harm in letting anyone who wishes it, do as you suggest."

Freddie, looking at Eileen Cressage, saw her shoot a glance at Morchard; but as she turned her head to do so, he could not see her expression. When she turned back again he had no difficulty in reading consternation in her face. She detected that he was watching her and endeavoured, with very little success, to assume an indifferent attitude. Westenhanger also had caught the by-play, and his face clouded.

"Suppose you begin, then," Freddie suggested to Morchard.

Morchard seemed rather annoyed at being directly attacked, but he gave a nod of acquiescence.

"Most of us went upstairs together, you remember. That would be about a quarter to twelve or so. I didn't look at my watch, so I can't make it closer. Anyway, it must have been about then. We've always been pretty early at Friocksheim. Then I undressed and went to bed—midnight, say. And I woke up as usual in the morning. That's all. Help you much, Stickney?"

Freddie ignored the query and glanced round to see if anyone else would volunteer. Mrs. Caistor Scorton sat up in her chair.

"I went to my room as usual—about a quarter to twelve, as Mr. Morchard says. Some people came up a little later. I heard steps in the corridor and the sounds of doors shutting. There was some talking in low voices and more doors shut. Then the whole house was quiet. I looked out of the window for a short time, wondering if the storm was coming at last. Then I heard a noise as if someone had stumbled on the mat outside my door. I opened the door quietly and looked out. It was Miss Cressage. She was carrying a lighted candle and by the time I got the door open she was a good distance down the passage. I didn't call after her, but just shut my door again. I looked at my watch to see how late it was, and I remember it was a quarter past twelve. After a time I undressed and went to bed. The next thing I can remember is waking up as usual."

Westenhanger was completely taken aback by this evidence. What could a girl be doing, wandering about the house at that time of night? Almost without thinking, he swung round on Mrs. Caistor Scorton and put a question.

"You're sure it was Miss Cressage?"

"Quite sure," said Mrs. Caistor Scorton, composedly. "She was wearing her dressing-gown and bedroom slippers. No one else has a silk dressing-gown of that shade."

Eileen Cressage had gone very white during Mrs. Caistor Scorton's evidence, but she made no comment. Westenhanger, looking at her momentarily, saw that she had been completely surprised. At the same time, her attitude suggested that she might have something in reserve, though she was not very confident about it. Freddie Stickney in his turn put a question to Mrs. Caistor Scorton.

"You said she was 'going down the passage.' What does that mean?"

"Miss Cressage's room is beyond mine. She was going away from it when I saw her."

"Oh, I see," said Freddie. "You mean that she was going along the corridor in the direction of the bachelors' wing?"

Westenhanger saw Eileen start in her chair at this elucidation by Freddie, but she evidently held herself in with an almost physical effort.

"Why on earth doesn't she say something?" he wondered to himself. "I'd stake any money that she's straight, and yet she lets that little swine go on unchecked with his insinuations. I can't understand it."

Whether she wished it or not, Mrs. Caistor Scorton had

changed the whole atmosphere. Up to the moment when she began to speak, the affair had been handled in an almost frivolous spirit. Freddie Stickney had been making a fool of himself, and no one liked him sufficiently to feel troubled by that aspect of the matter. Even the Talisman theft had not weighed over heavily as a personal thing, for nobody had any formulated suspicions in his mind. But Mrs. Caistor Scorton, in half a dozen sentences, had brought them face to face with a new problem, and the silence of the girl made it difficult to find innocuous explanations. Something ugly had reared up in the midst of what, to most of them, had been little more than a joke Eileen's white, strained face, and her attitude of a creature at bay, had taken away all humour from the situation. Freddie Stickney had achieved a masterpiece in the creation of discomfort. Westenhanger could see Douglas Fairmile's face, and in its expression he read the twin of his own feelings.

The American broke the silence, before its awkwardness grew too obvious.

"You mean that Miss Cressage was going towards the head of the main staircase, I suppose?"

Mrs. Caistor Scorton nodded without speaking.

"I understand it better when it's put in that way," said Wraxall, bluntly.

Eileen Cressage threw him a glance in which Westenhanger recognised gratitude. The American had taken the edge off the situation, to some extent, by his intervention. But a moment's reflection showed Westenhanger that Wraxall had merely turned the matter into a fresh and difficult channel. Down the staircase was the way to the Corinthian's Room and the Talisman.

Before anyone else could interpose comments, Wraxall again threw himself into the breach:

"My tale's more elaborate than these two. It'll take longer to tell, I expect. I went upstairs to bed with the rest of the party, but I didn't undress just then. I felt that storm coming up, and I like storms. I wouldn't miss one. So I just sat at my window. My room's the second on the corridor in the bachelor's wing, as you go along from the staircase. Yours is the first, isn't it, Mr. Westenhanger?"

"Yes, I'm next you."

"Your room was empty, that night, so anyone going along the corridor had to pass my door before they got

to any other room. I was wide awake, at my window.
I've pretty sharp ears, and I was listening hard for the
first of the thunder. I heard nobody pass my door. I'd
have heard anyone in the corridor. Make a note of that,
Mr. Stickney. It seems important."

He broke off and glanced contemptuously at Freddie.

"At almost exactly half-past twelve," he went on, "the
storm broke. I looked at my watch at the first thunder-
clap. It was a good storm. I've seldom seen better.
But from my point of view it was rather a failure, just
then. I couldn't see well enough out of my window. I
was losing half of it. So I got up—I hadn't undressed—
and I took my candle with me because I didn't know where
the corridor switches were. Nor the switches in the hall
below. I'd failed to make a note of them."

He paused for a moment as though expecting comments,
but no one said anything.

"I went downstairs. I wanted to get outside if I could.
I didn't mean to lose any of that storm. At the main door,
I had a glance at the burglar alarm. It's the same pattern
as I use in my own house, so I put it out of action and
opened the door. It was quite dry outside then. The
rain hadn't started. So I went out."

Westenhanger was struck by an idea.

"Just a moment, Mr. Wraxall. That meant you left
the door open behind you, didn't it? Could anyone have
got in without you seeing him?"

Wraxall nodded approval.

"No, nobody could have got in. I had my eye on the
door all the time. I was never away from it. To continue:
The whole house-front was dark when I went outside,
except for some windows in the little tower above the
Corinthian's Room. They were lit up."

"That's Eric Dangerfield's room," interjected Westenhanger.

"Quite right. You'll hear more about that when I
come to it, but let's take things as they happened. Almost
as soon as I got outside there was a terrific flash—blinding.
And then the father and mother of all the thunder-claps.
I found in the morning it had struck one of the trees near
by. That was at twelve thirty-nine p.m. exact—I looked at
my watch by the next flash which came immediately after."

"That must have been the peal that frightened me,"
Nina interjected. "It was the loudest I ever heard."

"Within a minute or two," continued Wraxall, "a light went up at the end of the east wing."

"That was in my room," confirmed Cynthia Pennard.

"We can ignore it for the present, then," said Wraxall. "I'm just giving you what I saw. About five minutes later—that would be about ten minutes to one by rough reckoning—a light appeared in the Corinthian's Room——"

"Ah!" exclaimed Freddie Stickney. "This is getting hotter."

"Only another of your mare's nests, Freddie," explained Douglas. "It was I who switched that on."

Wraxall continued without taking any notice.

"I saw a light in the Corinthian's Room and—as I was about to say when Mr. Stickney cut in—in the library which leads out of the Corinthian's Room. Five minutes later, say about one o'clock in the morning, the rain drove me indoors. I bolted the door and put on the alarm again. As I came back into the hall, someone switched on the lights, and I found young Dangerfield there. I said something about having been out looking at the storm and he nodded. Then I went upstairs and back to my room. The best part of the storm was over, so I went to bed, perhaps round about quarter past one. Like the other people I woke up as usual in the morning. That's all I can remember at present."

The American's narrative, whether intentionally or not, had brought a relaxation of the tension in the room. By his purely objective treatment of the matter he had produced an unconscious change in outlook among his audience. Westenhanger was relieved to see that even Eileen's face had taken on a less strained expression. She was anything but at her ease, yet there was something in her face which suggested that she had passed the worst.

Douglas Fairmile was the next to volunteer an account of his doings during the night.

"I'm no great hand at exact times and seasons," he began. "You'll just need to take what you get. And I'm no amateur in storms, either. If lightning leaves me alone I'll never trouble it. But that storm forced itself on my notice—and not in a quiet insinuating way, either. To be frank with you, it kept me awake. After a while I got fed up listening to it, so I thought I might as well read, since I couldn't sleep. So I padded off downstairs to get a book from the library. Mr. Wraxall says it was just about one o'clock, and he knows more about it than I do. The only thing that strikes me as important in the affair is that when I switched on the lights in the Corinthian's Room, I happened to notice that the Talisman was still in its place. So that means it disappeared after one o'clock in the morning."

He glanced at Eileen as he spoke. Westenhanger felt a wave of relief at this evidence, since it seemed to clear the girl completely; but on looking at her, he was surprised to see that she showed no sign of elation. Her expression hardly indicated that she had appreciated the force of Douglas's statement.

"I picked up a book," continued Douglas, "and just as I was leaving the room, Eric came down his stair. We exchanged a few bright remarks about the storm—nothing worth recording—and I left him writing something at the table in the library. I must have got through the hall— I didn't bother to switch on the lights—before Mr. Wraxall came inside again. And so to bed. And may I repeat, Freddie, lest you failed to catch my whisper last time, that I did *not* steal the Talisman as I was passing. Make a note of that. It seems important, as Mr. Wraxall says."

"I'm afraid my story doesn't help much," said Nina Lindale, shyly, "and it makes me out to be a terrible coward. But I've always been nervous of thunder since I was a kiddie. I didn't mind the beginning of this one —at least I tried not to mind it. But then there came a terrific flash and a perfectly awful peal of thunder, and my nerves went to pieces altogether."

"That must have been the time the tree was struck, I expect," said the American. "Say twenty minutes to one?"

"Oh, don't ask me what time it was. I had other things to think about. After that, I felt I simply couldn't be alone for another minute. I got up and went next door into Eileen's room. I wanted company at any price, even if I had to knock up half the house to get it. But Eileen wasn't there. Her bed hadn't been slept in. So I thought perhaps she was in the same state and had gone to someone else's room. I rushed along to Cynthia's bedroom and burst in on her. And after that I didn't dare to go back to my own room again, so I just stayed with her all night."

"That accounts for my light being switched on, you

see, Mr. Wraxall," said Cynthia to the American. "I've really no idea of what time it was that Nina came along to me; but it was just after that awful thunder-clap; and I expect that was the one you made a note of. Nina and I fell asleep after a while, once the storm had gone down. I don't know what time that was, either. Do you generally fall asleep with your eyes on your watch, Mr. Stickney? It seems very hard to fix any definite times for things which happen at night."

Freddie smiled in a superior fashion.

"As it happens, I did look at my watch in the middle of the night. I went to bed at the same time as the rest; and went to sleep, too, which is more than some of you seem to have been able to do. I slept through the storm. But later on the wind got up. My window-blind began to flap badly; and that woke me up. I looked at the time to see if it was worth while getting out of bed and fixing it, or whether it wasn't worth while. That was at twenty minutes to three, I remember distinctly."

He glanced at Cynthia triumphantly. She took up the implied challenge at once.

"Yes, Mr. Stickney, you've given us *one* time. But you haven't told us when you went to sleep. It seems to me you're no better than the rest of us, really."

Freddie ignored her and continued his tale.

"I made up my mind to get up and fix the blind. That was at twenty minutes to three, as I said. While I was at the window, I looked out. My room looks right across the court-yard to the windows of Miss Lindale's room. As I was standing at the window, a light went up in the windows next to Miss Lindale's."

He paused, and Westenhanger saw by his expression that he hoped to spring a surprise. Freddie swung round suddenly upon Eileen.

"That's your room, isn't it, Miss Cressage?"

The girl's face showed that this was the piece of evidence which she had been dreading; but she managed to keep her voice under control as she answered.

"My room is next Nina's, and I did switch on my light sometime in the small hours. I didn't look at the time, but no doubt you're quite right about it."

Again the atmosphere had grown tense. Westenhanger swiftly scanned the girl's face, and he was distressed to see how haggard she seemed. "She looks just like a trapped animal," he thought in the first flash. Then some unidentifiable trait in her expression brought a second idea to the fore. "She looks as though she knew she's in a very tight corner; but she expects to pull out of it somehow in the end. She's pretty nearly desperate—but not quite."

Freddie, having drawn general attention to Eileen's attitude, contented himself with completing his story.

"I looked out of my window for a short time after fixing the blind so that it wouldn't flap again. After that I went back to bed again and fell asleep almost immediately. I waked up at the usual time."

He waited for a moment and then added:

"Now if we had Miss Cressage's story we should have had everybody's version of the affair."

Eileen rose to her feet, and they could see that she was trembling, though she kept herself under control. Westenhanger instinctively leaned forward in his chair. If the girl had some trump card in her hand, now was the time to play it. If not, then undoubtedly Freddie Stickney had put her in a bad position. She had left her room at a quarter past twelve. Freddie's evidence pointed to her coming back again at twenty minutes to three in the morning, and switching on her light as she re-entered her room. What could any girl be doing out of her bed at that time of night, and for two hours at a stretch? And, undoubtedly, from the evidence of Douglas, the Talisman might have disappeared during the time she was moving about the house. No matter where she had been, it looked a bad business; and yet Westenhanger could not help feeling that there must be some explanation.

"That girl's straight," he repeated to himself. "She's over-straight, if anything, by the look of her. And yet she's got herself into some deadly hole or other."

Then an idea suddenly flashed into his mind.

"Suppose she's shielding someone else! I never thought of that! But it would need to be a pretty strong motive that would make her take the thing as she has taken it."

Before he could follow out this train of thought, Eileen's voice broke in on his reflections.

"I really haven't anything to say. It's quite true that Mrs. Caistor Scorton saw me in the corridor after twelve o'clock. I didn't know she had seen me then. And it's quite true that I switched on my light when I came back again. I don't know what time it was then, but probably

Mr. Stickney is quite right. It doesn't matter much. I wasn't near the Talisman during the night. That's all I can tell you."

Her control suddenly broke, and she moved hastily towards the door. Douglas Fairmile sprang up and opened it for her to pass out. As she passed him, she could read in his face that he at least was quite prepared to take her word.

As the door closed behind her, the atmosphere of strain grew more intense. The realisation that they had narrowly escaped a nasty scene weighed upon the group; and no one seemed eager to break the silence. At last Westenhanger, feeling that the first note struck was of importance, swung round on Freddie Stickney. He ignored the events of the last few moments completely.

"Well, Freddie," he said, coldly, "your inquest doesn't seem to have led to much. I can't congratulate you. Speaking purely as a bystander, I can't say that you've achieved anything. Take your own case. You went to bed at some unspecified hour. You say you slept through that storm. That's quite possible; though some of us might have difficulty in believing you, if I can judge from the accounts I've heard of the thunder. At any rate, you tell us you waked up shortly before three o'clock and were actually out of bed at that time—*just the period when the Talisman was stolen*. You were up and about for some unspecified time. Then you went back to bed and fell asleep again. Quite all right, no doubt."

His voice grew more incisive.

"But if you think you've cleared yourself of suspicion by telling that tale, I may as well sweep away your illusions. If a detective were working on this case, he'd simply ignore your whole yarn—except one solid point. He'd take Miss Cressage's word that she switched on the light in her room, and he'd believe you when you say you saw that light go up. That's the only point where there's the slightest confirmation. And Miss Cressage is the only person who could clear you, if it happened to turn out that the Talisman disappeared about three o'clock in the morning."

He shrugged his shoulders contemptuously.

"You seem to have the foggiest notion of evidence, Freddie. Anyone could have foreseen this sort of thing. Even a child would know that at night, in a house like this, it's almost impossible to establish a decent alibi. Nina and Cynthia are the only two of you who have established cast-iron alibis; and that was due to a pure accident—the thunderstorm."

"That's true," said Wraxall, before Freddie could reply. "That's quite correct, Mr. Westenhanger. Nobody could get an alibi under these conditions, in the normal way. I quite agree with you that this little playlet hasn't been a success. By no means. I think we'd be well advised to forget all about it."

Douglas Fairmile laughed at the sight of Freddie's expression; and with that laugh, the tension was released again. Douglas's mirth seemed infectious, following so closely on the strain of the last quarter of an hour.

"Well, I'm glad you can't suspect *me*," said Nina Lindale with a faint smile. "I never thought a thunderstorm would clear my character. I suppose I ought to be thankful."

"Ditto!" added Cynthia, lightly.

Westenhanger returned to the attack in a sardonic tone.

"One thing I noticed, Freddie; you didn't go the length of denying that you stole the Talisman yourself. An oversight, probably. Oh, don't trouble to do it now; it would look rather too much like an after-thought. Besides, no detective would take your word for it—with that look on your face."

"'Detected Guilt, or The Sinner Unmasked'—what?" jeered Douglas. "Freddie, you'd make the fortune of a problem painter if he got hold of you just now. 'Did He Do It?' That would be the title. Picture of the wily fellow who takes charge of the whole investigation and then leads all the sleuths on the wrong scent while he makes off with the swag, eh? Priceless!"

The three men had turned the tables on Freddie, and he had the wit to recognise the fact. The whole effect of his efforts had been nullified by this last touch of ridicule, which made a special appeal after the earlier tension. He nodded sulkily, as though admitting an error; but he made no direct reply to Westenhanger.

Nina Lindale gave the signal for the company to break up.

"I'm off to bed," she announced, unsuccessfully trying to conceal a yawn. "I got very little sleep last night, and if I stay up any longer I shall doze off in my chair."

"That's a sound idea, Miss Lindale," said Wraxall. "I begin to remember that I lost some sleep too, last night."

Morchard and Mrs. Caistor Scorton joined the group which was moving toward the door. Cynthia linked her arm in Nina's and was turning away when Douglas called her back and spoke to her in a low voice.

"What a thoughtful child it is!" they heard her say, in mock admiration. "And did you imagine I hadn't thought of that long ago? Don't worry!"

She hurried after her companion. Freddie Stickney, left alone with Douglas and Westenhanger, shuffled for a moment or two and then retired to the door.

"I'm going to bed," he said, reaching for the handle.

"Right, Freddie," said Douglas, making a pretence of consulting his watch. "I've taken the time. Set your alarm clock every quarter of an hour and jot down that you were in bed each time when you woke up. It'll be an invaluable memorandum if anything happens to go astray to-night. Bye-bye. If you feel one of your ears burning, don't fret. It will probably be me saying what I think of your exploits."

Freddie suppressed a snarl and went out. Westenhanger dropped into a big lounge-chair and pulled out his pipe.

"Sit down, Douglas; it's early yet."

Douglas picked out a convenient seat, near enough to allow a low-voiced conversation.

"I asked Cynthia to drop in to Eileen's room and tell her what we thought of things. Couldn't leave the girl imagining we believed she was a wrong 'un, could we? And she might have thought that, cutting off when she did. Cynthia was going to see her off her own bat, it seems. Sound girl, Cynthia; she'll do it tactfully. Some people might make a bad break in a case like that."

Westenhanger acquiesced silently, and filled his pipe before he spoke again.

"Damnable business, that," he said at last. "And if we'd stopped it, there would have been some sort of scene. Everyone's nerves were on edge. Anything was better than that. But what actually happened wasn't so very much better after all. That girl was as near cracking up as she could be. If it hadn't been for her grit, we might have had a much nastier affair on our hands."

"One would like to wring Freddie's neck, of course," Douglas mused aloud; "but that would mean a row. We can't have rows. With luck, we can stifle this business;

but a row would make it anybody's news. Freddie gets off this time, I'm afraid."

"He does. I'm sorry."

"The infernal thing is that the little sweep's right, you know, Conway. We *are* all under suspicion. I don't suspect anyone myself—not my line. But there's no getting away from it. Someone did take that damned Talisman."

"Afraid so. The only hope that I have is that it may have been a practical joke after all, and that the joker was afraid to own up. Trusted to putting the thing back again without being spotted."

"Possible, of course," conceded Douglas. "But I can't identify the prize idiot."

"Nor can I. Well, take the other thing and see if it leads you any further—theft, I mean. I'm out of it, by pure luck. You've all the money you want. Morchard has more than's good for him. The Scorton woman is rolling in it. I take it that the girls don't come into question?"

He glanced interrogatively at Douglas, who nodded his agreement.

"Then that leaves the American and Freddie as a residue. Know anything about Wraxall, Douglas?"

"Nix, as I suppose he'd say. He's a collector, of sorts, and rolling in money, I've heard."

"H'm!" said Westenhanger, pausing for a moment.

"Well, pass Wraxall," he continued. "That leaves us with Freddie. I don't like Freddie. I've nothing against his morals, for I know nothing about them. I do know he's hard up, though. But I've been hard up myself at times. That doesn't necessarily make a black mark on one's record."

"True," Douglas agreed. Then after a few seconds he added: "Know the Scots verdict *Not Proven* Conway? 'The accused was discharged with a stain on his character. All saved, bar honour.' That's how you feel about Freddie, perhaps?"

"I'm not very friendly. The way that girl was baited to-night was enough to sicken any decent person. But there's a difference between feeling like that and calling the little beast a thief, you know."

"Not Proven; that's so."

Westenhanger considered for a few moments as though

he found it difficult to choose words for what he had to say. At last he put down his pipe.

"There's one thing, Douglas—that girl has got to be cleared. We're all mixed up in *that* affair, thanks to Freddie's infernal manœuvres; we can't shirk responsibility. I don't know what possessed her to go roaming about the house at that time of night. Still less can I imagine why she couldn't tell us what she was after. But she's a straight girl, if ever I saw one, and we simply can't afford to let things rest as they are. I don't want to know what she was doing—and I don't much care. But the only way to clear her is to find out who actually did the trick. It'll be a stiff business."

Douglas looked serious.

"Stiff enough, if you ask me. If you want a Watson, I'm your man; but you'll need to supply the Sherlocking yourself. I simply haven't the brains for it. The whole affair is a complete mystery—and likely to remain so, for all the help I could give."

"I'm not hopeful," confessed Westenhanger at once. "The only detecting I ever did was guessing what cards were in my opponents' hands. It's not so much I expect to get anything out, Douglas. I feel one has to turn to and do what one can, or else I shouldn't be comfortable. That girl's face wasn't a happy sight to-night. It's got rather on my nerves, if you want to know."

He took up his pipe again. Douglas said nothing, but his face showed that he understood Westenhanger's account of his feelings.

"What do you make of Wraxall?" Westenhanger demanded abruptly.

"Decent soul, I thought. Backed us up well in the matter of sitting on Freddie."

Westenhanger made no comment. Douglas let him smoke in silence for a while before inquiring:

"What do you think?"

"Wraxall was the only one of you who had a complete story ready to account for all his doings during the night. That's my impression about Wraxall, Douglas."

71

CHAPTER VII

CYNTHIA PENNARD moved slightly to avoid a spot of light which had crept across the cushions of her hammock until it reached her face.

"Douglas," she said lazily, "has a hippopotamus got a tougher hide than a rhinoceros? I'd like to know."

"I've heard them both well spoken of—highly commended, in fact. I'd hate to draw an invidious distinction and cause trouble at the Zoo. But why this lust for general information? It's not like you."

Following her glance across the broad lawn, Douglas caught sight of Freddie Stickney sitting on the grass beside Mrs. Caistor Scorton's garden-chair. Cynthia turned her head again.

"That's quite the thickest-skinned creature I ever heard of," she explained, "and I was only wondering which animal ought to come after him."

"Can't you spend the day better than in thinking up insults to rhinoceroses and hippopotami? They'd wilt with shame if they dreamed you ·were putting them in Freddie's class. No flies on Freddie, as they say. Why so? Because they'd merely blunt their beaks if they tried to get through his hide. His fair companion's pretty tough on the surface, too. Perhaps that's why all the gnats have moved over here. Suppose we disappoint 'em by going to the tennis-courts?"

Cynthia slipped neatly out of her hammock, and they went off together.

There was more than a grain of truth in their comments. Freddie Stickney prided himself—and justly—upon one knightly quality: he never showed a wound. The most brutal snubbing left him quite unabashed. Coming down to breakfast after the fiasco of his "inquest," he had encountered Eileen Cressage at the head of the stairs, and he had insisted on chattering trivialities to her all the way down. At table, his beady eyes had wholly failed to see the marked coldness with which he was treated by everyone, and he took no notice of the fact that all conversations into which he inserted himself were apt almost immediately to fade out into silence. Only Mrs. Caistor Scorton seemed to recognise his existence, and when breakfast was over, he had sought her out on the lawns.

"What do you think about this affair of the Talisman, Mrs. Caistor Scorton?" he demanded, as he sat down on the turf beside her chair.

Mrs. Caistor Scorton seemed to ruminate for some moments before replying. Then she glanced shrewdly at Freddie. Evidently she thought it worth while to draw him out.

"Oh, I don't know, Mr. Stickney. I'm not clever, like you; and I can make nothing of it, one way or the other. But I'd like to hear what you think. You've been putting two and two together, I'm sure, and I expect you've got a good idea of things."

Freddie rose to the bait without hesitation.

"If it would interest you, I'm delighted to give you my inferences. You've got all the facts already."

Mrs. Caistor Scorton nodded, but said nothing. Freddie corrected himself immediately.

"No, I was wrong in saying that. I've been hunting out some more evidence—things that didn't come out last night. One or two points seem to be important."

Mrs. Caistor Scorton became more alert.

"That sounds interesting, Mr. Stickney. I'd like to hear it."

Freddie considered for a few moments.

"I was just trying to arrange it in my mind," he explained. "The easiest way will be to take each person in turn, and examine the evidence we have about that person in particular. Take Eileen Cressage first. I think it's obvious that some of us know more about her affairs than came out last night."

He looked up into Mrs. Caistor Scorton's face inquisitively as he spoke, and his voice had a hint of interrogation in its tone. Mrs. Caistor Scorton stared down at him unwinkingly.

"One would almost think you were connecting me with her, Mr. Stickney. I hardly know her."

"Well, correct me if I am wrong," said Freddie, brightly. "I admit some of it's guesswork; but I believe I'm right.

We'll see. Now to start with, she's hard up. That's common knowledge. People invite her to their house out of good nature, and she 'stays with them to save money, living on the cheap."

No one would have imagined, from Freddie's semi-indignant, semi-pitying tone, that this description accurately fitted his own methods during part of the year.

"I believe that's true," said Mrs. Caistor Scorton, in a judicial voice. "It's common knowledge, as you say. What next?"

"She lost a lot of money to you at bridge the other night."

"That's common knowledge too, Mr. Stickney. Everyone in the room knew that. Are these your wonderful revelations?"

The quite perceptible ring of disappointment in her tone touched Freddie on the raw. He was put on his mettle, just as she intended.

"Wait a moment," he begged. "Let's take things as they come. She didn't pay you at the time? No. She gave you a cheque. I was watching her face closely just then. I'm a bit of a physiognomist, you know. It was plain as print to me. That cheque was no good, Mrs. Caistor Scorton."

Mrs. Caistor Scorton regarded him with a rather malicious smile.

"Indeed, Mr. Stickney?" she laughed. "Then how do you account for the fact that the cheque was met when it was presented? I paid it in immediately and my bank collected it at once."

Freddie Stickney held up his hand, asking permission to interrupt her.

"Yes," he said rapidly. "I suppose the cheque *was* met the next day. But all the same, she hadn't a spare £200 in the world that night. I know the signs: you can't deceive me. She hadn't the cash that night. But she had it next day. What happened in between?"

"How should I know?"

Freddie took no notice. His question had been merely a rhetorical one. He continued, marking each point with emphasis.

"The Talisman disappeared; that's what happened in between. And during the night, we know that Miss Eileen Cressage was out of her room at a time when the Talisman might have been stolen. There's no denying that, is there? And what happened first thing next morning? Long before half of us were up, she went off to town. And where did Westenhanger run across her in town? Coming out of Starbecks the jewellers, the place where they'll make advances on any little trinket you've no immediate use for. And your cheque was met all right."

He paused for a moment, and Mrs. Caistor Scorton looked down at him curiously.

"You seem very good at putting two and two together, Mr. Stickney. Do you enjoy it?"

Freddie seemed rather annoyed at the interruption. It ruined the dramatic pause he had planned to make before his summing up.

"Of course I enjoy it," he replied, rather crossly. "I like using my brains. Well, there's the case. If seems to me to need more explaining away than we've had so far."

"It's very ingenious," said Mrs. Caistor Scorton, in a non-committal tone, "but isn't there some other possible explanation of things? One mustn't look at a thing from one side too much, you know."

Freddie was not a person who welcomed criticism of his pronouncements; but he felt that his reputation as a man of ideas was at stake. Swiftly his mind reverted to an incident of the previous night.

"There is another possible explanation, I admit," he said, in a rather grudging tone. "Morchard has plenty of money. A matter of £200 would be nothing to him. Now he's very keen on Miss Cressage's looks. I've watched him, and I know the signs. Perhaps the money came from him. You said last night that when you saw her she was going towards the bachelor's wing."

"I said nothing of the kind," Mrs. Caistor Scorton interrupted sharply. "I said she was going along the corridor."

"Which leads to the bachelors' wing, of course," persisted Freddie.

"And to the main staircase. Besides, Mr. Wraxall said he heard no one pass his door."

"How could he?" demanded Freddie triumphantly. "You said she was wearing bedroom slippers. She wouldn't make a sound."

"Do you know, Mr. Stickney," Mrs. Caistor Scorton commented in a colourless tone, "you seem to have an unwholesome mind, if I may say it without offence." Her voice became indignant. "You know precious little about girls if you think Eileen Cressage would raise money in *that* particular way. I'm not talking about morality; I'm speaking of fastidiousness. If you'd suggested Douglas Fairmile, it might have been credible; but it's quite beyond believing if you drag in Mr. Morchard. She simply wouldn't dream of it. There are some things a girl of that type won't do; and a cash bargain with Mr. Morchard's one of them."

"Very well," said Freddie, sullenly, "you can have the other alternative if you prefer it."

"It's far more likely; I can tell you that," declared Mrs. Caistor Scorton, coldly.

"Well, let's leave her alone and go on to the rest."

Mrs. Caistor Scorton nodded an abrupt consent.

"Wraxall's the next on the list," Freddie went on, recovering his good humour in the eagerness of his dissection. "I've picked up some facts about him too. He came here for one purpose, and one purpose only. Do you know what this was? To get the Talisman for his collection. That's all he's here for. Now I found out—no matter how—that on the night of the storm he approached old Dangerfield and offered to buy the thing. Offered a gigantic price for it. It didn't come off. They wouldn't sell. So there he was, knowing he'd failed to get what he wanted. You know what these collectors are? Sort of monomaniacs on their hobby."

"Are you suggesting that Mr. Wraxall took it? Absurd!"

"I'm not suggesting anything. I'm simply marshalling the evidence. What is there? We know Wraxall was out and about in the house for the best part of the night. What made Eric Dangerfield come down from his room? Perhaps he heard Wraxall wandering round near the foot of his stair and frightened him off the first attempt on the Talisman. Perhaps Wraxall came back again and had a more successful try. All we know is that the motive was there; the opportunity was there; the theft was committed. Draw your own inference."

Mrs. Caistor Scorton seemed to have recovered her earlier mood.

"Oh, I'm not so clever as you are, Mr. Stickney. I'm quite content to hear your own views. Let's take the next person on your list."

"Take Douglas Fairmile," continued Freddie, quite restored to good humour by the scrap of flattery. "My deliberate judgment is that Douglas is not guilty. First, there's no motive. Douglas has any amount of money; he doesn't need the Talisman for the sake of turning it into cash. Second, he hasn't the initiative to carry through a thing like that. He's just one of these would-be funny fellows. No, in my opinion, it wasn't Douglas."

"I agree with you," concurred Mrs. Caistor Scorton. "Let's pass on."

"Morchard's the next. Same thing. No motive. No evidence. Morchard didn't take it."

"Anything to say about Mrs. Brent, Mr. Stickney?"

"Ah," said Freddie importantly. "I have a piece of fresh evidence about her. Two nights ago, I happened to be passing outside her window when she was discussing storms with that Yankee; and do you know what I heard her say?"

"No," said Mrs. Caistor Scorton. "I don't know. I wish you wouldn't go on asking these questions when you know I can't possibly answer them."

Freddie ignored the interruption.

"I heard her say this," he went on, impressively. "'After a really bad storm I'm hardly normal. I might do something wild. *I might steal my best friend's spoons.*' That's what she said; I heard it distinctly. Now what was the state of affairs on the night the Talisman was stolen? Wasn't it the worst storm you've known for years?"

"It was," agreed Mrs. Caistor Scorton, "quite the worst But remember that you slept through it yourself. You told us so last night. So perhaps Mrs. Brent did the same."

"You're trying to laugh at me." Freddie's tone showed that he was hurt. "I'm sure Mrs. Brent didn't sleep through it. She hasn't got my strong nerves. No, I expect it drove her nearly out of her mind. What if she stole something even more important than her best friend's spoons? Her room was quite near the place where the Talisman stood. What if she got up in the night with all her nerves in rags, stole the Talisman, hid it somewhere— and forgot all about it? And next morning she goes off on the *Kestrel*, nobody knows where. What do you think of that?"

"Not much," said Mrs. Caistor Scorton, gently. "Try again."

Freddie looked at her dubiously for a moment or two before continuing his survey.

"That leaves the two girls. But they have a complete *alibi*, luckily for them."

Mrs. Caistor Scorton looked at him quizzically as he stopped.

"Your list isn't complete yet, Mr. Stickney. You've left out quite a number of possible people. Myself, for one. Yourself, for another. And you've forgotten the four Dangerfields. Let's be quite fair all round. What about these people?"

Freddie, for once, was completely taken aback.

"That's only a joke, isn't it? You didn't actually think . . ."

"Oh, don't let us stumble over a trifle like that. Let's be fair all round." Mrs. Caistor Scorton's eyes twinkled, but their expression was hardly kindly. "Since you won't do it, I'll show you that you've had a diligent pupil just now. I'll follow your own methods and you'll criticise my efforts."

Freddie uttered some protesting noises, but she took no notice.

"First, there's Mrs. Caistor Scorton. She had an opportunity of stealing the Talisman. What about motive? I understand she's plenty of money. She'd hardly be tempted by that. No motive? Then shall we agree to pass Mrs. Caistor Scorton? Very good."

Her voice grew slightly acid.

"Then there's Mr. Stickney. Opportunity? The same as Mrs. Caistor Scorton's. Motive?" She turned on him swiftly. "You're hard up, aren't you, Mr. Stickney? Yes? So I've heard people say. People do talk, don't they? Well, then, what do you say about Mr. Stickney's case? He had the opportunity. He had a motive, we'll say. And he admitted last night that he was up and about just at the very time when the Talisman was stolen. Pass Mr. Stickney? Well . . . hardly, I think. He'd better go back for further examination, hadn't he?"

Her laugh had a sarcastic ring in Freddie's ears. But before he had time to interrupt her, she had passed on down her list.

"Now for the Dangerfields. All of them have opportunity. What about motive? (You see how apt a pupil I am, don't you?) So far as the two old people go, there's no motive. They have the Talisman already; they don't need to steal it. Then there's Helga. Her fiancee's big game shooting in Africa just now. She's going to get married when he comes back. Big game shooting costs money. I happen to know that he has plenty. Helga wouldn't need to steal the Talisman. Pass Helga Dangerfield, I think."

She glanced ironically at Freddie, who was somewhat mystified by the turn of the examination.

"That's the whole list, except for Eric Dangerfield. Do you happen to have picked up anything about him, Mr. Stickney?"

Freddie seemed to feel that his reputation as an authority was at stake. His beady eyes took on a meditative expression as he ran over his memory for information.

"He's Helga's cousin, of course. And he's the nearest living male in the family. I suppose he's an heir-male or whatever they call it. Friocksheim goes down the male line, I've heard."

"Nothing very new in all that, Mr. Stickney. Don't you know something about him personally?"

"Not much," Freddie replied, doubtfully. "I've never met him before I came here this time. He's been abroad till quite lately. A bit of a rolling stone, from all I've heard. Remittance man, or something like that."

"A ne'er-do-well, then?"

"I think so. Most likely."

"Any other pleasant characteristics you can think of?"

Freddie hesitated for an instant, then apparently he made up his mind to divulge something.

"Of course, Mrs. Caistor Scorton, this is absolutely in confidence. You won't repeat it?"

She shook her head, and he continued.

"He's very hard up. I know that for a fact. I happened to be walking in the garden that night he was playing bridge with you. He and the old man were talking; and I chanced to overhear some things they said. Of course, I wasn't listening on purpose; but sometimes one can't help catching a sentence or two."

Without giving his neighbour time to interrupt him, he hurried on to his revelation.

"I gathered that Eric couldn't pay up that night, either. He was dunning his uncle for cash to square up with Morchard. Old Mr. Dangerfield wasn't pleased. He said something about this being the last time. At any rate he said 'last time'; but perhaps he was speaking of some other time, before that. He seemed very hot about it. Eric wasn't looking very comfortable."

"You seem to have heard a good deal," said Mrs. Caistor Scorton indifferently.

But Freddie hardly seemed to notice her aloofness. He was off on a fresh scent.

"I'd never thought of that," he volunteered. "Of course, that throws a fresh light on things. Let's see if we can put two and two together. Fact number one, he's hard up. Fact number two, he's a ne'er-do-well. Fact number three, he couldn't pay Morchard that night. Number four, he may not have been able to persuade his uncle to pay. Number five, he did pay after the Talisman disappeared—I happen to know that. Problem, how did he manage to pay? Well, suppose he took the Talisman. He wouldn't need to sell it. He could raise some cash on it easily enough, being a Dangerfield. He could get an advance and let them notify his uncle. Old Mr. Dangerfield would be forced to pay up in order to get the thing back. Or he might even simply hide the thing and blackmail his uncle for money—hold the Talisman to ransom, so to speak."

"You have a wonderful imagination, Mr. Stickney. I hope you'll go on looking into the whole affair. Perhaps you'll be able to clear it up for us. It's certainly been most unpleasant to feel that this cloud of suspicion is hanging over the place. You'll do your best, I'm sure."

Freddie tried to appear modest under this testimonial to his capacity.

"That's what I've felt all along," he admitted. "One really owes it to everyone to do one's best to clear the thing up. It's so awkward for all of us."

Mrs. Caistor Scorton gave him what appeared to be a grateful glance. Then, with more interest than she had shown for some minutes, she put a direct question.

"Whom do you really suspect, Mr. Stickney?"

Freddie apparently had been tabulating his conclusions as he went along, and he was able to answer her without a pause.

"Three people. I can't get nearer than that."

"And they are?" inquired Mrs. Caistor Scorton with just a touch of eagerness.

"Miss Cressage, of course," responded Freddie at once. "I think her doings need looking into. I'll pay special attention to her."

"Quite true. There's a good deal that would be all the better of some explanation. I don't pretend to see through it myself. Now, the next person?"

"The American, obviously. If we knew all that he knows we might know a good deal more than we do know," explained Freddie, with the air of a Sibyl uttering some profound monition.

"Possibly. And the third person?"

"Eric Dangerfield. Curious that I hadn't thought of him before, isn't it?"

"Very strange," agreed Mrs. Caistor Scorton. "You're usually so quick at conclusions, Mr. Stickney."

She rose to her feet with an air of dismissal.

"Well, I mustn't detain you," she said. "Be sure to let me know if you discover anything else that's interesting."

As she moved across the lawn she glanced over her shoulder and smiled encouragingly; but if Freddie had been a thought-reader he would hardly have felt flattered.

"What a malicious little reptile," she reflected. "He makes me feel shivery. Luckily he's not likely to do any real harm. Nobody will pay any attention to him."

CHAPTER VIII

CONWAY WESTENHANGER had no very high opinion of his own ability to unravel the Talisman mystery, and the more he thought over the subject the less could he see any simple solution. One point, however, seemed beyond dispute: the method of elimination, as handled by Freddie Stickney, had been given a trial and had led to absolutely nothing whatever. The net result of Freddie's efforts was that everybody had been made to feel uncomfortable, while not a single gleam of light had been thrown upon the problem. And yet, given the conditions of the case, the elimination method seemed to promise results. If the servants were put on one side, and if no thief had got into the house in the darkness, then only thirteen persons remained who had any possible means of access to the Corinthian's Room that night. One of them must be responsible for the vanishing of the Talisman. That seemed an inevitable conclusion.

But here his train of thought was crossed by another. He could not quite dismiss from his mind the impression made upon him by the way in which old Rollo Dangerfield had taken his loss.

"The thing's worth at least £50,000," Westenhanger reflected. "The Dangerfields may be well enough off, but a loss on that scale is something more than a flea-bite. And yet he doesn't seem disturbed in the slightest. One could bet that he really believes the Talisman will turn up again in a few days. If it isn't cold confidence, then it's the best acting I ever saw. I could almost take my oath that he meant what he said."

He turned the matter over and over in his mind for a time; but although a number of suggestions offered themselves, none of them seemed satisfying.

"It may be a case of rank superstition, but I don't read him so myself. Who believes in that sort of stuff nowadays? It can't be that. Of course, he side-tracked all the talk about the Dangerfield Secret. He's probably half-ashamed of that business—likely it's some old ritual about informing the heir that in 1033 or so the head of the Dangerfields sold his soul to the Devil. The Dangerfields Secret has nothing to do with the case anyway."

But Westenhanger was wrong on that point, as he was to discover at no distant date. However, dismissing that line of thought, he sought for other possible explanations of the mystery.

"The old man may know who took the Talisman," he suggested to himself. "If that's so, then perhaps he means to put the screw on the culprit quietly, without saying anything to the rest of us. Most obviously he doesn't want a scandal at Friocksheim. But in that case he must have spotted the wrong 'un immediately; because first thing in the morning, he was quite certain that the Talisman would turn up again—he wasn't worried in the slightest degree. If he tracked down the thief between one a.m. and breakfast-time, it was a lightning bit of detective work. But if it wasn't a case of detection, then the only possible explanation is that he actually saw the theft committed."

Westenhanger paused only for a moment on this idea, however, for its inherent improbability struck him at once.

"That's no good. If he'd caught the thief in the act, he'd simply have threatened to expose him; got the Talisman back from him, and replaced it in its cabinet without giving rise to all this trouble."

Then a new thought occurred to him.

"But suppose old Rollo couldn't trust the thief not to have a second try, with better luck the second shot? That's a possibility. If I'd been in old Rollo's shoes under these conditions I think I'd have pocketed the Talisman and kept it safe until that particular guest's visit was up. Then he could put it back in the cabinet with a comfortable mind. That's a possibility, too, and Wraxall might fit the case."

But here again his knowledge would hardly fit the hypothesis.

"No, that won't work, either," he admitted to himself. "Old Rollo's a chivalrous old bird. He knows Miss Cressage is under suspicion now—Freddie's sure to have let that leak out. If the old man knew the identity of the thief he certainly wouldn't stand aside and let the girl bear the brunt of things for a moment, I'm sure. . . . Wraxall isn't even a friend of the Dangerfields; he's the merest casual caller, so far as they're concerned. There's no reason why they should shield *him*."

He cudgelled his brain for another alternative hypothesis.

"Suppose the old man didn't spot the thief, but managed somehow to discover where the Talisman was hidden after it was stolen. He may be keeping a watch on the hiding-place, waiting for the thief to give himself away by going after the thing at last."

He brooded for a time on the various ideas he had evolved; but in the end he put them all aside.

"Damn it!" he said, irritably, "if I go on like this, I'll end up by being as bad as Freddie. That's not the way to go about the business at all. What's wanted is new facts, not a lot of futile ideas. One must begin somewhere. I'll go and have a look at the Corinthian's Room and see if anything suggests itself when I'm on the actual spot."

Westenhanger had learnt that no change had been made in the Corinthian's Room since the theft. The cabinet had been untouched, just as the thief had left it. They had all been asked not to tamper with anything.

"The Talisman will come back by the way in which it went," Old Dangerfield had said, with a faint mockery in his voice. "Let us leave the door open for it to get into its case again."

Without any very strong hope in his mind, Westenhanger made his way to the Corinthian's Room, which, to his relief, was untenanted. He felt a certain shamefacedness in actually embarking on this attempt at detection, and he was glad that he could examine the place without betraying his purpose. As he entered the door his eye was caught by the chess-board set in the floor pattern, and he examined it curiously.

"These little holes at the corners of the squares are rum," he thought, as his eye was caught by one of them. "I begin to wonder whether Wraxall wasn't near the mark when he talked about some kind of man-trap for protecting the Talisman. But no, that's obviously rubbish, because the Talisman's gone, and yet none of us shows much in the way of visible damage. Besides, old Rollo declared there was no man-trap—you could lift the Talisman and come to no harm. He volunteered that. And if there's one thing certain in this business it's that Rollo isn't an aimless liar. That notion has nothing in it."

He stepped across the chess-board and halted before

the empty cabinet which had held the Dangerfield Talisman. It stood on its stone pillar so that the glass front was breast high, and he examined it minutely in the hope of detecting something significant. The central plate-glass slab, through which he had inspected the armlet three nights before, was intact. On the velvet floor of the cabinet he could see the clearly marked ring made by the long-continued pressure of the bell-cover of tinted glass which now stood in a fresh position a little to the right, almost behind the closed door of the cabinet. The other door stood half-open, and he noticed that it had no lock but only an ordinary spring-catch. Idly he tried the strength of the spring, using his nail to avoid leaving any finger-marks, and he found that the catch was in good order. The handles of the doors were simple in pattern like miniature cork-screw handles. Conway Westenhanger studied the glass surfaces with care, but after a time he abandoned his self-imposed task.

"Not much use bothering about finger-marks there," he commented. "There's no saying how many of us had our paws on it, that night he showed us the Talisman. Some of them are bound to be there, even if the case has been dusted by the servants. Most likely there's a set of my own amongst them. Nobody could be incriminated by that, certainly. There's nothing in it."

He stepped back a pace to look at the cabinet as a whole, and suddenly a keen expression crossed his features. He had seen the thing he wanted.

"Well, *that* limits it down considerably!" he said with relief. "What a bit of pure luck! And I believe I'm right too."

He thought for a moment or two before deciding on his next step.

"This isn't going to be so easy, after all," he concluded, with more hesitation in his manner. "I can't go running round them, asking that particular question bluntly, or the thief will be put on his guard long before it comes to his turn. This affair will need careful handling—very careful. And I'll need to try a blank experiment first with someone who is absolutely above suspicion. I know how I'd do the thing, but I'm prejudiced subconsciously, probably. I'll need some subject who doesn't know what I'm after."

He ran over in his mind the list of the house-party.

"Douglas, of course! He's the man. He offered to

help if I needed him, and he's able to keep his tongue quiet."

Then a fresh thought occurred to him. A picture of Eileen Cressage's strained face came up in his memory and changed his immediate purpose.

"I'll see her first, and try it," he decided. "After all, the main thing is to clear her and get her out of this affair if possible. Once that's done, there will be time enough to think about Douglas."

It took him longer than he expected to hit upon a line of procedure that satisfied him. More than once he was forced to discard an idea which proved faulty after consideration and think out something fresh. At last, however, his plans seemed to be sound so far as he could see. He closed the door of the Corinthian's Room and made his way into the hall. Freddie Stickney was sitting beside the main entrance, evidently deep in thought.

"Wake up, Freddie!" Westenhanger brutally interrupted the reflections of the amateur detective. "Seen Douglas about anywhere?"

"I think he's been playing tennis. Most likely he's still down at the courts."

"Oh! Seen Cynthia and Miss Cressage since breakfast?"

Westenhanger was careful to couple Eileen's name with Cynthia's in his demand. He had no desire to let Freddie know that he was in search of Eileen in particular.

"Cynthia's probably down at the tennis-courts with Douglas," Freddie assured him. "I saw them go off together in that direction. Miss Cressage went away by herself some time ago, towards the shore—over yonder."

Westenhanger nodded his thanks curtly and descended the steps leading down into the gardens. He sauntered along while he was within range of Freddie's eyes, but as soon as he got out of sight of the door, he quickened his steps. Ten minutes brought him to a spot from which he could see the nearer coastline, and, looking from point to point, he at last detected a girl's figure on a tiny headland which ran out to form one horn of the bay.

He made his way indirectly towards her, and before he reached the ridge of the headland he slackened his pace, so that when he actually came into her neighbourhood he seemed to have arrived there by pure chance in the course of an aimless walk. He wished, above everything, to avoid giving her the impression that he had deliberately sought her out; for the test he meant to apply depended for its success on her being completely off her guard. He had not the slightest doubt as to the result, but his scientific caution demanded that he should play his game with absolute fairness. If the test was to establish anything whatever, it would have to be applied without fear or favour.

As he drew nearer he tried to read something from her attitude. She faced the sea, and from time to time he saw her glance along the horizon, only to look down again when her eyes found nothing but the skyline.

"That girl's got a bit of personality somewhere," Westenhanger reflected, as he advanced. "Every line of her figure shows some emotion, just as clearly as if I were looking at her face. But what particular emotion is it? She looks dejected, but that isn't everything. There's something else there as well."

Enlightenment flashed across him.

"That's the way Robinson Crusoe might have looked when he was hoping for a sail and yet felt certain it wasn't coming that day. It's hope deferred that's wrong with that girl. But what's she hoping for?"

By this time he had come quite close to her, and at the sound of his steps on the turf she turned her head.

"Not disturbing you, I hope?" he said, casually, as he came up. "I came up to have a look at the view for a moment or two. May I sit down?"

She nodded assent, seeming to accept his company with indifference. He seated himself a couple of yards away and for some minutes he gazed over the bay without saying anything.

"May I smoke?"

She gave him permission, and he rose and stepped across to offer his case. She took a cigarette, but he seemed to change his mind, closed his case and put it back in his pocket. Then he re-seated himself in his old position.

"That's stupid of me," he exclaimed, as the girl looked at her unlighted cigarette. He drew out a little silver box and tossed it over to her. "Catch."

He threw it so clumsily, that though she snatched at it in the air, she missed it, and was forced to reach over and pick it up.

"Sorry," Westenhanger apologised, as she struck a match for herself.

He waited for some minutes before saying anything

further. Eileen Cressage seemed to feel no desire for talk. She smoked slowly, and from time to time her eyes followed the tiny blue clouds as they drifted seaward on the faint airs which came from the land. Westenhanger was not deceived. She was still scanning the horizon-line in search of something. Suddenly he realised what the thing must be.

"I wonder how Mrs. Brent is getting on," he said, watching the girl's face as he spoke. "She hasn't made any sign since she left."

"How could she?"

"Oh, wireless. Most boats have it."

"I wish the *Kestrel* had. But she hasn't."

Something in the girl's voice surprised Westenhanger— an intensity of feeling which seemed quite uncalled-for by the subject. Of course, Eileen was watching for the *Kestrel's* return. That was why she had come up to the headland; that was why she looked out to sea so eagerly. Anyone could put two and two together to that extent. But why should she be so eager to get into touch with the yacht? Obviously she wanted to do so; the reference to the lack of wireless could mean nothing else. And the tone of her voice was enough to betray the intensity of her desire.

Of course the *Kestrel* meant Mrs. Brent; there was no one else on board except the crew. But that meant that the return of Mrs. Brent was the thing Eileen Cressage was awaiting with such eagerness. Where did Mrs. Brent come into the affair? The only thing that mattered now to the girl was to be extricated from the position she was in. Had she been shielding Mrs. Brent in something? Had she given Mrs. Brent some promise of secrecy and was she now waiting for the *Kestrel's* return so that she might take back her promise and clear herself? It sounded unlikely. Mrs. Brent could hardly be mixed up in the Talisman mystery. But if she was not, why should Eileen be so eager for the coming of the yacht?

He watched the sea again, avoiding the girl's face with his eyes. After a time she finished her cigarette and threw away the stub.

"Another?" he suggested, drawing out his case.

She refused, and he took a cigarette himself and felt for his match-box. Eileen had let it slip down to the ground beside her after using it, and she now picked it up and tossed it across to him. Westenhanger deliberately lighted his cigarette, blew out the match carefully, and pitched it away before saying anything.

"Nobody suspects you of taking the Talisman, Miss Cressage," he said at last.

The girl started as though she had been stung, and made a gesture as though she wished to stop him saying anything further. Westenhanger continued without appearing to notice her action.

"If that was all I had to say, Miss Cressage, I think I would have left it to your imagination. No decent person thinks you had anything to do with that business; and I expect you know that without my telling you. What I wanted to say was a shade more interesting."

He looked out to seaward, so as to let the girl see that he was not watching her.

"I *know* you didn't take it, and I think I'll be able to prove that fairly conclusively to any reasonable person."

To his surprise she showed very little relief at his statement. Her voice had no particular ring of pleasure in it when she replied. It seemed almost as though she regarded the matter as of slight importance in comparison with something else that was in her mind. Westenhanger was frankly puzzled by her attitude—even a little nettled to find that his efforts on her behalf led to so little acknowledgment.

"It's very kind of you, Mr. Westenhanger. I know I have some very good friends here at Friocksheim. But there are some other people here too. I know perfectly well what some of them think. Even if I were cleared of the Talisman theft, they'd go on repeating other things about me. Oh, I know what they've been saying. I'm not a fool, Mr. Westenhanger. I know quite well what that miserable little beast Stickney has been hinting about me."

She raised her eyes again to the sky-line, looking over the empty sea.

"Oh, I *do* wish the *Kestrel* would come!"

For a few moments Westenhanger also scanned the horizon, giving her time to pull herself together again. When she broke the silence, it was in another tone.

"I'm sorry, Mr. Westenhanger. That was ungrateful of me. You've been very kind. Don't take that seriously. You know I've got very raw nerves just now, and you mustn't blame me too much."

Westenhanger's smile reassured her.

"Now I'm all right," she went on. "I don't deserve it; but I wish you'd tell me just what you meant by what you said just now. How can you clear me in the Talisman affair? Of course I knew all along that you never believed I took it. I could see that in your face—and in Douglas's too. But proving it's a different thing, isn't it?"

Westenhanger smiled again, in genuine amusement this time; and his expression helped the girl in her struggle for the control of her nerves.

"I'm going to play the mystery-man for another quarter of an hour," he said, "then I'll explain the whole affair to you. We'll need Douglas's help also. But just to tantalise you, I can tell you that I got absolute certainty on the point since I came up here half an hour ago. Now, if that excites your curiosity, let's gather in Douglas and clear the ground for my explanation. It's so simple that you'll probably think you saw it yourself, really."

She rose to her feet and gave a last glance round the sea-rim; but no smoke showed on the horizon. Then they made their way down the headland and back into the Friocksheim grounds. Douglas had finished his tennis, they found when they reached the courts; and as Cynthia had gone into the house to write a letter he was easily persuaded to go with Westenhanger and Eileen. As they walked through the gardens, the engineer puzzled Douglas by a request.

"Have you a thick scarf, Miss Cressage?"

"Yes."

The girl's face showed that she had no idea of what lay behind the inquiry.

"Well, would you mind getting it—and a pair of gloves. And then would you come to the Corinthian's Room?"

She nodded without saying anything, and Westenhanger turned to Douglas.

"Your outfit, my lad, will be a pair of thin gloves, if you have them. Bring 'em to the Corinthian's Room, and don't keep Miss Cressage waiting. I'm going there myself direct."

In a few moments they rejoined him.

"Now Douglas," he said, "your business is to stand in the corridor at present and detain any possible intruder by the charm of your conversation. Nobody's to get into this room for the next five minutes. You're peaceful picket, you understand?"

Douglas grinned and retired into the corridor.

"Now, Miss Cressage," said Westenhanger, pushing the door until it was almost closed, "would you mind putting on your gloves."

The girl did so and then looked at him with a puzzled expression.

"What's all this about, Mr. Westenhanger? I don't understand."

"I'm afraid you must bear with it for a minute or two more and then it will be quite obvious. Do you mind if I blindfold you with this scarf? I know it looks like a child's game; but I really am serious."

He wound the scarf round her head and fastened it gently.

"Can you see?"

"No; you've been quite efficient."

"It's most important that you shouldn't see anything. Quite sure you're absolutely blindfolded?"

"Quite."

"Very good."

She heard a click like the closing of a pocket-knife, then Westenhanger's voice in a low tone near her ear.

"I've just shut the door of the cabinet. Now let me lead you over to it."

He guided her carefully for a step or two.

"Now," he continued in the same low tone, "you're standing right in front of the centre of the cabinet. If you lift your hand you can open the door. Try it."

Obediently Eileen put out her hand, groped and caught the handle and, after turning it, opened the door.

"Now," said Westenhanger again, "suppose you try to reach the place where the Talisman was. Wait! You might knock over the bell, being blindfolded. Don't move an inch after I say Stop! . . . Stop!"

She brought her hand to rest immediately.

"Now, bring your hand back to your side and then take a step backwards. I'll see you don't trip."

As she stood, after completing the movement, she heard another slight click.

"That's all, Miss Cressage. Now I'll take the scarf off."

He did so and she looked round slightly dazzled by the sunlight which streamed into the room. Nothing seemed to be changed; and she failed to understand what his manœuvres meant. Then her eyes ranged over the cabinet and something caught her attention.

"You've been playing some trick on me, Mr. Westenhanger," she said, indignantly. "I'm sure I opened the right-hand door of the cabinet, and now it's the left-hand one that's open!"

Westenhanger, as soon as she began to speak, had crossed the room swiftly and closed the door leading into the corridor completely. He turned back with a vexed expression on his face.

"My fault entirely," he said. "I ought to have shut that door. You nearly gave the show away to Douglas. Didn't I tell you it was obvious?"

Eileen looked from him to the cabinet and then back again to his face, which showed a mixture of triumph and amusement.

"But it isn't obvious," she protested. "I don't understand what you're driving at."

"We'll repeat the whole performance with Douglas, and you'll see the point."

He went to the door again and summoned the picket.

"Douglas, come inside. I strongly recommend to your attention the genuine antique carving on the back of this door. It's well worthy of study. Study it."

Douglas Fairmile obediently stepped into the room, faced the door and fixed his eye on the carving.

"I know it by heart, old man," he asserted. "You can't puzzle me with any of your parlour games."

"Got it well into your mind? All right. Miss Cressage will now blindfold you."

The girl, still more puzzled by this procedure, put the scarf over Douglas's eyes and fastened it in position.

"Blind as a bat, Douglas?" demanded Westenhanger. His tone changed. "I'm serious. You can't see anything?"

"Not a thing."

"Right."

Westenhanger took out his pen-knife and opened it silently. He drew Eileen's attention to it with a glance.

"Oh, half a jiff," he exclaimed, as if he suddenly remembered something. "One of the cabinet doors is open. I'll shut it." He shut his pen-knife with a click; but to Eileen's surprise he made no attempt to close the open door of the cabinet.

"Now, Douglas, this way. I'll lead you."

Again he gave the same series of orders as he had given to her. She saw Douglas put out his right hand, grope for the handle of the right-hand door, open it, and then inserting his arm into the case, reach to the left towards the place where the Talisman used to lie.

"Stop! . . . Now come out again, gently. Don't upset the glass bell."

Douglas withdrew his arm cautiously.

"One pace to the rear, and stand fast."

Douglas stepped back obediently. Westenhanger went up to the cabinet.

"I'm shutting the door. Hear the click?"

He suited the action to the word, closing the door which Douglas had opened. Then he turned round to Eileen.

"*Now* do you see, Miss Cressage? That'll do Douglas. You can take off your turban. It doesn't suit you."

Douglas disentangled himself from the scarf, blinked for a moment or two, and then looked at the cabinet.

"What's your little game?" he demanded. "The left-hand door's open now. It was the right-hand one that I opened."

"Exactly," said Westenhanger. "The left-hand door's been open all the time—*just as the thief left it*. Neither of you touched it. That's why I blindfolded you both. I wanted you to think both doors were shut; and I didn't want to close that left-hand door. Much better to leave things exactly as they are. The Dangerfields may want to call in the police after all, you know; and we mustn't destroy any possible clues. Hence the gloves I asked you to put on—you've left no finger-marks."

Eileen broke in with a trace of excitement in her voice.

"Now I *do* see. You wanted to test which hand I used when I opened the cabinet. Both Douglas and I are right-handed. The thief was left-handed because he opened the other door—not the one we opened. Is that it?"

"That's it." admitted Westenhanger. "I told you it was obvious. And of course all that by-play was just meant to keep your mind off the crucial action, so that you'd do it perfectly naturally, without giving it a thought. See it, Douglas? Don't forget the pattern on the back of the door; it's most important, you know!"

"You had me there, I'll admit," confessed Douglas.

"You wandered me completely, so that I hadn't a notion what you were after. And so the thief's left-handed, is he?"

"Looks like it, doesn't it?"

Eileen stepped over to the cabinet and examined it for a moment or two.

"How, exactly, did you come to think of it, Mr. Westenhanger? I suppose it was the left-hand door that gave you the key?"

"There's some confirmatory evidence," Westenhanger explained. "Will you stand in front of the case, Miss Cressage? Now notice that you've the choice between the two doors if you wanted to get at the Talisman. You're right-handed, so you choose the right-hand door, naturally. Besides, it's always easier to turn a handle clockwise than counter-clockwise; and that favours the right-hand again, subconsciously. To open the cabinet you turn the right-hand handle as you turn a corkscrew, which is easier than turning the left-hand handle counter-clockwise."

Eileen put out both hands and imitated the motion of opening the doors.

"That's true enough," she said. "I remember that sometimes a door handle gives one trouble if it works in the opposite direction from the usual way."

Westenhanger continued his explanation.

"Now look at where the bell has been placed. That's the really important point. The thief might have been a right-handed man and used his right hand to take the Talisman; then, after he had got it, he might have closed the door he had used and opened the left-hand one. But the bell gives him away."

Douglas examined the case closely.

"The bell's slightly to the right of its old position. Is that what you mean?"

Westenhanger nodded.

"That's it. A right-handed man goes in at the right-hand door, just as you both did. Then he crooks his elbow towards his chest to get his hand over to the Talisman. That brings his hand to the centre of the case. It's a narrower case, you notice. Not much room to manœuvre in it."

"I see," said Eileen. "He'd pick up the bell; and he'd have to put it down again—clear of the Talisman—in order to pick up the jewel. If he put it down on the right-hand side of the case, it would be in the way of his arm in getting out again, so he'd set it down *beyond* the Talisman towards the left of the case. Then he'd pick up the Talisman and take his hand and arm out of the case. Is that it?"

"Yes," confirmed Westenhanger. "That's what a right-handed man would do. And since the bell's been set down towards the right hand of the cabinet, it's obvious that there's been a left-hander at work, isn't it?"

"That seems right," Eileen admitted. "It's very clever of you to have noticed it."

"You noticed it yourself. It just happened that I was lucky enough to spot the thing almost at once."

Eileen reflected for a moment, then she addressed Westenhanger directly.

"There's just one other thing I don't quite understand. Out on the headland, you said you'd made certain about the matter after you met me there. That means you weren't quite sure before. What did you mean by that?"

Westenhanger laughed.

"That's obvious, too. Don't you see it now?"

The girl went over in her memory the talk which she had had with him half an hour previously; but quite evidently it suggested nothing to her mind as a solution.

"No," she admitted at last, "I can't think of anything."

"It's simple enough. Think of the things I did; don't bother about anything I said to you."

After a moment Eileen recalled something.

"You offered me a cigarette."

"Yes. I held the case so that you could reach it with either hand; but you used your right hand to pick out the cigarette."

"Was that all?" She put on a judicial expression. "That doesn't seem much to go on in a thing like this—does it, Douglas?"

"Look at him grinning," said Douglas, in sham disgust. "He's laughing at us. He's got more up his sleeve, of course."

Westenhanger admitted it with a nod.

"Of course I have. What happened next, Miss Cressage?"

"I smoked for a while."

"Do you usually smoke unlighted cigarettes?"

Eileen laughed at her omission.

"No, of course not. I remember now. You gave me your match-box."

"Hardly correct in detail. I was rude enough to pitch my match-box across to you, so that you could catch it with either hand. What I wanted to see was which hand you would use. You made a snatch at it—with your right hand."

"I didn't imagine I was being watched so closely as all that, Mr. Westenhanger. Is that all, now?"

"Oh, no. There's more to come. You finished your cigarette and threw away the stub. You tried to fling it over the cliff-edge on your right side, if you remember."

"I think so. One does these things without thinking about them."

"That's just why I attached importance to them in this case. Now think. It was a fairly long distance to throw a cigarette, wasn't it. You just failed to send yours over the edge. So you had to pitch it to the best of your ability. If you'd been left-handed you'd have used your left hand, swinging it across your body. What you actually did was to use your right hand in an awkward attitude. Evidently your right hand, even used awkwardly, was better than your left used in a natural gesture. Obvious conclusion—you were right-handed."

"That was rather neat, wasn't it, Douglas?"

"Oh, Conway always had the name of a smart lad, even among the great brains like myself. Don't let's interrupt him. I can see he's still bursting with news."

"How do you strike a match on a box, Douglas?" demanded Westenhanger, suddenly.

"How should I know? This way, of course."

Douglas fished a match-box from his pocket, took out a vesta and struck it.

"That's what you did, Miss Cressage. You held the match in your right hand and the box in your left, just as Douglas is holding them now. A left-hander reverses the positions and strikes the match with his left hand. I remember noticing that once."

"Anything more, Mr. Westenhanger?"

"Just one thing. After a while, I took out a cigarette myself and you had to throw my match-box across to me. You used your right hand again. That made five things, in any one of which even partial left-handedness might have come out. What settled it, to my mind, was the snatch at the match-box when I tossed it over to you. That's an almost instinctive movement, when you've no time to think. One uses the hand that's had most practice, provided one has a free choice between the two hands; and I was careful to pitch the box so that you might have used either hand for it."

"Well, you're a good actor, Mr. Westenhanger. I never suspected anything at all; and the whole time you must have been watching me like a cat watching a mouse."

"It wouldn't have been much good if you had suspected," said Westenhanger. He turned to Douglas. "Now, Douglas, does that evidence seem enough to prove that Miss Cressage had no hand in the Talisman's disappearance? I promised her I could do that. It's for you to say."

Douglas Fairmile had no doubts.

"Of course it does. I may not be an impartial judge, of course; for I never believed for a moment that Eileen had the least connection with the Talisman affair. But that evidence would convince most people. Smart of you to spot these things, Conway."

Conway Westenhanger glanced from one to the other.

"It's for Miss Cressage to say what we ought to do next," he pointed out to them. "My main reason for going into the thing at all was simply to clear her of suspicion."

Eileen gave him a grateful glance and seemed inclined to say something. Then quite evidently she changed her mind and chose a fresh subject.

"What do you think, Douglas?"

"Never suffered from doubts in my life. Seems to me the first thing is to put a stop to any more chatter with your name in it, Eileen. Call another general meeting. Let Conway make a few remarks. That would finish it."

Eileen looked from one to the other doubtfully. She reflected for a moment or two, while Douglas and Westenhanger waited for her to speak. At last she gave them her view.

"No, you're wrong, Douglas. That wouldn't finish it. It would simply turn it into something worse. Both Mrs. Caistor Scorton and that little creature Stickney were accurate enough in what they said last night. I was out of my room, just as they made out. If I wasn't stealing the Talisman, then they'd have their own ideas about where I was during that time. Mr. Westenhanger knows what I mean; and so do you, Douglas. And I can't clear myself. I really can't."

She deliberately caught the eye of each man in turn

and held it long enough to show she was not avoiding them; then she looked down, as if thinking carefully.

"You certainly mustn't say anything about this, just now. It wouldn't do me any good. And there's a better reason. Our one chance of catching this thief is to find the left-handed man amongst the people here. If you bring out this evidence, he'll be on his guard at once and cover up his left-handedness somehow. He could cut his right hand badly, or something like that."

"I know that," admitted Westenhanger, "but the main thing still seems to me to get you cleared. Don't you want to be?"

Eileen studied his face in silence for a moment.

"I'll tell you something," she said, at last. "When you came down this morning and began to talk, I thought you were just trying to be sympathetic; but I didn't take it at face value. I believed you were only trying to cheer me up, and that your talk about proving things wasn't meant to be taken seriously. Now I know you really did mean what you said. What's more, I've learned that somebody did more than just sympathise. You didn't stop there, Mr. Westenhanger: you did something practical to clear me of suspicion."

"I happened to be lucky, first shot—that's all."

She waved that aside and went on:

"You really *did* something, no matter how you choose to describe it; you didn't simply stand round, pitying me. Do you know, that's made things ever so much easier for me, now that I know about it. I can't explain why; it's just a feeling. I don't feel absolutely isolated now, as I did this morning. Don't think I'm ungrateful to you and Cynthia, Douglas, or to Nina either. You were all as kind as you could be. But somehow nobody seemed to be doing anything to help; and I was feeling the strain of it all horribly. Now it seems all right again, somehow."

She stopped for a moment, then added doubtfully:

"I don't suppose I've made it clear; but it is so. I feel as if a weight were off my mind. I don't care how long it is before the *Kestrel* comes back."

"What's the *Kestrel* got to do with it?" asked Douglas.

"I can't tell you," she said, in a lighter tone. "It's my turn to play the mystery-man, Mr. Westenhanger. But everything will be all right when the *Kestrel* drops anchor in the bay. I feel sure of that."

"Are you talking about the Talisman?" demanded Westenhanger.

"No! What's the *Kestrel* got to do with the Talisman?" Eileen asked in surprise. "I only meant my own affairs. I can't tell you anything about the Talisman. I know nothing about it."

Westenhanger accepted her statement without comment.

"Then I take it that you think we ought to use this affair"—he indicated the cabinet—"to track down the fellow who stole the Talisman? Things are to be left as they are, so far as you're concerned? You don't want us to say anything to the rest of them?"

"No, certainly not." There was no hesitation in her tone. "You've got a trump card with this thing, Mr. Westenhanger. You know that well enough. And the thief must be found. One has to agree even with Mr. Stickney at times. He's quite right. We *are* all under suspicion until this thing is cleared up; and I think it ought to be cleared up. I know just exactly how it feels to be under suspicion. You must see it through to the end and catch the thief. I'm sure you can—you're quite clever enough for that—and it's the only way to clear the rest of us completely. I wouldn't hear of it being used and wasted merely to clear me personally and leave all the rest in the lurch. We've got other people to think of as well."

"Very sporting of you, Eileen," said Douglas. "I think you're right. But if you change your mind, of course you'll let us know?"

"I'm really all right again, thanks. I shan't worry a bit now. Things are quite different—and I can wait for the *Kestrel*."

CHAPTER IX

For almost a week, Friocksheim had been under strain. First had come the sultry spell, days of oppressive heat which set sensitive nerves on edge and brought a certain lassitude to even the most active of the guests. The storm, though it cleared the physical atmosphere, had coincided with the creation of a fresh tension. A cloud of suspicion, heavier than the cumulus in the sky, had settled down upon the house; and as the days passed without any sign of its dispersion, its influence showed more and more clearly among the house-party. Even Douglas Fairmile's normal high spirits were unable to resist it entirely.

"Something will have to be done about this business, Conway," he complained, as they sat smoking in the Corinthian's Room in the afternoon. "It's gone on for three days now, and everyone's feeling it more or less. We're all getting off our feed, metaphorically of course."

Conway Westenhanger nodded without taking his eyes from the tapestry on the wall. He seemed to be studying it closely; but in reality Diana's hunting hardly impinged on his attention. Like Douglas, he was feeling the strain, although personally he was free from any suspicion.

"Unrestful atmosphere, right enough," he commented, shortly.

Douglas made a gesture of impotent irritation.

"Everything's at sixes and sevens," he went on. "Even old Rollo—decent bird—is getting too much for me. If the talk drifts round towards the root of the trouble, he just smiles that far-away smile of his—as if he was thinking about something else entirely—and one almost expects him to tell us again that it's all right, that the damned thing will turn up again in due course, and that we needn't worry over it. Politeness carried to that pitch is enervating, Conway. That's a fact."

"I feel the same myself. But somehow, he's almost beginning to make me believe he really means it. A kind of hypnotic susggestion, I suppose. It's impressive, whether you like it or not, to see a man take a loss like that so quietly. I couldn't do it."

"Nor I. But he'll have the lot of us in the jumps if this goes on. I'm not a suspicious oaf like Freddie, but it irks me all the same. It's not so much that there's a thief among us that bothers me. We've mixed with all these people before—bar Wraxall. What really puts my nerves on edge is that I don't know *which* of 'em's the thief. I want to see the rest of us cleared."

Westenhanger's eye travelled incuriously over the group of Diana's nymphs and passed on to the stag at the other side of the tapestry; but it was evidently merely a mechanical movement. His thoughts absorbed the whole of his attention. Before he made any reply to Douglas the door opened and Helga Dangerfield came into the room. She nodded to them as she passed, and went into the library.

"Where's Wraxall to-day?" asked Westenhanger, merely to avoid leaving an impression on the girl that they had stopped talking on her account.

"Digging up megatheriums or flint arrows somewhere in the neighbourhood," said Douglas, taking the hint. "Or else he's chaffering for the oldest nutmeg-grater in Frogsholme. He seems really keen on that sort of stuff."

Helga Dangerfield came through the library door with a book in her hand.

"You like this room?" she asked, pausing for a moment as she passed. "So do I. It used to be my playroom when I was getting beyond the crawling stage."

"Nice floor for building castles on," Westenhanger suggested, with a glance across the smooth marble pavement. "You must have had rather a jolly time. Plenty of room."

"Sometimes I wish I had it all over again." She smiled at her own idea, then added: "I must hurry off; Nina and Cynthia are waiting for me."

As soon as she had left the room Douglas returned to the point at which the conversation had been interrupted.

"Can't you think of anything, Conway? I admit I'm not the star performer in the thinking orchestra. It's up to you to play a solo while I do the grunts of approval down in the bass."

Westenhanger shook his head.

"Eliminate and eliminate, that's the only way. And the only thing we have to eliminate with is this left-handed affair. It's none so easy, Douglas. The real bother rises out of the fact that most left-handed people are partly ambidextrous."

"I get your meaning up to the word 'fact,'" said Douglas, apologetically, "but it seems to slip a cog after that somehow. What about words of one syllable? I seem to remember seeing special clubs for left-handed golfers. Not much ambidexterity about that, surely?"

"That's just the point," explained Westenhanger. "I've been thinking about one or two left-handed people I know, and in most things you wouldn't spot that they were left-handed at all. If it's a one-handed job they're doing, they may use their right hand oftener than their left. It's only in two-handed things, like golf, or cricket, or billiards, or cutting hay with a scythe, that they give themselves away completely. It's the arm-motion rather than the hand that seems to come in. This Talisman affair is a case in point. The thief was using his whole arm to get inside the case."

"That's probably so," conceded Douglas, reluctantly. "It isn't so easy as I thought."

Before Westenhanger could elaborate his views, Eileen Cressage came hurriedly into the room. Her face was flushed with excitement; her eyes were bright; and her whole carriage showed that she had thrown off her load of difficulties at last. Westenhanger had never seen her looking so care-free.

"The *Kestrel's* back at last!" she announced breathlessly. "She's making for the bay. I saw her from the headland, and hurried back to the house to tell you; that's why I'm out of breath. I wanted you to hear the news at once, because it's all right now. I'm sure Mrs. Brent will clear everything up when she comes ashore."

"That's the best of news. I am glad, Eileen," said Douglas, before Westenhanger could say anything. "You've stuck it out like a good 'un, but it's about time it stopped."

Westenhanger added nothing to Douglas's words. His

expression spoke for him better than anything he could have said.

"I can't wait here," Eileen explained rapidly. "I must get down to the beach and get on board as soon as the yacht comes in. I began to think she'd never come back. These three days have been like centuries for slowness."

"We'll put you on board," said Westenhanger. "Come along, Douglas."

"Thanks. But really I'd rather go by myself, if you'll put the boat into the water for me."

They walked down to the boat-house, got out one of the boats and brought it round to the tiny jetty for her. She stepped lightly aboard, waved her thanks, and pulled with easy strokes to the *Kestrel*, which had just let go her anchor. The two men watched her get safely on board the yacht and then turned back towards the house.

"I suppose we'll hear all about it to-night or to-morrow," hazarded Douglas, as they left the jetty. "You seem a bit relieved, Conway; and I feel rather that way myself. It's been a stiffish three days for a girl, thanks to Master Freddie."

"I *am* relieved," Westenhanger acknowledged. "I've had her troubles very much on my mind, and I'm only too glad to see light ahead. But you needn't expect to learn much about the Talisman business, Douglas; she never had anything to do with that, you know."

"At least one part of this infernal mix-up will be straightened out, though, and that's always something."

Westenhanger made a gesture of assent.

"One never knows what may come out, once people start talking," he said, hopefully. "It's quite on the cards we may hit on a new idea, after we've heard Mrs. Brent. She's the missing witness, the only person who hasn't had a chance to tell her story of what happened that night."

"Who's that coming up in the car, I wonder," said Douglas.

Westenhanger looked across the lawn and saw a motor with a single passenger at the front door of the house.

"Seems to be Eric Dangerfield."

"Something wrong with him, then," Douglas commented. "Look at him hobbling up the steps with a stick. Seems as if he'd lamed himself a bit."

Eric Dangerfield's figure laboriously ascended the steps and disappeared into the house.

"Sprained ankle, or something like that," was Westen-hanger's verdict. "Well, Douglas, we'll just have to be patient. There'll be no 'orrible revelations for an hour or two at least."

His guess was quite accurate. Eileen and Mrs. Brent came ashore from the yacht only in time to dress, and neither of them appeared until the remainder of the party had assembled. Eric Dangerfield limped into the dining-room, still using his stick.

"Nothing much," he explained in answer to a question. "I twisted my ankle rather badly and had to rest it. That's why I didn't get back here sooner."

Mrs. Brent took very little part in the conversation at the dinner-table, but when the servants had left the room after serving coffee, she glanced round to secure attention and then addressed the company in general.

"I understand," she said, with a certain sub-acid tone in her voice, "that during my absence, Mr. Stickney has been organising a symposium of sorts. It seems a pity not to give my contribution to the common stock, even if it is slightly belated. Suppose we all go into the drawing-room after dinner for a few moments. I shan't detain you long."

It was impossible to learn from Rollo Dangerfield's face whether or not he understood her reference. Much to his regret, he explained, neither he nor his wife could be there. They had a meeting in the village that evening which in courtesy they must attend.

"I quite understand, Rollo," Mrs. Brent hastened to reassure him. "You won't miss much here, and in any case I can explain the whole thing to you to-morrow. It's of no consequence."

She made no further reference to the matter until the whole party, with the exception of their host and hostess, had gathered in the drawing-room. Choosing her favourite chair, she made a sign to Eileen to sit down beside her, and then waited until the others had grouped themselves.

"It appears," she began, frowning in Freddie Stickney's direction. "It appears that privacy has gone out of fashion since I went away. That's a new phase for Friocksheim, and I don't feel I'm much to blame for not anticipating it. Certainly, I didn't foresee such a state of affairs, and to that extent I'm responsible for some events which ought never to have occurred."

She stared at Freddie as though he were some curious animal which she was inspecting for the first time.

"It seems," she went on acidly, "that no one can have any private affairs now, so I think the best thing is to have a complete clearing-up of some misunderstandings—is that the right word, Mr. Stickney?—which have got abroad. I don't wish to leave any ground for such things in future. Miss Cressage agrees with me."

She turned to the girl.

"Tell them the whole affair from start to finish, Eileen."

Eileen Cressage looked up, but paused for a moment or two before saying anything. Westenhanger could see that she hated the business, but was determined to go through with it.

"Some of you know," she began, "that the other night I lost a lot of money at bridge. I didn't realise during the game how big a loss it was. Very foolish of me, I admit."

Mrs. Brent interrupted her sharply.

"I think the facts will be quiet sufficient, Eileen. I shouldn't make any comments, if I were you."

Eileen accepted the correction, understanding the underlying motive.

"I was taken aback," she went on, "when I heard how much I owed Mrs. Caistor Scorton. I don't wish to keep anything back now. It was far more than I could pay in any reasonable time. I lost my head, I'm afraid; I wanted at any cost to avoid a public explanation. So when a cheque was suggested, I filled one in and handed it over, intending to explain to Mrs. Caistor Scorton how matters stood, as soon as I could get her by herself.'

Westenhanger let his eyes wander to Mrs. Caistor Scorton's face, but it was absolutely expressionless.

"I felt that was the best thing to do," Eileen continued. "It avoided public explanations and unpleasantness for everyone, and it really made things no worse."

She paused, and Mrs. Brent took up the story, as though their parts had been pre-arranged between them.

"I seldom interfere in other people's affairs. I was brought up to believe that one shouldn't be a busybody. But some things seem to me outside the rules of the game, and then an outsider can take a hand. I noticed a thing that evening which seemed to me outside the rules. Taking advantage of a girl in a tight corner is . . . well, I needn't comment on it."

She darted a contemptuous glance at Morchard, without taking any pains to disguise it.

"That was what happened that evening. Naturally, I stepped in."

Morchard's face showed that he had not known this before. He made no comment, and Mrs. Brent continued.

"I asked Eileen to come to my room after everyone had gone to bed. I wanted to have a good talk with her; strike while the iron was hot, you see, and get a promise out of her that she wouldn't gamble in that way again. If I'd waited till next morning I wouldn't have been able to make such a strong impression."

She glanced towards Freddie Stickney again.

"I asked her to come to my room without letting anyone know she was coming, because things like that are better done without the chance of any other party poking his nose into the affair. It seemed to me quite a private matter, with which no one else had any concern. Curiously enough, Mr. Stickney, my views on that point are still unchanged."

Freddie's beady eyes were fixed on the carpet. He refused to be drawn. At a gesture from Mrs. Brent, Eileen continued the narrative.

"I waited until I thought everyone was out of the way. Then I took my bedroom candle, slipped on my dressing-gown, and made my way to Mrs. Brent's room. That was where I was going when Mrs. Caistor Scorton saw me."

The girl had got over the worst of her story; she reached a point where no blame could attach to her, and her voice showed the difference. At last she was able to shake herself free from suspicions. Westenhanger noticed that she did not even look in Freddie's direction. He had ceased to be of any importance.

"I went down the staircase and along the corridor to Mrs. Brent's room. She had been sitting up waiting for me. I'd like to tell you how kind . . ."

"No comments, please, Eileen," interjected Mrs. Brent again. "Let us have the facts."

The girl's eyes met Mrs. Brent's, resisted for a moment, and then dropped.

"Very well," she assented. "It's for you to say. They'll

know how I feel without my putting it into words.' I'll go on. Mrs. Brent told me she would pay my debt. She gave me some advice. And she made me promise two things. The first was that I wouldn't play bridge again for stakes higher than I could afford. I promised that. I'd had my lesson. The second promise was that I wouldn't mention to anyone anything that had happened that night. I promised that, too. It seemed little enough to promise, after her kindness. She laid a good deal of stress on it. She said she hated to have anything of the kind known."

"I do," confirmed Mrs. Brent. "I've no desire to publish things of that sort. It's a private affair. Of course, I'd no idea then that privacy was a back number. I've learned."

Eileen took up her narrative again.

"Mrs. Brent hadn't £200 in notes with her. She gave me a cheque and told me to go up to London first thing in the morning and pay it into my account, so as to meet the cheque I had given Mrs. Scorton, in case it was paid in immediately. Meanwhile, the thunderstorm began."

Mrs. Brent interposed once more.

"I found the storm was getting rather too much for my nerves after the first peal or two. Having someone in the room with me helped to steady things a little; so I asked Miss Cressage to stay with me until the thunder passed off. She waited with me till some time in the small hours. Then I let her go; for she had to get some sleep, and she had to be up in order to catch the first train."

She broke off and invited Eileen to continue.

"I left Mrs. Brent's room and went back to my own. Just as I got out of Mrs. Brent's room, Helga passed me . . ."

Helga Dangerfield's face showed complete amazement.

"You saw me?" she demanded. "You must have made a mistake. It was someone else, surely. Why, I fell asleep at the tail-end of the storm and didn't wake up again till morning."

Eileen looked puzzled.

"You were going towards the Corinthian's Room, Helga. I thought perhaps you were looking for a book to read, if the storm had kept you awake. You were past before you noticed me, I thought; and I was quite glad you hadn't seen me, since Mrs. Brent didn't want anyone to know I'd been down to see her. You had your blue dressing-gown on. Don't you remember?"

Helga Dangerfield shook her head definitely.

"You must have been dreaming, Eileen."

"Well, it doesn't matter," said Eileen. "I'll go on with the story. I went up to my room, blew out my candle, switched on my light, and crept into bed. I didn't sleep for quite a long time. I was rather shaken up, you know, between the storm and the things that had happened. But I dropped off at last, and just wakened in time to catch the first train."

She looked round the circle till her eye fell on Eric.

"You remember we went up to town together?"

Eric nodded, but said nothing. Eileen took up the thread again.

"In town, I went straight to my bank and paid in Mrs. Brent's cheque. After that I did some shopping. Then I suddenly remembered something. I never wear jewellery, but I have some things. It struck me that I might raise something on them and so be able to repay Mrs. Brent part of her cheque at once. It would be a kind of relief to my mind. She'd know I was taking things seriously. So I went back to my bank, where I kept them; took them out; went to Starbecks with them. I've dealt with Starbecks for years. They know me quite well, and they made no difficulty about it. I didn't get enough to repay Mrs. Brent entirely, but I felt it was always something done. As I was coming out of Starbecks' door I met Mr. Westenhanger, and we had just time to get to the station and catch the train."

Mrs. Brent made a gesture to stop the girl at this point.

"I think that covers the whole question," she said. "Now I've just a word or two to say. If I had imagined what was going to happen, of course I'd never have asked Miss Cressage to give me that promise. But I hardly supposed that any sane person could have foreseen what was coming. It passes all reasonable bounds. I've nothing to say about Miss Cressage's views on the matter. Apparently she believed in keeping private affairs confidential even under very great strain. She'd given her promise, and she kept it."

"What I felt," explained Eileen, "was that I'd given you two promises together. If I broke one of them straight away, what reliance could you have placed on my word in the second affair? I had to keep both. And, of course, I had only to wait for you to come back. Then you'd let me off my promise and I could explain everything. It only meant waiting, I thought. But I hadn't quite counted on the construction that would be put on things."

Her eyes flashed indignantly as she turned to Freddie Stickney.

"I haven't enjoyed giving these explanations. Probably most of you haven't enjoyed listening to them; but I'm sure you'll understand why you had to hear them."

There was an almost inaudible murmur of sympathetic assent from most of the circle. As it died down, Mrs. Brent closed the incident in a phrase or two.

"That's all. Miss Cressage had one serious fault, apparently. She was over-straight. I shouldn't have blamed her in the slightest if she'd told the whole story when she was asked. She preferred to keep the very letter of her promise. I don't envy some people their feelings just now. But perhaps they haven't any. Toads and so forth are said to be very insensitive creatures, and the reptiles generally feel little discomfort. So I am told."

She took Eileen's arm gently, and they left the room together. Undoubtedly, as a creator of discomfort, Mrs. Brent ran Freddie close. Westenhanger caught Douglas's eye, and they followed Mrs. Brent.

"Let's try the garden?" suggested Douglas. "Air in there seems a bit sultry for my taste. That last whang of Mrs. Brent's wasn't perhaps tactful; but it was nothing to what she might have said if she'd really let herself go. I've never seen her even peeved before; and to-night she was boiling underneath the surface. Even the trained observer, Freddie, can hardly have failed to notice the weather signs."

"Well, I suppose we'll be rid of some of them by the first train to-morrow."

"No we shan't! Nobody can leave Friocksheim till this Talisman business is cleared up. Your ways are not ours, Conway. All the rest of us are still under suspicion and we've got to hang on until the 'All Clear' signal goes. Pleasant prospect, isn't it? Well, we needn't talk to 'em more than's needful."

Westenhanger looked gloomy.

"There's only one way out of it, then. We've got to find the thief, if we can, and as quick as we can."

"Right you are, but easier said than done." Douglas's voice did not sound very hopeful. "Another canter in the Elimination Stakes to begin with?"

"All right. We'll be rigid this time. To start with, we can out aside as completely cleared: ourselves, Mr. and Mrs. Dangerfield, Mrs. Brent, Nina, Cynthia, and Eileen Cressage. Do you O.K. that?"

Douglas acquiesced with a nod.

"No doubt in these cases. I'm going on character as much as alibis and so forth. Let's sit down."

They found a garden seat which was dry and seated themselves.

"Mrs. Scorton? No motive that I can see. I think she drops out also."

"Agreed."

"Then there's Morchard." An angry tone came into Westenhanger's voice. "He's out of it too. You see why? Well, naturally he was the man Mrs. Brent was getting at. Didn't you see he offered to give Eileen the money if she'd come to his room? He'd be waiting there for her, not roaming about the house picking up the Talisman. Obvious, I think. Unless—— Could he have taken it and meant to throw suspicion on her? No, he wouldn't know she had been out of her room at all that night. No, that's wrong. We can leave Morchard out of it."

Douglas kicked angrily at the ground.

"The infernal thing is that one can do nothing to Morchard. The least row would lead to the devil of a scandal, and Eileen would suffer. It's Freddie's case over again, only fifty times worse. Our hands are tied."

"That's so," said Westenhanger, shortly. "Let's go on."

Quite evidently he disliked the whole subject.

"That leaves still in the net,' he continued, "Wraxall for one. I'm prejudiced in favour of Wraxall; but if he'd planned that theft beforehand, he'd have fixed up some very neat, circumstantial story to account for all his night's doings, you may be sure. And he undoubtedly had the most complete tale of the lot. I'm morally sure he didn't do it; but there's a loop-hole all the same. Besides, we can't afford to ignore possible motives, and there's no question that he came here for one purpose only—to get the Talisman. Leave Wraxall in, eh? We're trying to be inclusive, remember."

"Wraxall's a good sort," was Douglas's verdict. "I can't think he's the man we're after. But leave him in, since we can't count him as definitely cleared."

"Freddie?"

"I'm all for keeping Freddie under observation. I don't say he took the thing, of course. Can't go that length. But the line he's followed all along has been just the sort of thing he might have been expected to do, if he were the man we want. Who would suspect him, when he volunteered as a sleuth from Sleuth Town? Good bit of camouflage for a criminal, I think. And he had a very poor account to give of himself when it came to the pinch, very thin. Freddie stays in, so far as I'm concerned."

"My feeling too. Well, that leaves only two more, both Dangerfields: Eric and Helga. I'm not an enthusiast for Eric. Rather a rotter, it seems to me. But there's nothing very definite against him; we agreed on that before."

"Leave him in, then," Douglas decided. "We can't say more than 'not proven' for him, can we?"

"That brings us to Helga. I say, Douglas, did you make anything of that affair to-night? The girl wasn't lying. Neither was Eileen."

"That was what I felt," concurred Douglas. "Neither of 'em was lying, to my mind. And yet the thing seems flatly impossible unless one of them was giving the truth a pretty wide miss."

"It might have been someone else in a similar dressing-gown," suggested Westenhanger, half-heartedly.

"No good, Conway. The only other women available are Mrs. Dangerfield and Mrs. Scorton. They're both rather under middle height. Helga's a well-built girl, taller than the average. There could be no mistake about it."

Westenhanger cogitated for a time.

"I've got it!" he said, at last. "It's self-evident. Eileen was wide awake, obviously. But suppose Helga walks in her sleep? She wouldn't know she'd been there at all, if she got back to bed eventually without waking up. That would account for the affair, wouldn't it? It's the only simple solution. It might even explain other things as well."

He ruminated for a few more seconds before continuing. "I'll ask Eileen about it to-morrow. She was excited at that time, or she'd probably have spotted it as somnambulism at once. Perhaps she'll remember something if she thinks over it. This may turn out to be the key to the whole damned thing."

CHAPTER X

MRS. BRENT'S intervention did nothing to relax the tension in the social atmosphere of Friocksheim; on the contrary, it increased the general discomfort of the situation. Up to the moment of her reappearance, some attempt had been made, by common consent, to smooth over the awkwardness of things; but after her revelations it was inevitable that the guests should separate into inimical camps. On the surface a casual observer might have detected nothing amiss, since any display of open animosity would have made inevitable the scandal which all of them wished to avoid. Freddie Stickney and Morchard were treated with a distant and rigid courtesy which in itself emphasised the existence of new conditions. Beyond that, they were ignored by almost all the others. Mrs. Caistor Scorton alone seemed to keep them on the old footing, and she thus served as a link between the two parties.

How much Rollo Dangerfield knew—or suspected—Westenhanger was unable to conjecture. Mrs. Brent, Helga, or Eric might have opened the old man's eyes. Whether they had done so or not, his old-fashioned courtesy seemed to make no distinctions among his guests; and Westenhanger was left in doubt as to whether Rollo was still in complete ignorance or else, knowing the facts, he put his duties as a host before his private feelings as regarded Morchard and Freddie.

On the norming after the *Kestrel's* arrival, Westenhanger attached himself to Eileen and persuaded her to go with him to a quiet part of the gardens, where they were unlikely to be interrupted. He was anxious to secure what information he could about the appearance of Helga Dangerfield on the night of the storm, and he lost very little time in coming to the point.

"I was rather puzzled by that incident you mentioned last night," he said, as they picked out a secluded seat.

"Your meeting Helga in the corridor, I mean. Anyone could see that you were both telling the truth, and yet it sounds a bit impossible, doesn't it?"

"I was puzzled, too. I saw her quite plainly, hardly much further off than you are just now."

"Had you both got candles?"

"No, she had none; but I saw her quite distinctly by the light of my own."

"The electric lights weren't on?"

"No. But I could see perfectly plainly, except that a draught made my candle flicker. I recognised her dressing-gown. And no one could mistake her height and her walk—you know that way she carries herself, quite unmistakable, so graceful. Oh, it was she, undoubtedly."

"Did you see her face, by any chance? Did she look towards you?"

"No. She passed by as if she hadn't noticed me. I thought she hadn't."

"With your light in your hand? Curious, isn't it?"

Eileen considered the matter for some seconds without replying. Then her face lighted up.

"Oh, now I see what you mean! Of course! It was stupid of me not to think of that immediately. She was walking in her sleep?"

"It would account for the affairs, if she were? I mean, that idea fits with what you remember, does it?"

"Of course it does! I ought to have thought of it for myself, at once. But I never knew anyone who walked in their sleep. It's always been outside my experience, and I rather disbelieved most of the tales I've heard about it. So it didn't suggest itself to me until you mentioned the candle in my hand. Of course, then I saw at once that she couldn't help seeing me if she had been awake."

"Suppose we assume she's a somnambulist. She doesn't know she walks in her sleep. That's evident. For if she knows she's subjects to it, she'd have seen the explanation for herself at once; whereas she was just as puzzled as you were over the thing. Now doesn't that suggest something further to you?"

Eileen knitted her brows for a moment or two before she saw his meaning.

"The Talisman?" she asked finally.

"Yes. Suppose she took it away that night. She

may have concealed it somewhere and clean forgotten—
or never known, rather—that she had ever touched it."

The girl's face showed her surprise at this suggestion.

"Do you know, that's wonderfully clever! I really
believe you've come very near the mark. And wouldn't
it be a relief if it turned out to be true? There'd be no
thief after all."

"If some of them turned out to be thieves, I don't know
that it would lower them much in my opinion now,"
Westenhanger observed, elliptically.

Eileen avoided a direct reply.

"What I meant was that this cloud of suspicion would
be swept away and most of us could get back to normal
again. It's no use pretending that we're enjoying Friocksheim just now."

Before Westenhanger could say anything further, Nina
Lindale appeared, crossing the lawn before them. Eileen
beckoned to her.

"Nina, did you borrow my mirror by any chance?"

Nina Lindale shook her head.

"No, never saw it. You mean your silver one with
your initials on the back? It was on your dressing-table
a couple of days ago."

"Perhaps Cynthia's got it," Eileen conjectured.

"She's just behind me," Nina told her. "You can
ask her when she comes along. Tell her I've gone down
to the cove, if she asks. We're going to bathe."

She nodded her thanks and took the path leading to
the bathing-place. A few minutes after she had gone,
Cynthia appeared in her turn; but she also failed to throw
any light on the matter of the mirror.

"Sorry I can't help, but I never set my eyes on the
thing. Most annoying to have it go amissing, Eileen.
Take mine any time you want it."

"Thanks. I can't imagine what's become of my own,
though. It's not the sort of thing one mislays."

"Oh, it'll turn up all right. I shouldn't worry. Won't
you people come down and bathe? It's just the morning
for it."

They allowed themselves to be persuaded.

Westenhanger paid little attention to the incident of
the mirror. His mind was busy with a scheme which had
been concerted between himself and Douglas on the previous night. The list of suspects had now been reduced

to four; and it only remained to discover the left-handed person in this limited group.

A midday change in the weather favoured their plans. During lunch a thin rain began, and it soon became evident that the afternoon would be wet. With a little tactful management, the two men succeeded in carrying off Wraxall and Eric Dangerfield to the billiard-room.

"What about it?" inquired Douglas, indicating the cue-rack.

Eric shook his head with a smile.

"Leave me out," he said, indicating his lame ankle. "I can't stand on two feet with any comfort yet, much less lean over the table."

"You, then Wraxall?" Douglas suggested.

But the American declined his offer.

"I've seen you play. I'm not in your class."

"Give you a reasonable number of points to make a game of it."

It was quite obvious that Wraxall did not care to play, and Douglas refrained from pressing him. Westenhanger looked out of the window.

"A soaker of a day! We'll have to put in the time somehow. Come along, Douglas. We're bored stiff. Trot out some of your parlour tricks and keep us amused. Anything's better than nothing."

"I don't quite like the way you put it, Conway," protested Douglas, with a grin. "You haven't just got the knack of the felicitous phrase, as it were. You mean well, and all that; but somehow you don't just bring it off."

"Produce your latest, anyhow. The only stipulation I make is that you don't try to interest us in Find the Lady or the Elusive Pea. These are barred. But if you can make any money off me by other methods you're welcome to it."

He sat down and the others followed his example. Douglas considered for a moment and then took a Swan vesta box from his pocket.

"My sleight of hand's a bit rusty, I'm afraid," he apologised. "But perhaps I might manage to pull off this one if you haven't seen it before. Got a florin by any chance, Wraxall?"

The American searched his pockets.

"A florin," he inquired, "that's what you call a two-shilling piece, isn't it? This coinage of yours always makes me want to think before I can be sure about it."

He found his florin and handed it across to Douglas, who refused it.

"No," he explained, "I don't want you to say I palmed the thing. Observe carefully."

He slid the match-box half open and, holding the box so that they could all see plainly, he placed a florin of his own among the matches.

"My coin's under the picture of the Swan, you see?"

He closed the box and handed it over to Wraxall.

"Now put your florin in at the other end of the box. You can mark your coin, if you like."

Wraxall contented himself with noting the date of the florin before putting it in.

"Now shut the box," directed Douglas, "and hand it over to me. Just chuck it across."

Wraxall did so. Douglas caught it and held it out so that it was well away from his sleeve.

"This is the sticky bit," he announced. "Are you all sure that both coins are in the box? Quite sure? Well, seeing's believing. Have a look."

Holding the box in one hand, he slid the inner case forward with his finger until one coin showed. Then, without using his left hand, he reversed the box and showed the other end open, so that they could satisfy themselves that the two coins were still there.

"All content? Four bob in the box? I'll just show you them again."

He did so. As he closed the box for the last time, his voice changed as though he were trying to suppress his satisfaction at having got through his sleight of hand without detection.

"Now, Wraxall. I'll sell you the box as it stands for three bob. Take the offer?"

Wraxall pondered for an instant.

"It's this coinage bother," he explained. "Three bob? That's three shillings, isn't it?"

"Yes. I'm offering to sell you the thing for three shillings. You think it contains four shillings—two florins. I don't guarantee that. I simply sell the box, matches included with the other contents. Going . . . going . . ."

"I take you!" snapped Wraxall, certain that he would have detected any legerdemain.

117

"Right-o!" agreed Douglas, pleasantly. "You win. Here's the box. I'll just go through the formality of collecting your three bob, though."

He tossed the box over to Wraxall, who caught it and paid Douglas three shillings. The conjurer grinned mockingly.

"Quite satisfied with your bargain? Have a look inside the box. Both florins present and correct? You'll be glad to see *your own one again*!"

Wraxall saw the point almost immediately.

"Confound you, Fairmile! You've had the nerve to sell me my own florin! So I've paid three shillings for *your* florin. Is that it? And you muddled me up with all this talk about sleight of hand. That's neat. That's very neat indeed."

"Well, here's your three shillings," said Douglas, tossing them across one by one. "Now I'll take my florin and we're back at the start again. I'd be ashamed to rob anyone by that trick."

"You mean you'd hate to take advantage of the weakminded?" corrected the American, accepting his discomfiture with a smile.

"No. That trick's really an obstinacy corrector. You'd be astonished to see how often it comes off—five times out of six at the lowest, I've found. Well, here's another."

He turned to Eric Dangerfield.

"Got four pennies by any chance."

Eric searched his pockets and found the required coins.

"Now to avoid disputes later," Douglas explained, "you'll count 'em out one by one on to the table beside you."

Eric carefully counted out the four coins, putting them down one at a time.

"Four, I make it," he stated.

Douglas held out his hand with the fingers outspread.

"See it? Quite empty? No trap-doors or magic cabinets concealed anywhere? See the back too? Well, put your pennies into my palm. . . . I now close my hand. I take out my handkerchief. I shake it, showing that no coin is concealed in it. I cover my hand. Now, I say I've got *five* pennies in my hand. You can take off the handkerchief, if you like. *Five* pennies. Give me a bob if I'm wrong?"

Eric Dangerfield had been watching closely.

"All right," he agreed.

"Well, then. I *am* wrong, and you owe me a bob. I didn't bet a bob I was right. I said, 'Give me a bob if I'm *wrong*.'"

Eric Dangerfield fished out a shilling, but Douglas refused to take it. He was about to continue the prearranged series of tests when, to his surprise, Westenhanger introduced a variation in the programme.

"Before I forget, Douglas, you might give me the name of the place where you got that new racket. I want to make a note of it."

He felt in his pockets, then applied to Eric.

"Got a fountain pen, by any chance, Dangerfield?"

Eric took one from his waistcoat pocket and offered it to Westenhanger, who had pulled out a piece of paper. Westenhanger put out his hand and then withdrew it again.

"I hate using any one else's pen for fear of spoiling the nib. I write heavier than most people. Would you mind jotting the address down?"

Eric wrote down the address which Douglas gave, and both men noted that he used his pen in the normal way. Westenhanger put the paper in his pocket and again surprised Douglas by going to the window and looking out.'

"It's clearing up a bit. What about some fresh air, Douglas?"

This was the prearranged signal for breaking off operations; but Douglas was puzzled by its coming so early.

"Oh, all right," he agreed. "If you want to get soaked, I don't mind."

Eric could not be expected to join them, and Wraxall, for the sake of politeness, had to stay behind to keep the lame man company. As soon as they were well away from the house, Douglas showed his surprise.

"You broke that off a bit soon, Conway. Of course, I'm quite satisfied. They're both right-handed. Wraxall handed the box and grabbed at the shillings quite according to plan; and Dangerfield counted his lot of coins in the normal way. But I'd like to have worked a few more stunts on them, just for certainty's sake."

"Not worth while," Westenhanger said. "I've got

something absolutely certain to go on. As it happens, you're wrong, Douglas. Wraxall is right-handed. But the other fellow is ambidextrous. He uses his right hand for hand-movements; but when his arm comes in, he's left-handed."

"How do you make that out?" demanded Douglas in surprise.

"Just an accidental observation. He carries his fountain pen in his right-hand waistcoat pocket. You and I carry ours in the left pocket, so as to get at it easily with our right hands. He uses his left hand to take it from his pocket, and then he passess the pen to his right hand before he uses it. You see he uses his arm in taking it out, and he's left-armed. That's absolutely conclusive to my mind, and I didn't want to run any chance of arousing suspicion by going through the whole programme. I think we've got our man."

"That was pretty cute. I was watching him, but I didn't spot the thing, although I was on the look-out for it."

"It was just a bit of luck. Nothing to boast about."

Douglas considered for a time.

"Well, where do we stand? Motive? He's hard up and lost a lot at cards. Opportunity? He was wandering about the house late that night. Besides, his room is close to the one the Talisman was in. He's left-armed—the type we're looking for. He went up to town next morning—possibly to get the thing out of the house for fear of a search, even if he didn't dispose of it in some way then—pawning or some such business. And, by the way, he's got lamed in some way. I wonder if there is a man-trap after all, and he got mixed up in it slightly."

Westenhanger listened to this catalogue with a gloomy face.

"There isn't an atom of real proof in the whole lot. We could never satisfy anyone on the strength of that stuff alone. I'd never mention a word to anyone about it, Douglas; because we must have definite proof. And I don't quite see our next move."

"Watch him, and keep on watching, on the chance of something turning up, I suppose."

"It's a poor chance," said Westenhanger.

That idea remained with him for the rest of the day. The step-by-step process of elimination had been carried through with complete success; but it was useless to pretend to himself that the result was conclusive evidence. At the best it became a case of "Not Proven": a moral certaintly, perhaps, but nothing more. Something further was needed to establish the identity of the culprit beyond doubt. And the more he puzzled over the problem, the less chance could he see of bringing the thing home. One might devise a scheme for trapping a fellow-guest; but how could one out-manœuvre a man working on his own ground with complete knowledge of all the possibilities of the environment?

Even when he went to bed, Westenhanger lay awake seeking some solution of the problem. At last he realised that he was unlikely to get any farther forward; but by that time he had fretted himself into a state of complete wakefulness.

"No use going on like this," he reflected at last. "I must get something to take my mind off the thing. It's infernally tantalising to be so near it and yet not to hit on the right track. I'll go down to the library and get a book. I can read myself to sleep all right—push the affair out of my thoughts. If I lie here I'll simply worry at it till morning."

He got up and put on his dressing-gown. His watch showed him that it was in the small hours; and all the house was quiet. He opened his door cautiously, took his candle with him, and went down the stairs.

When he reached the hall below, he was surprised to find a light shining from the open door of old Dangerfield's study; and as he came opposite the room he looked in. Rollo was sitting, fully dressed, beside the fire; and at the sound of Westenhanger's approach he glanced up. Westenhanger, feeling that his midnight perambulations demanded some explanation, turned into the study. Rollo showed no surprise, but invited him to sit down on the opposite side of the hearth.

"Got a touch of insomnia, to-night," explained Westenhanger, "so I thought I'd come down for a book and see if I could read myself to sleep. I was just on the way to the library when I saw the light in here."

Rollo's face expressed some concern.

"I hope you aren't subject to it," he said. "Anything going wrong with one's sleep is a terrible thing."

Westenhanger detected more feeling in the comment than he had expected; and for a moment he was surprised.

Then it flashed across his mind that Rollo probably knew of Helga's somnambulism and had thus a keener interest in such matters than most people. He hastened to reassure the old man.

"No; it's not chronic. Just a touch of it one gets at times."

A fleeting expression changed Rollo Dangerfield's face for an instant; but it was gone before Westenhanger could identify it.

"I sometimes get it myself when I'm worried," said old Dangerfield. "It's a bad business if it gets a firm hold on one. You're not worried about anything, I hope?" he added, sympathetically.

Westenhanger hardly cared to tell a downright lie.

"Oh, nothing in particular, nothing to do with my own affairs," he said, trying to pass the matter off lightly.

But Rollo fastened upon the tacit admission.

"You are worried, then? I'm very sorry. Nothing serious, I trust?"

Then, as if suddenly struck by a thought, he demanded: "It's not this Talisman affair, is it?"

Taken by surprise, Westenhanger's face betrayed him. Rollo's eyes missed nothing.

"You really mustn't worry about that. The Talisman is all right, I assure you. If that were the only worry I had, I should count myself fortunate."

He broke off in order to listen for something; and Westenhanger could see that his ears were strained to catch some faint sound which he evidently expected. After a few seconds, the old man's vigilance seemed to relax; his eyes still turned to the open door, but apparently he was satisfied that nothing was coming. Westenhanger had little difficulty in reading the situation. Rollo was on guard to watch over his daughter if she found her way downstairs during her sleep-walking. Then, suddenly, it occurred to him that Rollo's post lay on the road to the Corinthian's Room. Could it be that the old man had some idea that Helga's somnambulism was connected with the loss of the Talisman? She might have taken it during her sleep, and he might be watching her to discover, if possible, where she had concealed it. He resolved to push his inquiries, even at the cost of some failure in courtesy.

"I believe, Mr. Dangerfield, that you know all the time

122

what has become of the Talisman. Is that why its disappearance doesn't worry you?"

Rollo's eyes grew suddenly stern.

"Do you suggest that I am shielding anyone?" he demanded, bluntly. "That's rather a grave charge."

"It wasn't brought by me," Westenhanger exclaimed. Put in that precise form, the matter took on an aspect which he had not considered at all. "Certainly I never suggested such a thing! I never so much as thought of it."

Rollo acknowledged this with a slight inclination of his head. Then, after a time, he spoke again.

"I could hardly complain if some such idea came into your mind. But no matter how strong the motive, I doubt if I would yield to it in this case. I would never dream of letting a guest of mine lie under suspicion when a word from me would clear up the matter. Never. Besides, whom could I shield?"

He met Westenhanger's eye frankly.

"There are only two possible people: Eric and Helga. You might suspect either of them; but what does it amount to? Eric could have taken the thing, undoubtedly. He may have reasons for taking it. He's left-handed, like the thief . . ."

"You knew the thief was left-handed?" asked Westenhanger in surprise.

"So did you, evidently," the old man retorted, unmoved. "It was obvious to anyone who saw how the cabinet was opened."

"Yes," admitted Westenhanger, rather crestfallen to find that another person had arrived at the same conclusion by the same line of reasoning.

"But Eric didn't take the Talisman," the old man continued. "You will have to take my word for that. I can't, of course, prove it to you. It's a difficult business, proving a negative. But I give you my word of honour that Eric didn't take it. Eric knows what he knows. He wouldn't take it."

"You mean the Dangerfield Secret?" demanded Westenhanger, astonished to find that matter cropping up in this connection.

"If you choose to call it so," said old Rollo, dismissing the matter by his tone. "But if I am not supposed to be shielding Eric—and I am not shielding him, as I told you —then it must be . . ."

He broke off sharply and held his hand in caution. Westenhanger, listening with all his ears, heard the faint sound of a step on the staircase. Rollo rose silently to his feet with another gesture of warning, and stepped lightly over to the door. Almost as he reached it, Helga's figure appeared in the corridor. She passed without a look aside, though the glare of the lighted room fell full on her face as she went by.

Old Rollo softly switched on the corridor lights and fell in behind her. Westenhanger, picking his steps with caution, followed. Helga, unconscious of their presence, led them down to the door of the Corinthian's Room, which she entered. Westenhanger had a hope that possibly her movements might throw light upon the mystery; but when he reached the door, Rollo had switched on the lights, and it soon grew clear that she had no interest in the cabinet. She wandered aimlessly about the room for a time, then returned to the door and came out again, the two men standing aside to let her pass.

Rollo waited until she had gone some distance down the corridor, then he whispered to Westenhanger:

"Please put out the lights; I must see her safely back to her room."

Their figures retreated down the stretch, turned at the staircase and disappeared. Westenhanger waited for a time. Then, remembering the original object of his journey, he passed into the library, selected a book, and went upstairs to his room, after extinguishing the lights. But his book helped him very little.

"Old Rollo was speaking the truth, I'm sure. He doesn't believe Eric's mixed up in the thing at all," he mused. "But that doesn't necessarily prove that Eric didn't take it after all. We've eliminated everyone except Eric. He's the only one who fits the facts. And yet old Dangerfield spoke as if he had absolute certainty. What was it he said? 'He knows what he knows.' But what does he know? This Dangerfield Secret? Is there some deadly business connected with the guarding of the Talisman, so dangerous that no one would risk touching it 'if he knows what he knows'? The old man, if I read him right, isn't a mystery-monger for the sheer love of it. There never was a less theatrical person; he's natural all through, and absolutely straight."

His thoughts turned to the scene he had just witnessed.

"No wonder the poor old chap's worried. A sleep-walking daughter is enough to worry anyone. There's no saying what mischief she might get into."

A fresh line opened up in his mind.

"He said he wasn't shielding anyone. Did he mean merely that he wasn't covering up a theft? If Helga took the thing while she was asleep, there would be no question of 'shielding' at all. I wish that girl hadn't arrived just when she did. She interrupted him just at the critical moment. Perhaps he knows she took it and is simply waiting to get it back eventually. That would account for all this coolness under a huge loss. It wouldn't be a real loss at all. The thing's bound to be somewhere near by; it's only a case of laying hands on it eventually. She'd be sure to give it away sooner or later if she goes on sleep-walking. And that's one of the reasons why he was watching for her to-night, perhaps."

125

CHAPTER XI

ON the following day, Westenhanger took the earliest opportunity of informing Douglas about the developments in the night. He had been strongly impressed by old Dangerfield's denial of Eric's responsibility, and he felt it would be unfair to suppress this information and so leave suspicion afloat in his friend's mind.

"Well, we can take the old man's word for it," was Douglas's verdict, when he had heard the whole story. "He wouldn't tell a lie, I'm sure of that. And apparently, from what you say, he thought he had good enough grounds, though he didn't throw much light on them."

"He convinced me. I'm quite satisfied, now, we're on the wrong track."

"Then the great elimination stunt has been a wash-out?"

Westenhanger gloomily accepted this estimate.

"It's landed us with the wrong man. I can't help feeling that," he said. "By the way, Douglas, is Helga left-handed by any chance?"

"No. I've played golf and tennis with her, and she's as right-handed as anyone, as far as I can see."

"Then we can exclude her."

"So it's a case of the Ten Little Nigger Boys—'and then there was none'?"

"It looks like it. Elimination's a sound enough system; but we've gone off the track somewhere, evidently. We started with three tests, didn't we? Left-handedness—Motive—and Opportunity. I still believe in the left-handedness. It's the only definite thing we've got, even if it has proved a wash-out in this Eric affair."

Douglas nodded assent to this.

"Then there must be something wrong with the others, evidently. Suppose we drop the opportunity factor. Really, anyone might have been abroad that night and no one would know about it except by chance."

"Right."

126

"That leaves motive. I don't see how we're going to get beyond our earlier notions on that point."

"Slipped a cog, somewhere, then? Just what I was thinking. And I think I know where it slipped. I've seen something that made me sit up somewhat. Let's stick to left-handedness as a sure winner, for a change, and see if I can't throw some light on things."

"What did you see?"

Douglas lit a cigarette before replying.

"Last night," he went on, "while you and Eileen were wandering round outside, admiring the moon after dinner, our three pariahs—Freddie, Morchard, and Mrs. Scorton —got up a little game of cut-throat. I expect they felt a bit chary of asking any of the rest of us to make up a four. At any rate, they were playing three-handed, and I happened to be sitting across the room. I wasn't so engrossed in Cynthia's conversation that I couldn't keep one eye on their table now and again."

"Get on with it," advised Westenhanger.

"Now this is what I saw," continued Douglas, seriously. "Freddie and Morchard· are normal, beyond a doubt. I watched 'em very carefully, and that's a cert. But the fair lady deals with her left hand. Strange I never noticed it before; but one seldom looks at a dealer, except casually, I suppose. However, there it is."

Westenhanger considered the matter for a time without comment.

"There's no motive," he concluded. Then his memory spontaneously threw up the incident of Eileen Cressage's mirror. "But perhaps that's where we went wrong. We've been on the hunt for a motive the whole time, Douglas. What about scrapping that notion and trying kleptomania for a change?"

"I was just working up to that point myself."

"Well, Eileen's silver mirror was taken from her room the other day. That's another motiveless affair—even more so than the Talisman."

"Ah, that puts a new face on things. I didn't know about that. And I can put something else in the kitty, judging from that. Mrs. Brent's gold wrist-watch has gone astray. She's been hunting for it all over the place. Of course I never thought of it having been taken. But this mirror-affair connects 'em up nicely. It's just the pointless sort of snatching that one might expect, if your notion's right.'

"Well, don't let's be in too much of a hurry this time," cautioned Westenhanger. "We made average asses of ourselves with our last dip in the lucky-bag. It looks as if we might be nearer the centre this time; but we're up against the same old bother. How're we going to prove anything?"

Douglas moved uneasily in his seat.

"I'm not over-keen on the job, Conway, and that's a fact. The only way of clearing the thing up is to watch her. And I don't quite fancy the job of spy."

"No more do I. But if her hands are clean, watching won't do any harm so long as nobody else knows about it. And if she's the thief, she deserves all she gets. She did all she could to put the blame at Eileen's door—don't forget that, Douglas. And if you do, I'm not likely to let it slip my memory. That was outside the rules of the game, as Mrs. Brent says."

Somewhat ruefully, Douglas admitted the justice of this view.

"I suppose you're right, Conway. I see your case all right. But," he added, firmly, "not even the best of causes is going to make me put on false whiskers or reach-me-downs. Worming one's way into people's confidence is also barred. Likewise overhearing conversations. Anything in the way of measuring foot-prints or hanging round pubs will be cheerfully carried out; but nothing of an ungenteel nature will be handled by this firm. That's that!"

"Don't worry, Douglas. It won't even run to a false nose. All I propose to do is to keep my eyes open."

"Dashed moderate, I call it. Trade Union hours, then. You can have the night shift if you like. I feel generous this morning."

Westenhanger guessed what was at the back of Douglas's reluctance.

"Get one thing clearly into your mind, Douglas. You're not spying on a woman—you're watching for a thief. Give chivalry a miss. It's quite out of place after what's happened."

"Very well," Douglas conceded, "if you put it that way I suppose it can be done. I'll regard it partly as a medical case: Kleptomania—its Cause, Detection, and Cure. That makes it seem a bit more respectable. Frankly, Conway, it's not a job I like much."

"I don't revel in it," Westenhanger admitted, gruffly.

"But I'm going to see it through, if I can. Somebody ought to pay for the trouble they've caused."

Douglas looked away.

"Well," he said, at last, "I suppose if it had been Cynthia instead of Eileen I'd be inclined to go in with both feet. I see your point, Conway. I'll keep my eyes open."

Westenhanger made no reply.

When he considered the matter later on, Conway Westenhanger had to admit to himself that he had embarked upon a forlorn hope. Nothing but pure luck was likely to bring the thing to success. And the chances against any result seemed tremendous. He could not dog his quarry continuously for any length of time, since that would inevitably lead to a disclosure of his intentions. For a large part of the day and during most of the night Mrs. Caistor Scorton would be outside his sphere of observation, and that left him very little chance of success. The possibility of enlisting assistance he rejected immediately. None of the party was likely to be useful. Eileen was the only one whom he might have approached in the matter, and the relations between her and Mrs. Caistor Scorton made her worse than useless for that particular purpose, apart from all other objections to the idea. Westenhanger resigned himself to waiting for the help of chance, with a full appreciation of the odds against success.

That night he and Douglas sat up later than usual. All the other guests had gone earlier to bed and the house was dark. As the two men came out into the corridor they found the door of Rollo Dangerfield's study wide open, and a beam of light shone from it across the floor.

"The old man's on guard again," Westenhanger hazarded to Douglas in a low voice. "He's having a worrying time, I'm afraid. Hard lines having a thing like that on one's shoulders."

But when they passed the open door they found Eric on the watch instead of his uncle. He wished them good night as they went by, but showed no desire for their company.

"They're taking it in turns, evidently," Douglas guessed as they went up the stairs. "Ah! perhaps that accounts for Eric being about in the small hours, that night of the storm. It may have been his turn for duty. We don't know how long this affair has been going on."

"That's probably it," Westenhanger agreed. "But if he

were sitting up how did the thief get into the Corinthian's Room undetected?"

"Oh, I expect Helga only walks about once in the night; and once they've seen her safe back to her room they can go to bed themselves. After that, the coast would be clear. You remember I saw the Talisman in its place about one in the morning?"

Westenhanger went to bed that night with the conscious- ness that he had accomplished absolutely nothing during the day. He had trusted to luck, but luck had not served. His hopes were gradually lessening as time went on.

"Something may turn up," he reflected, without optimism, as he undressed.

Something did "turn up"; but it was the last thing that he could have foreseen. On coming down to breakfast next morning he found Freddie Stickney busily spreading the news to Nina, Cynthia and Douglas.

"Heard the latest?" Freddie demanded as Westenhanger entered the room. "The Talisman's turned up again—safe in its cabinet once more, just as old Dangerfield prophesied."

"Who told you that?"

Westenhanger was completely taken aback by the news.

"Oh, it's all right," Freddie assured him. "You don't catch me swallowing things on mere hearsay. I've been along to the Corinthian's Room myself and had a look. And there it is, as large as life. Stuck under the glass bell, just as it used to be."

Westenhanger took his seat at the table without com- ment. This latest episode in the chain of events seemed beyond understanding. Given that a thief had taken the Talisman, why had the thing come back at all? All that the thief had to do was to leave it in its original place of concealment, if he feared detection. To put it back in the cabinet was to run a second risk of being discovered, especially now that one of the Dangerfields was on guard over Helga each night. And if it was not a case of theft, why remove the thing at all? Before he could continue his line of thought he was interrupted.

"What do you make of it?" Freddie was taking up his rôle of general inquisitor once more. "It seems a bit rum, doesn't it? And old Dangerfield's had the laugh, after all. He swore it would turn up again—and here it is! Queer, eh?"

"Very strange," Westenhanger agreed coldly.

Freddie was outside the scope of suspicion now, but Westenhanger had other reasons for disliking him. And what infernal impudence of the little brute to start this kind of thing again after the fiasco of his last effort in the business. Freddie, however, was not to be discouraged by coldness. His bright little eyes flickered from face to face, and he continued his remarks quite unpertubed by the obviously hostile atmosphere.

"What's that old tag about the man who finds a thing being the one who knows where to look for it?" he went on. "I begin to think it's a practical joke after all. The old man's been pulling our legs! He laid off all that stuff about the Talisman being able to look after itself. Then he took it away himself that night, eh? And now he brings it back again, and he laughs in his sleeve at us. How's that, umpire?"

He glanced round the table for applause, but received none.

"If you ask me, Freddie," Douglas pronounced bluntly, "it proves two things up to the hilt. One is that you have the nerve to sit down at breakfast and criticise your host behind his back. The other is that you don't know Mr. Dangerfield. He's the last man who'd play a silly game of that sort. Anyone with two ounces of grey matter in his skull would see that."

Douglas's rebuke would have silenced most people, but Freddie's skin was proof against even this attack.

"Think so?" he asked blandly. "Well, what better theory have you got yourself?"

. Douglas took no notice of the query.

"Well, I'm very glad Mr. Dangerfield has got it back," Nina said, ignoring Freddie's remark. "It's been so uncomfortable all the time to feel that he'd lost a thing like that—a thing he cared for so much."

"He didn't seem to worry over it," Freddie reminded her.

"Mr. Dangerfield's a thoroughbred," Cynthia commented. "No matter how he felt about it he'd never show it to us."

"You think not? No? Well, perhaps not," the irrepressible Freddie conceded graciously. "That's one way of looking at it, certainly."

Westenhanger took no part in the talk. His mind was busy with the task of fitting this new evidence to the earlier events. If a thief had taken the thing, why had the Talisman come back? The only possible explanation was that the thief had taken fright. But why should he take fright? So far as Westenhanger knew, nothing had come out which made the solution of the problem any clearer, and only imminent exposure could have forced the culprit to disgorge. Days had passed since the loss of the Talisman. There had been plenty of time to get it into a place of safe concealment. Why take the risk of replacing it in the cabinet? There seemed to be no plausible answer to that question.

But if it wasn't a thief, then it must have been one of the Dangerfields. One could leave old Rollo out of the business. He was the last man to play a practical joke on his guests—especially a practical joke which carried a tang as nasty as this affair did. Helga was another possible agent, and an innocent agent if it did turn out that she had a hand in the thing. Westenhanger began to incline towards this solution. But then Helga, according to Douglas, was right-handed, while the Talisman had been removed by someone who was obviously left-handed. Perhaps one turned left-handed in one's sleep. But on recalling fragments of his dreams, Westenhanger had to admit that he remembered himself as right-handed during his sleep. That seemed to exclude Helga.

Then it flashed across his mind that Eric had been on the watch on both nights, on the date of the Talisman's vanishing and—last night—when it returned. He had the place to himself on both occasions, and could do as he chose. He was left-handed, too. But against this, there was old Rollo's statement, evidently made in good faith.

Eileen Cressage came into the room as he reached this point in his cogitation. She sat down beside him, and he hastened to clear up an item which had occurred to him.

"Had young Dangerfield sprained his ankle before he left here with you that morning?"

"No. He was all right. He sprained it in London, somehow—getting out of the way of a taxi, I think he said."

"Funny thing to happen, surely?"

"Oh, he slipped on the kerb-stone, or something like that."

Westenhanger's half-formulated idea broke down. 'It was quite evident that Eric had not got his injury in connection with the theft of the Talisman. It was not a case of his having been half-caught in the man-trap. Probably there was no man-trap at all. Rollo had denied its existence, and one could take Rollo's word for things. At any rate, Westenhanger felt he had given every possibility a fair examination.

Mrs. Caistor Scorton came into the room, and Westenhanger glanced up as she entered. Freddie broke out at once.

"Heard the latest, Mrs. Caistor Scorton? The Talisman's come back!"

Westenhanger had his eyes on Mrs. Caistor Scorton's face as Freddie spoke; and he was amazed to see the effect of the words. Incredulity, stupefaction, and fear, swept in succession over her features almost in an instant. Then she regained command of herself, her thin lips tightened, and she walked to her place without showing any further sign of emotion. Only Westenhanger and Freddie seemed to have noticed anything abnormal, so quickly had she recovered her self-control. The other members of the party had not looked up as she came into the room.

"Now we've got something," Westenhanger commented inwardly. "That shot took her absolutely off her guard. She knows something about the business—anyone can see that. She was absolutely taken aback by Freddie. She'll want to know all about it, and then perhaps she'll have to do something. If we can only keep an eye on her through to-day we may get to the bottom of the business at last."

He dawdled through his breakfast, lending an ear to Freddie's repetition of the tale of the Talisman's return. Mrs. Caistor Scorton listened eagerly, he could see, and her breakfast remained almost untouched. Westenhanger learned nothing further. When Eileen rose from the table he accompanied her out of the room.

"You're not doing anything important this morning, are you?" he questioned in a low voice, as soon as the door closed behind them.

"Nothing in particular."

"I want you to put yourself in my hands, then. Don't ask questions, please. I wish you to be an absolutely unbiassed witness, if anything turns up. But keep your eyes open. I want you to pay special attention to Mrs. Caistor Scorton to-day. It's most important. Watch everything she does closely, and we'll compare notes afterwards."

He led her to some seats near the main entrance, from

which they had a view of the corridor, and when they had
ensconced themselves he began to talk of indifferent
matters, so as to give a semblance of naturalness to their
attitude. Very soon Mrs. Caistor Scorton, accompanied
by Freddie, came out of the breakfast room and passed
along the corridor towards the Corinthian's Room.

"Quick! I want to overtake them," ordered Westenhanger.

He and Eileen came up with the others just before
reaching the end of the passage. Westenhanger stepped
forward and opened the door, so that he could see Mrs.
Caistor Scorton's face as she entered, but he learned very
little. She seemed to have regained complete control of
herself.

All four crossed the chess-board and approached the
cabinet. Freddie had made no mistake. There on its
velvet bed lay the Talisman, protected by the bell of tinted
glass which had been moved back to its old position.
Both doors of the cabinet were closed. Everything seemed
to have returned to its normal state.

Westenhanger, covertly scrutinising Mrs. Caistor Scorton's face, saw a flash of expression which took him by
surprise. She seemed to be witnessing some incredible
happening—something beyond the bounds of the possible.
It almost suggested that she had disbelieved Freddie and
had been staggered by the actual sight of the Talisman. In
an instant the signs of bewilderment vanished and she again
had herself under control. Freddie had evidently noticed
her amazement.

"Oh, it's come home again, all right," he said triumph-
antly. "Old Dangerfield was sound enough, after all.
But how it's got here is a mystery, isn't it, Mrs. Caistor
Scorton?"

"I don't understand it," she admitted, dully, and as she
spoke she allowed her face to reveal the stupefaction which
was evidently still her dominant feeling.

"Well, I'm very glad to see it again," said Eileen. "It's
a relief to find that it wasn't stolen after all."

Her glance made Mrs. Caistor Scorton wince. Neither
of them had forgotten Mrs. Caistor Scorton's evidence
against Eileen; and the older woman evidently had little
difficulty in reading the girl's feelings—she avoided any
recognition of the underlying meaning in Eileen's last
remark by turning to Freddie Stickney.

"I really hardly believed your story at first, Mr. Stickney; but one can't disbelieve one's eyes. It seems incredible that it has come back again. I feel almost inclined to doubt it even now."

"We can soon settle that for you," said Freddie. "I'll take it out of the case and you can handle it."

Westenhanger broke in with a violence which surprised them all.

"Paws off, Freddie! Don't lay a finger on it!"

He laid a rough hand on Freddie's shoulder and drew him back from the cabinet. Then, noticing their surprise, he went on in a milder tone:

"Mr. Dangerfield refused to allow any of us to touch it, the night he showed it to us. He objects to it being handled. That's enough for me. We can't go against his wishes behind his back. Understand?"

Freddie acquiesced sulkily. Mrs. Caistor Scorton relieved the strain by looking at her watch and discovering that she had something to do. As they left the room, Westenhanger lagged behind with Eileen for a moment.

"Keep her in sight at any cost. I'm going up to my room for a moment. I'll join you again."

When he returned, he found Eileen standing at the main entrance with Freddie Stickney. Mrs. Caistor Scorton had disappeared.

"Shall we go now?" Westenhanger asked the girl. She nodded and they shook off Freddie without much difficulty. He supposed they were going to play tennis. Eileen led the way down into the gardens.

"She went off almost as soon as you went upstairs," she told Westenhanger, as they hurried along. "I stood at the door and watched the road she took. We ought to make up on her in a moment or two if we hurry."

"I don't want to make up on her. I want to follow her without showing ourselves. She's making for the Pool, if I'm not mistaken. That will suit very well."

He took a pair of prismatic glasses from his pocket and slung them round his neck.

"We may want to watch from a distance. That's why I had to go upstairs for these."

Eileen nodded.

"It's the Talisman affair, isn't it?" she asked. "I don't quite see what it all means, but you know something, obviously. Why are we scurrying after her just now? The

Talisman's back again. I don't see what you expect to find out."

"No questions, Eileen!" Westenhanger smiled. "If I'm right, you'll see it all in a few minutes. I don't want to put any preconceived notions into your mind."

The girl studied his face in silence as they walked on.

"Very well," she said. "But to tell you the truth I'm getting rather wearied of Talisman mysteries. It seems to me I've had more than my share of them."

"This will be the last of them, perhaps, if we're lucky."

As he spoke they drew near the edge of the spinney which lay about the Pool, and he made a gesture of caution to the girl. They could see Mrs. Caistor Scorton's figure crossing the open glade in front of them.

"Now watch with all your eyes," ordered Westenhanger, lifting his glasses as he spoke.

Mrs. Caistor Scorton glanced round nervously once or twice; then, apparently satisfied that there were no on-lookers, she made her way to a pollard willow which over-hung the water. Still on the alert, she put her hand far down into a hollow in the tree-trunk and drew out something. It was too far off for Eileen to see more than the movement, but Westenhanger whispered a running des-cription of what his glasses showed him.

"She's taken something from the hole. . . . It's very small. . . . I can hardly make it out. Gold, apparently, by the glint. . . . Now she's putting her hand in again. . . . . Something bigger this time . . . Yes . . . Your silver mirror. . . . It's tarnished a bit, I'm afraid. . . . Now for it. She's trying again. . . ."

His tone showed a sharp disappointment.

"It looks like a silver-mounted paper-knife. . . . Yes, that's it. . . . Ah! I thought so. She's got more in that hoard of hers. . . . Something moderate-sized this time. . . . Confound it! She's turned away from us. I can't see it. . . . Now she's putting them all back again. Quick, Eileen! Back along the path and get in among the bushes. Hide! As quick as you can. Don't make a sound."

They managed to conceal themselves before Mrs. Caistor Scorton came back into the belt of trees; and from behind the bushes they watched her go past. Believing herself alone, she took no thought for her expression; and on her face they read the utmost bewilderment, faintly tinged with fear.

"She hasn't spotted it," Westenhanger thought to him-self. "She ought to have done. But I expect she's completely jarred up. Well, this is the end of her little game."

As soon as Mrs. Caistor Scorton had disappeared Westenhanger came out of his concealment and beckoned Eileen back to the path.

"Now that the coast's clear," he said, "we can have a look at the magpie's hoard. No questions yet!" he added as she began to frame one. "Facts, first of all; and you can draw your own conclusions."

They went down to the tree; and Westenhanger soon found the hollow which Mrs. Caistor Scorton had used as her cache. Putting his hand into it, he drew out in succes-sion the articles which he had seen through his glasses.

"There's Mrs. Brent's wrist-watch," he said, holding up his first trophy. "No! Don't touch it! I'll lay it on the grass."

Again he put his hand into the hollow. The second object gave him more trouble, but at last he managed to humour it up the channel in the tree trunk.

"Your mirror. What a pity it's in such a state! No permanent damage done, though. It'll clean up all right. You can have that."

He handed it to her and reinserted his hand into the hole.

"The paper-knife. Don't touch!"

"Why, that's the one that used to be on the library table."

"So it is," said Westenhanger. "Now for the star piece of the collection."

He drew out the fourth object, and at the sight of it Eileen exclaimed in astonishment:

"The Talisman! This is impossible, Conway! We left the Talisman safe in the house not a quarter of an hour ago. She can't have stolen it a second time."

She put out her hand for the armlet, but Westenhanger sharply drew it back out of her reach.

"Paws off, Eileen, as I remarked to Freddie not so long ago. Under no circumstances whatever are you to touch this thing until I give you permission."

"Let me see it, then. I won't finger it."

He held it out for her inspection and she examined it minutely.

"It *is* the Talisman!"

She thought for a time, while Westenhanger watched her in silence.

"Oh, now I see it, I think. There are two Talismans? Or there's a Talisman and a replica. Mrs. Caistor Scorton stole this one. The other one's up at the house now. She must have got a shock when she heard the Talisman had come back again. Is that it?"

Westenhanger's reply seemed irrelevant.

"Mrs. Caistor Scorton's not a very clever person like you."

"Ah! now I see what it means. She stole this one; and when she saw the other one in the case she was absolutely puzzled. She never thought of a replica. And so she thought she'd come up against magic and spells. Is that it? No wonder she was so staggered. I was completely puzzled myself for a moment or two, and I expect her conscience—if she has one—must have upset her a bit."

"That's how I explain it myself," said Westenhanger. "But proceed. What else do you make of it?"

The girl considered for a time; then at last she hit on a solution.

"Of course, it's obvious when one puts two and two together. The Dangerfields never kept the Talisman in the cabinet at all. They had a replica for show and they kept the real Talisman in a safe place."

"Yes," agreed Westenhanger, "and that would account for the bell of tinted glass. The tinge would conceal the fact that the stones in this thing are paste. Even an expert couldn't see anything wrong with the water of them, if he looked through that dingy cover."

"You think that's why Mr. Dangerfield wouldn't allow it to be taken out of the cabinet?"

"Quite probably."

"And that's why he has been so easy-going over the whole thing? He didn't stand to lose much—only a piece of sham jewellery."

"Obviously correct, I think. 'It's very clever of you to have noticed it,' as you once said to me."

Eileen laughed.

"How you seem to treasure my sayings!"

She examined the armlet again.

"So this is the thing that brought me into all that trouble. And it's only a sham after all! By the way, didn't Mr.

Dangerfield say something rather bitter about the original Talisman that night he told us the legend? Something about it's being a sham and a fraud from the very start?"

"It wasn't quite that. He said 'it was a memorial of lying and cheating."

"It seems an unpleasant sort of thing altogether. We'd better get it off our hands, I think. What are you going to do with it now?"

"Take it up to the house again. But that reminds me, you're still under the law of 'No Questions.' Everything shall be cleared up to your satisfaction in a very short time, if you'll only wait."

He wrapped the armlet carefully in his handkerchief and dropped it into his pocket, taking care to touch it as little as he could. The wrist-watch and paper-knife he put into his breast-pocket with less precaution.

"Now for the next act!"

"Wait a moment," pleaded Eileen. "Just one question. Why did Mr. Dangerfield put out the real Talisman this morning?"

Westenhanger had his answer ready.

"What happened? The thief got a nasty jar. I expect that was what he intended to do. He may have been on the look-out as well as ourselves."

They made their way up to the house. On the road they met Eric Dangerfield walking slowly.

"Seen Mrs. Caistor Scorton?" asked Westenhanger, casually. "She was just in front of us."

"Yes," answered Eric. "She's gone up to the house."

He walked on and they hurried forward towards Friocksheim.

"She's gone to have another look at the cabinet. expect," said Westenhanger. "Well, since she's in the house, we may as well strike while the iron's hot. I'll not keep you on tenterhooks much longer. As a matter of fact, there's no more mystery in the business."

CHAPTER XII

At the door of Friochsheim, Westenhanger gave Eileen his directions.

"I must get rid of these, first of all," he explained, tapping his binoculars. "While I'm upstairs, will you go along to the Corinthian's Room and wait for me there? I shan't be a minute."

When he rejoined her, he had a brown-paper parcel in his hand, and from its shape she inferred that it contained the stolen articles.

"Now we can get to business, Eileen."

With a gesture, he invited her to come with him to the cabinet of the Talisman, and to her astonishment, he opened one of the doors and withdrew the armlet from beneath the bell. Putting it aside with a warning not to touch it, he took from his pocket the replica which they had discovered in the hollow tree; and this he placed on the velvet bed, arranging it as nearly as possible in the position previously occupied by its duplicate. He then covered it with the bell and closed the door of the cabinet.

"Now the trap's baited," he said, putting the second armlet in his pocket with no particular precautions. "But we can't risk the chance of a fresh mouse nibbling the cheese before we're ready. I'll have to stay here on guard. Your business will be to go off, now, and collect all the people you can. It doesn't much matter who they are, so long as Mrs. Caistor Scorton's one of them. Bring half a dozen at least. Tell them anything you like to get them here. I'll guarantee to keep them, once they arrive."

Eileen went off on her errand without venturing to put the question which obviously was trembling on her lips. Westenhanger sat down to await the arrival of his audience.

The first to appear were Mrs. Brent and Wraxall. Mrs. Brent was plainly rather mistrustful.

"Is this another of these peculiarly unsatisfactory general

meetings, Mr. Westenhanger? I hardly expected to find you issuing invitations of the kind."

"Didn't my messenger reassure you?" countered Westenhanger, with a smile.

"Well, I hope my character's not going to be dissected this time," she retorted tartly. "If I'm dragged into it in any form, I warn you I shall simply go away."

Westenhanger's amusement grew more apparent.

"Don't make too rash promises," he advised. "I don't think you'll ask for your money back at the door if you manage to sit through the first act. This play gets brighter as it progresses."

Wraxall looked at Westenhanger quizzically.

"What particular brand of drama do you specialise in? Is it tragedy? Tragedy's hardly my line. Nor yet is sob-stuff. I don't seem to react much to sob-stuff. Or are you a Happy-Ender? I'd rather you were. It's preferable. I don't care about having an attack of catawampus as the curtains flips down."

"I'll hear your criticisms afterwards," Westenhanger said lightly.

Mrs. Caistor Scorton entered the room, but it was evident that she would have stayed away had she dared to do so. It was a very different Mrs. Caister Scorton from the one who had so calmly given her damning evidence against Eileen a few nights earlier. An air of bewilderment was still on her face; and Westenhanger saw that she was puzzled by his summons and uncertain as to its meaning. Quite obviously she was afraid, and afraid of something which she could not define even to herself. She walked across the room and seated herself with her back to the light. Westenhanger avoided looking in her direction.

"Just as I thought," he reflected. "She has no notion that she's been spotted; but the general complexity of the affair is giving her the jumps. She'll brazen it out if she can, when it comes to the pinch. Lucky I was careful."

Rollo Dangerfield followed close on Mrs. Caistor Scorton's heels. As he entered, he shot a glance at Westenhanger from under his white eyebrows, a glance in which doubt seemed to mingle with a certain hostility.

"He doesn't like being dragged into this affair," was Westenhanger's interpretation. "I suppose it jars on his notions about the code of a host. I can't help his troubles, though. He's got to go through it with the rest. We must get rid of that woman to-day, and he ought to be put on his guard in case he ever thinks of bringing her down to Friochsheim again."

Freddie Stickney lounged into the room a few minutes later. At the sight of the assembly, his eyebrows rose momentarily and he glanced inquisitively from one to another as though he hoped to discover from their faces the secret of the meeting. Westenhanger curtly invited him to sit down. He augured little good from Freddie's presence, and was inclined to blame Eileen for having dragged the creature into the affair at all. But then, remembering that she probably wanted Freddie to see the final clearing-up of the affair so as to leave him no chance for tittle-tattle, Westenhanger had to admit to himself that she was right in her choice.

Almost at once, Eileen and Cynthia came throught the door together. Cynthia looked round the room in some surprise. Eileen had evidently brought her there without explanation.

"Who's in the chair this time?" she inquired languidly, when she had inspected the company. "You, Mr. Westenhanger? Well, that's a relief!"

She and Eileen chose seats near Mrs. Brent. The gathering now seemed complete, and Westenhanger was about to begin, when the door opened again. Eric Dangerfield came into the room. It was evident that he had not been summoned like the others, and that he had no idea of what was afoot. He seemed wrapped in a brown study, for when he raised his head and caught sight of the company, he was obviously surprised. He made no comment, however; but Westenhanger saw him glance swiftly round the group until he picked out his uncle. Eric's face was glum, and the message which his eyes telegraphed was evidently unsatisfactory, whatever its purport. Old Rollo's expression showed that the silent communication had taken him completely aback. Incredulity, followed by something like dismay, flashed for an instant across his features before being effaced by the return of the old man's normal expression of aloofness. Westenhanger was at a loss how to interpret the incident. Eric, having delivered his message to his uncle, looked again at the company and then seated himself in the nearest vacant chair. He seemed to be brooding over some problem which puzzled him, and he appeared to pay little attention to Westenhanger's opening words.

"I think we're all rather *blasé* of these meetings, by now," Westenhanger began. "It'll be a relief to you to know that this one is positively the last. Most of us have had evidence of sorts dragged out of us on one pretence or another. It seems a pity to be out of the fashion, so I'll give you mine. And that will finish the business."

Mrs. Caistor Scorton shifted slightly in her chair; but Westenhanger could make nothing of her face. If anything, she seemed more bewildered than ever.

"As you know," Westenhanger continued, "I was away from Friocksheim on the night of the Talisman's disappearance. I've nothing fresh to say about that. Not to drag things out, I have suspicions"—he dragged out his words slowly—"which amount to . . . almost . . . a certainty . . . with regard to the disappearance of the Talisman."

To avoid glancing at any particular person, he fixed his eyes on the tapestry of Dian's hunting, as though that chase engrossed his whole visual attention for the moment.

"Somebody suggested that this business' has been a mere practical joke," he continued. "If so, then this is the last chance for the perpetrator of it to own up. Anybody volunteer?"

Nobody accepted his offer. At last Freddie Stickney broke the silence.

"Anyone can see it's a practical joke. There's the Talisman staring you in the face! It's not been stolen at all."

"Think so, Freddie? Perhaps you're right. But some other things have gone amissing: Miss Cressage's mirror, Mrs. Brent's wrist-watch, and"—he glanced at Eric for confirmation—"a silver-mounted paper-knife from the library table."

Eric nodded his confirmation of this. He was paying more attention to Westenhanger now.

"There's no question of a practical joke in these cases, for the articles have not been returned."

"That doesn't prove anything about the Talisman," Freddie objected with an air of acuteness. "It was returned; they weren't. Obviously the cases are different."

"If you insist on their reappearance," answered Westenhanger, "it's easy enough to gratify you."

He unwrapped his paper parcel and took out its contents one by one.

"Your wrist-watch, Mrs. Brent? No, don't touch it, if you please. And Miss Cressage's mirror. And the paper-knife with the silver handle, which most of us know well enough."

Eileen was surprised to find that he had not included the Talisman in the series.

As he drew out article after article, Westenhanger had shot a sidelong glance at Mrs. Caistor Scorton. With the appearance of the stolen goods, her figure had grown rigid, and her face now showed fear as its dominant note. She waited breathlessly for Westenhanger's next move.

"These things," Westenhanger went on, "I recovered this morning from the place where they had been hidden."

His eyes happened to light on Eric's face as he spoke, and he noticed an expression flit across it as though this evidence had cleared up something. But immediately perplexity reappeared in Eric's features. A fresh point seemed to have arisen to puzzle him.

Westenhanger refrained from dragging out the agony.

"The thief was Mrs. Caistor Scorton," he said, bluntly.

At the words, Mrs. Caistor Scorton rose from her chair.

"Mr. Westenhanger is very free with his insinuations," she commented. "So far, he has produced nothing to support that lie."

Westenhanger turned on her.

"These things were stolen from various places in the house. This morning, Miss Cressage and I watched you take them from the hollow tree down by the Pool. I think that's clear enough."

"Then it's simply your evidence against mine. Miss Cressage doesn't count, I'm afraid. She was under suspicion herself not so long ago."

Westenhanger went white with anger.

"Miss Cressage cleared herself of any charge that you brought against her. But you're mistaken if you think the thing rests solely on that evidence. The thief was left-handed; so are you."

"So are other people."

Westenhanger admitted this with a curt nod. He had tried to drive her into an acknowledgment without using the Talisman; but there seemed to be no way out of it.

"It's no use bluffing, Mrs. Scorton. Your finger-prints are on the Talisman."

Rollo Dangerfield interrupted him sharply.

"You are mistaken there, Mr. Westenhanger."

Westenhanger stepped over to Rollo's side and lowered his voice so that only the old man could hear.

"Take my word for it. I'm afraid I've stumbled on the Dangerfield Secret, and I'd rather say nothing to put other people on the track."

Rollo could take a blow without wincing. Apart from the dismay in his eyes, he showed nothing to mark that he had been touched on his most sensitive spot.

"Very well, Mr. Westenhanger. Do as you please. And thanks for your restraint."

He raised his voice and spoke to the company at large.

"I'm sorry that I inadvertently threw doubt on Mr. Westenhanger's statement. He knows best."

Westenhanger pressed his point.

"Do you deny that your finger-prints are there?"

Mrs. Caistor Scorton had seized on Rollo's intervention as a possible way opening to safety; but with his recantation she seemed to lose heart completely.

"Well, I took it, then," she admitted. "I couldn't help it. I'm a kleptomaniac. I can't help taking glittering things like these. I'm not a thief. I don't steal for money. I don't need money. It's simply I can't help taking some things. They fascinate me. I simply have to take them. I've fought against it, but it's no good."

"So I thought," said Westenhanger. "But that hardly excuses the way in which you tried to throw suspicion on other people. If you hadn't done that, it might have been possible to hush this up. But you made it impossible to stop short of complete exposure. I gave you every chance."

"Need we go any further?" interposed old Rollo. "I think the matter is now quite clear to all of us; and I'm quite sure none of us wish it to go any further. The main thing is that suspicion has been cleared away."

Westenhanger agreed.

"You've got off lightly, Mrs. Scorton. And you've Mr. Dangerfield to thank for it. If the police had been called in . . ."

Mrs. Caistor Scorton made no response. Nothing which she could have said would have lessened her defeat or gained her any sympathy. Westenhanger had put his finger on the main point of her offence when he spoke of her attempt to throw the blame on other shoulders: kleptomania might be forgiven as a morbid effect, but her effort to shield herself at Eileen's expense had put her in an even worse light. Without a look at anyone, she crossed the room, fumbled with the door-handle for an instant before Westenhanger could come to her assistance, and then went out.

With her departure, a sudden slackening of the tension made itself felt. Everyone seemed anxious to minimise the whole matter as far as possible. The third uncomfortable scene of the week was at last safely behind them, and obviously, as Westenhanger had predicted, it would be the last of the series. Friocksheim could get back to normal once more now that the cloud of suspicion had settled finally on the right person. In a few minutes Westenhanger's audience had filtered from the room, leaving him alone with Eric and old Rollo.

As soon as the last outsider had gone, Westenhanger put his hand in his pocket.

"Here's the real Talisman," he said, handing it over to the old man. "Before staging that last affair I exchanged it for the replica which Mrs. Caistor Scorton took, so that I could prove the thing by means of her finger-prints if necessary, and yet keep the rest of them from knowing that you were using a duplicate. I didn't wish to let outsiders into a secret which I'd stumbled upon myself by accident."

"Very thoughtful of you," Rollo said warmly. "Most people would have been less careful of our feelings, I'm afraid."

Westenhanger remembered something.

"Of course, Miss Cressage knows the state of affairs as well as I do; but you can trust her to keep other people's secrets. She's proved that already at considerable cost."

"Oh, one could trust Miss Cressage completely, I know."

Westenhanger took a chair, as though to show that he had more to say. Rollo Dangerfield, after placing the Talisman in the little safe in the wall, sat down in his turn. Eric took up his position in front of the fire-place.

"I'm not quite clear about the whole of this business," said Westenhanger to his host. "Perhaps, since I've blundered so far into it—unintentionally—you won't mind settling one or two points for me."

Again he noted with surprise that an expression of dismay seemed to flicker for an instant in Rollo's face. "Now what on earth is he jumpy about, at this stage in the affair?"

Westenhanger asked himself; but he could find no immediate answer to the question.

Rollo merely nodded in response to his guest's remark. He evidently intended to answer or not as suited him best.

"What has puzzled me, for one thing," Westenhanger continued, "is why you have been using a replica at all. Why not put the Talisman in a place of safety and be done with it?"

"Did you never think of a stalking-horse?" Rollo asked. "If we locked up the Talisman, then anyone who wished to steal it would concentrate his efforts on the thing itself, and we should have to take precautions. As it is—you've seen the process in operation yourself—the thief thinks it is all plain sailing. He concentrates on the sham Talisman and never thinks of anything else. If he's successful—it matters very little to us. All he gets is some gilded lead and a few bits of cheap paste."

"I hadn't thought of that," Westenhanger admitted. "It's certainly a sound piece of tactics. But doesn't the secret leak out if the thing happens to be stolen?"

"No," explained Rollo. "Suppose a thief takes the replica—it's been stolen oftener than we say in public— what does he do? He can't publish his information. Nobody learns anything about it."

"That's true, of course, when one thinks of it," Westenhanger admitted, dismissing the matter. "Now there's another point that puzzled me. Why did you suddenly put the Talisman back into the cabinet last night?"

This time it was Eric who took the matter up.

"Look at the position from our point of view, Westenhanger. The thing was stolen in the small hours, that morning. I was round the house in the earlier part of the night, watching to see that Helga came to no harm. By the way, Douglas saw me writing a note to Morchard, enclosing a cheque for my losses; and I think Wraxall must have seen me leaving it in the hall for Morchard to get in the morning."

"You seem to know a lot of details," commented Westenhanger.

"Freddie Stickney has his uses," Eric explained. "He gave my uncle a full and embroidered account of all that went on at that inquiry of his. Well, we come to the next morning. Of course my uncle and I went straight to the cabinet; and at once I knew the thing had been stolen

by a left-handed person. It was obvious to me, because
I'm left-handed myself, as you know."

He smiled ironically.

"You and Douglas were very ingenious, Westenhanger;
but as my own mind was running on parallel lines, I hadn't
much trouble in seeing what you were after with your
coin-counting and all the rest of it."

Westenhanger felt the home-thrust; but Eric seemed to
attach no importance to the matter.

"I had to go up to town that morning to pay in a cheque
to meet the one I'd given to Morchard, before he could
present it. Same case as Miss Cressage, in fact. So we
decided to postpone investigations till I got back in the
afternoon. As you know, I got scuppered in town—
twisted my ankle—and couldn't get back for a day or
two. My uncle didn't make much of a success at the sleuth
business. He was quite content to wait till I turned up
again and picked out the missing left-hander. You see, we
had a pull over you people in the fact that I'm left-handed
myself, and so I know the finer points in which a left-hander
differs from the normal. We had Mrs. Caistor Scorton
picked out in a very short time after I came home again—
a much shorter time than you took over the business,
naturally, owing to our handicap of special knowledge."

He sat down and began to fill his pipe.

"Meanwhile, of course," he went on, "Freddie had
muddled things up no end by his pranks. But Mrs. Brent
had cleared Miss Cressage the night I came home again,
so that matter didn't affect us. My uncle had been carrying
on his part of the show in my absence—producing an
atmosphere, if you see what I mean. All that stuff about
the Talisman always coming back—of course, it always
does come back!—and so forth. That was all meant for
Mrs. Caistor Scorton's benefit. We wanted to get her
into a state of uncertainty—general jumps, in fact, semi-
eerie atmosphere, you know, no saying what's going to
happen, and so forth. My uncle managed that side of it,
with special attention to her as soon as I'd picked her
out."

It was evident that old Rollo was half-ashamed of the
part he had played. He said nothing, however, and Eric
went on.

"Once we were sure of our effect, we brought the Talisman
home again."

He nodded in the direction of the cabinet.

"We took care that Freddie knew about it first thing. He passed it on to Mrs. Caistor Scorton. She's not a brainy person, really; and she fell right into the trap we had laid for her. Given her brand of mind, we counted that she would go straight off to where she had hidden the replica she had stolen; and we had only to keep an eye on her. It worked out quite according to plan. She lost her head when she saw the thing over there. She must have thought the world was upside-down or something. So off she scuttled at once to see what had become of her own Talisman. Mixed up with the general muddle in her mind there was probably the fear that we had found the thing and got it back. So away she went to make sure. That really seems to support the kleptomania notion. No thief with any constructive capacity would have dreamed of going to his cache in these circumstances. As soon as she left the house I was on the watch with a telescope from my rooms in the tower up above here. You can see every part of the place from there—bar the belt of trees round the Pool. You can see the Pool itself, and I watched her go down there and examine her hiding-place. As soon as she put the things back again I went off as quick as I could limp to secure them.

"I remember we met you on the road."

"Yes. I passed you and went right on to the willow. You can guess how I felt when I put my hand into the hole and found nothing there. I hadn't seen you and Miss Cressage through the telescope, you know; you must have hidden in the belt of trees when I was on the watch; and you only came out after I had come down from my post."

"So that's why you were looking puzzled when you came in here?"

"Well, how would you have felt? It seemed a bit weird to find the things gone, within a minute or two of my seeing them put back into the hole."

Westenhanger smiled.

"I'm glad you haven't had all the laughs on your side."

"I came in here," Eric continued, "just to see if the cabinet was all right; and of course I plunged into the middle of your At Home. You certainly took a nasty bit of work off our hands by your intervention. Well, I think that's all. Virtue rewarded and all that—just like a fairy tale, eh?"

"It's been a thoroughly unpleasant business," old Rollo spoke at last. "There's only one thing in it that gives me any satisfaction. It was our good fortune that the only people who fathomed the secret of the replica are you, Mr. Westenhanger, and Miss Cressage. We know that the matter is safe in your keeping."

"Mrs. Caistor Scorton must have some suspicions, surely?" Westenhanger suggested.

"Suspicions, yes," admitted the old man, grimly. "But I think she's hardly likely to mention the Talisman to anyone in future. She won't betray much."

"So that's why you wouldn't call in the police?" demanded Westenhanger. "I must confess that puzzled me badly. I began to believe you really thought yourself that the Talisman would come back of its own accord."

Rollo avoided answering the question.

"You may tell Miss Cressage exactly what you think fit about all this," he said. "Perhaps she ought to know the whole facts. We can trust her implicitly. We all know that."

"Well, Friocksheim will be a bit more comfortable to live in, now, or I'm mistaken," Eric said hopefully as they left the room. "We'll be three short at dinner tonight, no doubt; but I expect we'll bear up under the loss."

"Three?" queried Westenhanger.

"Mrs. Scorton's hardly likely to stay. Then Morchard was only down here trying to persuade us to sell him Friocksheim. Nothing doing, of course; we'd as soon think of parting with the Talisman itself. After what's happened, we shan't press him to prolong his visit. He's not a friend of ours, it was merely a matter of business."

"I wondered how he came to be here at all," confessed Westenhanger. "He seemed a bit out of his element. And who's the third?"

"Freddie. I have an idea that my uncle will politely but firmly hasten his departure. He's stirred up enough trouble to last us for a while, and we'll be happier without him."

As it turned out, Eric was accurate in his forecasts. Mrs. Caistor Scorton took her departure in the afternoon, without meeting anyone, and by the same train went Morchard and Freddie Stickney.

"Must have been an interesting scene at the station,"

speculated Douglas Fairmile as he joined Wraxall and Westenhanger in the evening, after most of the others had gone to bed. "The good lady would hustle into her compartment first of all. Seat facing the engine, no doubt. In her state of mind it would be better to look forward than to look back. Bury the past! Then friend Morchard would hop into a smoker. And Freddie would be left on the platform, wondering which of them he'd most like to worry with his company up to town. He's not the lad to feel himself *de trop* anywhere."

"Let's forget 'em," sugested Westenhanger. "They gave us enough trouble between them. I can feel the air of the place different, since they've gone."

"So can I," confirmed the American. "It's been a very awkward week for all of us; and it's been specially awkward for me, if I may say so. I was the outsider in the part. Your English hospitality's perfect, and you couldn't have done more to make me feel at home. But all the same, I was the one visitor that none of you knew personally before we met here. And I was the only one, bar the Dangerfields, who had a direct interest in the Talisman. I wanted the thing badly. The Dangerfields knew that quite well; I'd even made an offer for it the very night it was stolen. Old Mr. Dangerfield put that offer aside. Quite polite, of course; but you know that uninterested way he has, as if he were thinking of something else all the time. No good. But I'd showed him how keen I was on the thing."

He put down his cigar.

"And that very night, the thing disappeared! Collectors have the name of being an unscrupulous gang. I might have lifted it easily enough. And next day I got a notion he suspected me. It was very awkward. It was most awkward. And we've got you to thank, Westenhanger, for getting us out of it. I'm grateful. I'm very thankful to get my character cleared."

"But surely you didn't expect to buy the Talisman?" said Douglas. "The Dangerfields would never part with the thing."

"If you're ever hard up, Fairmile, you'll do a lot of things you wouldn't think of in your present state. I reckoned it out this way. The Talisman is the big Dangerfield asset. So long as they have it, they're all right. Their credit's good. But money's more use to them than

151

jewels just now. I have ways of finding out things like that, and I banked on it. My offer would have been a better spec. for them than the Talisman itself, from the credit point of view. I offered far more than the thing's worth in the open market—twenty-five per cent. more. But it seems this family pride comes in. They won't part with the thing. I was struck by that. I haven't met that so strong before."

"Perhaps your information's wrong about their finances. One would need to be in the last ditch before one would think of selling a thing like the Talisman. And I doubt if the Dangerfields are anywhere near the last ditch."

"That's where you're mistaken, Westenhanger. That's what made me so sure I was going to get the thing. They're right in that ditch now."

CHAPTER XIII

CONWAY WESTENHANGER had never pretended, even to himself, that he had a natural gift for detective work. He had quite frankly recognised that only good luck could bring him to success in his search for the taker of the Talisman and a retrospect over the events of the week served merely to confirm the idea. None the less, the history of the case caused him to feel a touch of chagrin. While he had been following out erroneous inductions, the two Dangerfields had gone straight to the mark; and if he had actually beaten them by a short head in the end. it was by good luck and nothing else. In fact, he had profited by their manœuvres in the matter of the Talisman's return. Without that incident, he would have been unable to discover anything at all.

Now, so far as he was concerned, the episode seemed to have reached its end, but when he thought over the whole affair, one point still remained a mystery to him. Why had old Rollo shown that touch of dismay at a reference to the Dangerfield Secret? The thing had been only momentary, but it had been unmistakable, and Westenhanger had seen it twice over within a very short period. The first time, he recalled, was when he had hinted to Rollo that he had stumbled on the Secret; the second occasion was when he had shown signs of asking questions which, possibly, might touch the same subject.

"Is this Secret of theirs merely the use of the replica as a stalking-horse to mask the real Talisman?" Westenhanger asked himself.

But a moment's reflection showed him that this explanation would not cover the facts.

"No, it isn't that. Old Rollo knew I'd tumbled to their use of the replica. That was what startled him the first time. But it was some time after that, when I began asking questions to clear the affair up, that he got really

153

worried. He couldn't have been troubled about his stalking-horse then, because obviously I knew all about it already. But he was quite evidently afraid I was getting near something. Ergo, the replica affair isn't the real Dangerfield Secret at all. There's something further, behind all this. And it must be something pretty big, too; for Rollo Dangerfield isn't a person one could easily jar off the rails."

Westenhanger hated to be puzzled. A problem worried him until he could get at its solution. And this affair at Friocksheim had given him more anxiety than he had expected, when he had first gone light-heartedly to Freddie Stickney's inquiry. Then, he had been in a completely detached position, the one person who could not come under suspicion. But the outcome of Freddie's operations had been to drag Westenhanger into the business on behalf of Eileen Cressage; and from that he had gone further in his attempt to clear up the whole affair and fix the blame on the right shoulders. And now, something seemed to lead him another step on the road; a fresh mystery confronted him, obscure and tantalising by its very vagueness.

With an effort he put it to the back of his mind.

"It's no affair of mine," he repeated to himself again and again.

But even that truism failed to exorcise his demon. Ever and again the Dangerfield Secret crept up out of his mental background and insisted on forcing itself upon his conscious thoughts, and with each appearance it took on a slightly different and more definite form. He gathered no fresh data, but things which he knew already began to fit themselves together in his mind, until at last, in a flash of illumination, he seemed to see' the whole puzzle completed.

"So *that's* the Dangerfield Secret!"

Then, as the fuller implications of the thing forced themselves upon him:

"No wonder they were afraid. Poor devils!"

He ran over the evidence once more, and found himself forced to believe that he had reached a correct solution. Everything pointed in the same direction. Not only so, but other things now fitted themselves into the scheme, things which he had noticed casually, and had not hitherto thought of, connecting together. And then a further conjecture shot across his mind, completing the whole history of the Dangerfield Secret.

"That's it, almost certainly," he reflected. "They've made nothing of it themselves, though they're cute enough. But I wonder . . ."

He paused, in doubt for a moment.

"It's a very long shot; but a fresh mind often sees a thing that other people overlook. Perhaps one might lend them a hand. Luck's been with me, so far. Let's press it while it lasts. If it's a wash-out there's no harm done."

His first step was to seek out Rollo Dangerfield.

"Might I have another look at that peculiar leather thing you showed us one night—the thing your grandfather left?"

Rollo looked at him suspiciously, but complied without any marked reluctance. They went together to the Corinthian's Room where Rollo opened the safe.

"I'd like to have a glance at the chess-board problem, too," said Westenhanger, as though struck by an afterthought. "I used to be rather keen on these things, and I'd like to see if I could solve that one."

The old man put his hand into the safe and withdrew the two objects. Westenhanger took them.

"I'll copy this, if you don't mind, and then you can put them back into safety. I'd rather not be responsible for them longer than's necessary."

He stepped over into the library, followed by Rollo, and copied down the wording of the document and the position of the chess-pieces under the old man's supervision. Then he took up the leather disc and inspected it closely.

"I thought, perhaps, that it might have been a leather washer for some mechanical contrivance," he said at last, handing the shrivelled object back to its owner. "But now that I've seen it again, I don't believe it can have been that, after all. It's certainly been used for some purpose or other, for the surface isn't smooth on either side. Shoemaker's leather sheets always have one side semi-polished, if I'm not mistaken."

"What made you think of a washer?" inquired Rollo, more from politeness than from interest, it seemed.

"You mentioned that your grandfather took some interest in mechanics—a bit of an inventor, I gathered. So

I thought possibly it might have some connection with machinery. But when one looks at it, I doubt if that's a possible explanation. It might be the washer of a pump-piston, of course, but I shouldn't think so. The hole in the centre's only big enough to take the twine. A piston-washer would have a bigger hole in it. No, it beats me."

Rollo took the thing back without comment. Westenhanger passed him the paper also; and old Dangerfield replaced them in the safe. He was turning to leave the room when Westenhanger spoke again.

"By the way, the Dangerfield Secret's only three generations old, isn't it, Mr. Dangerfield?"

By the startled expression on Rollo's face, Westenhanger saw that he had hit the mark. The old man was plainly astounded by the question. It was a few moments before he replied.

"You're somewhere near it," he admitted, looking distrustfully at the engineer. "How did you come to hit on that particular period?"

"Oh, just a guess," said Westenhanger, lightly.

Rollo seemed in doubt as to what he should say next. Then evidently he felt it best to keep off a subject which he seemed to think a dangerous one.

"If you find the key-move of that chess-problem," he said changing the topic with obvious intention, "you might make a note of it and tell me what it is. We may as well enter it up in the archives."

He smiled with little apparent amusement and left Westenhanger to his self-imposed task. The engineer plunged at once into the study of the chess-position. Two minute's scrutiny satisfied him on one point.

"That's no normal chess problem," he said to himself. "If it's White to play, he can checkmate Black by simply taking that pawn with his bishop. The old Corinthian evidently was an expert, from what old Dangerfield told us; and no expert would trouble to put down a thing like this on paper. And, by the same reasoning, Rollo's suggestion's rubbish, too. There could be no conceivable dispute over a position of this sort. The merest beginner would see at a glance that Black has lost the game. The Corinthian would never have troubled to jot this down, if that was all the matter at stake."

He looked at the diagram disgustedly.

"Of course, if one were full up to the back-teeth with port, it might look less obvious than it does. I shan't try the experiment, though. It's quite on the cards that he was completely dazed and didn't see the mate in one move. Let's leave it at that just now, and try the rest of the thing."

He transferred his attention to the inscription above the diagram.

"*Nox nocti indicat scientiam.* Night unto night sheweth knowledge, it's translated in the Bible, I remember. That's mysterious enough. I wonder why he chose the Latin instead of the English version. Perhaps he read the Vulgate and liked the sound of the Latin. Now what about these two texts: Matthew Sixth and Twenty-first; Luke Twelfth and Thirty-fourth. There ought to be a Bible somewhere on the shelves."

He hunted for a time and at last discovered the volume.

"Let's see. '*For where thy treasure is, there will thy heart be also.*' And the other one: '*For where your treasure is, there will your heart be also.*'"

He pondered over the texts for a time, but no enlightenment came to him.

"All the same," he assured himself at last, "these two texts seem more to the point than the rest of the stuff. I can't help feeling I'm on the right track. Suppose we put it all together and see if there's any traceable connection between the three links."

He began at the top of the paper.

"*Nox.* Darkness. Black. Does that mean, by any chance, that it's Black's turn to play and not White's?"

He mentally tried over the possible moves; but they led to nothing.

"No good. A bit far-fetched, in any case. But why use Latin in one text and English for the rest; for the text-references are obviously to the English Bible and not to the Vulgate—Luke isn't Latin. There might be something there, if one could only see it."

He stared at the paper as though hoping that some key-word would flash up from the inscriptions.

"The fresh eye doesn't seem to see much," he confessed ruefully, after a time. "I make neither head nor tail of it. And yet I'm dead certain that the thing's there, if one could only get a glimpse of it. What's wanted is someone I could talk it over with—one often gets a flash that way."

A recollection of Rollo's words passed through his mind: "You may tell Miss Cressage what you think fit. We can trust her."

Westenhanger hesitated.

"It's straining the meaning a bit further than old Danger-field meant, perhaps. But the principle's the main thing. She wouldn't let anything slip out. Besides, they've never taken me into their confidence. I'm not giving anything away they've told me. So why not?"

He folded up his paper, put it into his pocket, and left the room. It took him some time to discover Eileen, but at last he found her at the tennis-courts, watching Douglas and Cynthia playing a single.

On the departure of the three pariahs, the Friocksheim atmosphere had cleared, as the weather changes after the passing of thunder. Sudden relaxation of the long-drawn-out strain of suspicion produced a reaction among the remaining company; and the influence of Douglas Fairmile oon supplanted the morbid inquisitiveness of Freddie Stickney. Tacitly it was resolved to obliterate the whole incident from memory, and to make the house-party a success.

In this new medium Eileen Cressage had undergone an almost visible change. Relieved from the irritation of Freddie's suspicions and freed from the annoyance of Morchard's presence, she had recovered an enjoyment of life and high spirits which marked how much she had been repressed under the weight of mistrust. Westen-hanger had been surprised to find in her almost a new character.

"Care to walk down to the sea?" he asked, as he came up to where she was sitting.

She sprang up at once and joined him.

"Let's go to the headland again," she suggested, as they passed through the gardens. "I'd rather like to sit there for a while."

"The *Kestrel's* still in the bay," Westenhanger reminded her. "You won't have to sweep the horizon for her smoke this time, thank goodness."

"No. That's over. And I suppose you won't be worried over puzzles about whether I'm right or left-handed this time."

Westenhanger took up the challenge, much to her surprise.

"Don't be too sure of that! I've got another problem on hand now. Care to help?"

Eileen's face clouded suddenly.

"Not more suspicion, surely? And I thought we'd got rid of all that! Friocksheim's been lovely, since we put all that affair behind us. You're not raking it up again, are you?"

Westenhanger reassured her with a smile.

"No. That's the last thing I'd want to do. You know that quite well. This is a philanthropic effort, if it's anything."

"Oh, well, if it's merely a case of helping someone, I'll be delighted to do anything."

They had reached the headland, and he took a seat by her side before saying more.

"It's just a thing that's puzzling me," he explained. "You remember Mr. Dangerfield showed us those relics of the old Corinthian that night? I've had another look at them, and I feel sure there's something behind the business. I'd like to talk it over with you, just to see what you make of it. Of course, we say nothing to any one else about it—that's understood?"

Eileen nodded agreement.

"Go ahead then, Conway. But I shan't be much help, I know."

Westenhanger pulled out his copy of the Corinthian's document.

"This is the thing. I feel sure that it's the key to something or other. The Dangerfields evidently have made nothing of it, so I thought I'd try my hand—or our hands—at it."

Eileen took the paper from him and scanned it for a moment.

"You've come to the wrong girl. I don't know Latin and I don't play chess. What help could I be?"

"Well, ask any questions you like. Perhaps they'll suggest something. That's the way you can help."

Eileen looked again at the sheet in her hand.

"What does this Latin sentence mean, first of all? I've forgotten what Mr. Dangerfield told us."

"*Nox nocti indicat scientiam*? 'One night gives a tip to another night' would be a colloquial translation of it."

The girl looked puzzled.

"But I thought it came from the Bible. I never heard

knights mentioned in the Bible. Are you sure you're right?"

It was Westenhanger's turn to look blank.

"Your education's been neglected. Didn't it rain for forty days and forty nights about the time of the Deluge?"

Eileen's face cleared.

"Oh, I see what you mean. I thought you meant K-N-I-G-H-T when you said that one gave the other a tip."

Westenhanger's excitement was obvious.

"I knew you'd throw some light on the thing! That makes it clear enough. But who'd have thought of a pun?"

"What do you mean?"

"Look here, Eileen. 'Night unto night sheweth knowledge.' That's how it reads in English. These horse-headed pieces on the chess-board are knights—with a K. If the old Corinthian had put his text into English, it would have been fairly obvious: 'Night unto night' . . . and two knights on the board. So he used the Latin and concealed the thing. It could only be understood if one translated into English and took the sound of the words as a guide instead of the spelling."

"I think I see. So that really means that one of these knights on the chess-board has something to tell the other one? What is it he can tell? You play chess; I don't."

Westenhanger shook his head.

"It's not so easy as all that, Eileen. Chess doesn't help much here, so far as I can see. But suppose we go up to the house and get a board and the pieces. It'll be easier to see then, perhaps. If anyone comes across us, I'm teaching you chess, remember. We don't want this talked about."

"Very good." She rose to her feet. "Let's go now."

They went up to the house and Westenhanger unearthed a chess-board and men in the library. Soon he had set up a duplicate of the diagram with the pieces, and he and Eileen bent their heads over it.

"Even if you don't know chess, at least you know what a knight's move is: two squares on and then one to the right or left. You can make the move in any direction you please. Like this, or this."

He illustrated it on the board.

"Yes, I remember that. It comes into puzzles and things of that sort."

Westenhanger thought for a short time without saying anything.

"One knight gives a tip to the other," he mused at last. "There's only one tip worth having in chess: and that's how to checkmate your opponent."

He looked over the board once or twice.

"That's it!" he exclaimed. "One of these knights can mate the black king without the help of any other piece if he moves this way. One—two—three—four moves!"

He moved the white knight from the knight's square successively to the squares number 1, 2, 3, and 4 in the diagram.

"That gives checkmate. Now let's try the other knight."
He tried a move or two.

"This second knight can't get a mate in four moves by any chance. That looks all right, doesn't it?"

"You mean that the one knight could show the other one how the thing ought to be done?"

"Something like that. A bit far-fetched, of course; but so is the pun on the word knight—and I'm sure we're right about it."

"Well," demanded Eileen, eagerly. "What does it lead to? Do you see what it means?"

Westenhanger made a gesture of negation.

"No. In itself it doesn't mean anything to me. We'll

need to guess again. I'm afraid I'll have to think it over for a time. At present it suggests nothing to me."

Eileen's face showed her disappointment.

"Oh, I thought we were just on the edge of finding out something. What a nuisance."

Westenhanger thoughtfully folded up his paper. Then he replaced the chess-men in their box and put the box and chess-board back into their proper places.

"Well, let's go out and see if we can't find something else to do," he suggested. "Sometimes a thing occurs to one easier if one doesn't think too hard about it. Shall we take out one of the cars for an hour or two?"

They left the library and passed into the Corinthian's Room. Westenhanger's eye was caught by the Chess-board on the pavement and his face lighted up.

"I believe I've got it!" he exclaimed. "Didn't Mr. Dangerfield tell us, that night, something about the pieces being found in position on that Chess-board?"

Eileen recalled the scene.

"Yes," she confirmed. "He said that after the duel they found the document on his desk and the pieces in the same order on that big Chess-board. You remember he suggested that it might be the end of the game he and his friend had been playing."

Westenhanger's features showed the elation he felt.

"Well, I believe we've stumbled right on the solution. Our luck's holding, after all; for it was pure luck that I happened to look at that Chess-board as we passed. I'd forgotten about the thing—or at least I hadn't thought about it in that connection. But when my eye caught the board I remembered something else."

He knelt down and scrutinised the corners of one or two squares.

"Yes, they are oil-holes right enough. I was sure they were, the first time I saw them, but I couldn't make out what they were there for. They're all stopped up with dirt. We'll need a fine wire and a bottle of oil. Probably the whole affair's rusted up with age; for it can't have been working for years and years."

Eileen's eyes shone with excitement.

"You really think you've got to the bottom of it? Let's go at once and get the oil and the wire and whatever else you need. I do want to see you clear the thing up. This last bit sounds exciting."

"It may be all wrong, you know," Westenhanger warned her. "Don't imagine we're out of the wood yet."

"What do you think you're going to find out? The Dangerfield Secret?"

"If this turns up trump," said Westenhanger, "you and I will know more about the Dangerfield Secret than the Dangerfields themselves do. I'm pretty sure of that, at any rate. But there's an 'if' with a capital 'I' in it yet; so don't expect too much. It's quite on the cards that we're on a wild-goose chase with a mare's nest at the end of it."

"Well, do let's get the things you need and start as soon as we can."

Westenhanger had little difficulty in getting what he wanted. They came back to the Corinthian's Room and, with precautions against being surprised, set to work to clear the oil-holes of the accumulated dirt. After that, Westenhanger, with an oil-can, liberally dosed each channel.

"There," he said. "We'll need to give the stuff time to ooze into the bearings. Let's go and fill in the time with something else."

They played tennis for an hour and then came back to the Corinthian's Room. Westenhanger had refused to explain his purpose, and the girl was on tenterhooks to see what he meant to do. Westenhanger took out his paper, opened the cupboards containing the iron chessmen, and began methodically to set them up in the position marked in the Corinthian's diagram. In a few minutes he had the scheme completed.

"Now we come to the final stage," he said. "We'll play over the four knight's moves. I think that's the key to the thing."

With considerable difficulty he shifted the white knight from square to square.

"One—Two—Three. Now for it—four!"

The heavy iron figure dropped into its final position—and nothing happened! Westenhanger stared at the board in unconcealed discomfiture, and Eileen's face showed her disappointment.

"It hasn't worked!" she exclaimed. "That's hard lines, Conway."

"No, it hasn't worked," he answered, in a tone of perplexity. "And yet I feel absolutely sure that we're on the right track. It all fits together too neatly to be wrong.

Those four moves ought to have released some catch or other. I expected one of the Chess-board squares to spring up, or something like that. But nothing's happened."

He lifted the iron pieces one by one and restored each to its proper place in the cupboard.

"There's some step we've missed, evidently. I wonder what it can be."

Just as he closed the cupboard door, Cynthia came into the room.

"Oh, you're here, Eileen? I've been hunting for you all over the place. We want you, if Mr. Westenhanger can spare you just now."

She asked Westenhanger's permission with a glance; and he made a gesture of release.

"I'll think over it," he said to Eileen. "Perhaps I may hit on something."

After the two girls had left the room he stood for a time staring at the Chess-board; but it seemed to suggest nothing fresh to him. He returned to the library, pulled out his copy of the Corinthian's document and fell to studying it once more. As he opened out the paper, his eye was caught by the part of the inscription which hitherto he had neglected:

Matt. VI. 21; Luke XII. 34.

"That's got to come into it somehow," he admitted to himself. "But I can't see the relevancy as it stands. *For where the treasure lies, there will your heart be also.* It sounds like the only straight tip in the whole business— the key to the affair. But what the devil can it mean, exactly? It's very vague as it stands."

Feeling sure that up to that point he had been on the right track, he went over each link in his chain of thought; and then, in a flash, he saw what he had previously missed.

"That's it! Of course, the other text ought to have put me on the track. He wasn't so bemused after all, that old bird! A deuced good mnemonic—once one has the key. Now it all depends on one point. I'd better leave the old man alone. He's getting a bit tired of questions. I'll get hold of Eric. He's likely to know."

Luck was in Westenhanger's way that morning. He discovered Eric Dangerfield sitting reading on one of the lawns, at no great distance from the house. His ankle was still weak and kept him tethered within a short radius.

Westenhanger did not plunge immediately into the subject which interested him, though he had little fear of arousing any suspicion in Eric's mind. He was sure that at this time he had out-distanced the Dangerfields completely, and was nearer the solution of their family mystery than they themselves had ever been. Luck had stood him in good stead.

At last he led the conversation round to the point.

"I suppose you've made very few changes in Friocksheim in the last hundred years—elecrtic light, and so on, of course; but a lot of furniture seems good old stuff."

Eric nodded.

"We're a conservative lot," he said.

"That's a good bit of tapestry in the Corinthian's Room. I suppose it's hung there for long enough?"

"About a century and a half, I should think. It's taken down for cleaning, of course; but it's never been shifted out of the Room since it came here. It fits the wall space exactly; and there's no point in hanging it in a fresh place."

"You've got one or two pretty good pictures, too. I like the Dutch one in your uncle's study."

"Girl trying on jewels? It's not at all bad."

"What is it? Seventeenth century? I know next to nothing about these things."

Eric professed ignorance.

"You've come to the wrong shop. I know as little about these things as you do yourself. Try my uncle. He's got a turn for them; and he can tell you the history of most of them."

Westenhanger had secured the information he needed. He changed the subject, and, very shortly afterwards, he left Eric to his book.

"Now," he said to himself, as he walked back to the house, "is that absolutely everything linked up at last? I can't afford to have another fiasco through overlooking things. Let's see. The Latin text? Right! Then the chess problem? O.K. now, I think."

He went back to the Corinthian's Room and stood for a few seconds before the tapestry of Diana's hunting.

"Yes," he concluded, "I think that's all right also.

That's all, isn't it? No, it isn't! I'd forgotten that leather thing. The chances are it has nothing to do with the affair; but one ought to give it a trial."

He sat down and filled his pipe while he speculated.

"I'm pretty sure it isn't a washer, though that's what one might have expected it to be. Now what on earth does one use a leather disc of that size for, unless it's in connection with machinery. And the old Corinthian was a bit of an inventor—more than a dabbler in mechanics, if I'm on the right track. And yet from the look of the thing I'm almost certain it's got no normal use in a machine. The twine through it proves that almost conclusively. Hold on, though! It might be a valve of sorts. That might be it. But why leave a valve-piece along with the document? That must be wrong."

He thought over the matter without evolving anything which seemed to throw light on the problem. At last he took up a fresh line.

"Old Rollo suggested that it was a toy that the old Corinthian had made for his kiddie. But then, why leave it along with the document? That seems a silly sort of thing to do. And from the look of the leather, the thing had been used in some way. I don't know much about leather; but the way that disc was warped . . . It must have been wetted and allowed to dry, or something. That would crinkle it."

Then a final flash of illumination lit up the whole problem in his mind. He laughed partly at himself and partly at the simplicity of the solution.

"Why, of course, it's a kid's toy. I've played with the same sort of thing myself. And that's what he used it for. He was a bright old bird, right enough. No wonder we got no result with the Chess-board."

He stepped into the Corinthian's Room, drew aside the tapestry, and examined the panelling behind it. To the ordinary eye it showed nothing; but Westenhanger seemed satisfied with what he saw. He let the tapestry fall into place again.

"Now let's see! Nothing doing to-day, that's certain. I'll have to wait till to-morrow before I can try it out. But I'm dead sure of it this time. It's no wonder the Danger-fields never got near the thing. I'd never have been near it myself if it hadn't been for that talk with Eileen. Pure luck. No credit to any of us."

He turned away from the hanging and consulted his watch.

"Just time, if I take the car down. The Frogsholme cobbler first of all; and then a shop where I can get some long needles. That fits me out. And to-morrow I'll give old Rollo the surprise of his life. The bottom will be out of the Dangerfield Secret! What a relief for the old man!"

167

CHAPTER XIV

ON the following afternoon, having completed all his arrangements, Westenhanger ushered Rollo Dangerfield and Eileen into the Corinthian's Room.

"Mind if I lock the door for a short time?" he asked, turning to his host. "I'd rather not be interrupted by anyone in the middle of this affair. You'll agree with me when you've seen what I have to show you."

Old Rollo's face showed more that a trace of suspicion. Westenhanger had vouchsafed no information about his project; and the old man evidently felt mistrustful. However, he nodded his consent and waited while Westenhanger turned the key in the lock.

"What's the glass of water for?" Eileen demanded, pointing to a tumbler which Westenhanger had in his hand.

"You'll see before long," he assured her, putting the glass down on a table. "I think we'll take things one at a time."

Rollo seemed to think that he had been kept in the dark long enough.

"May I ask why you have brought us here?"

Westenhanger noticed the old man's glance at Eileen as he spoke, so he resolved to put matters on a plain footing at once.

"Miss Cressage knows almost as much about this matter as I do myself. Between us, we seem to have hit upon something which you ought to know at once. Miss Cressage, I may say, gave me the key to the mystery. Without her help I don't think I'd have hit on the thing at all."

At the word "mystery," a shadow gathered on Rollo's face. He glanced from the engineer to Eileen as though trying to read their thoughts. Westenhanger hastened to reassure him.

"When you've heard the whole story, Mr. Dangerfield, I think you'll agree with me that Miss Cressage has done you a very great service."

The old man again scanned Westenhanger's face keenly, before making any reply. Evidently his scrutiny satisfied him; for the distrust slowly faded out of his expression, and he turned to Eileen with a faint sketch of a bow, as though making acknowledgement and amends.

"I am entirely in your hands," he said. "It's quite clear that you have been acting for the best."

Eileen broke in as soon as he had finished.

"You mustn't take what Mr. Westenhanger says as being strictly accurate. I really did very little to help. In fact, I'm as much in the dark as you are, just now, Mr. Dangerfield."

Westenhanger intervened.

"I think it will be best to take the things step by step and let you see how we reached the kernel of the affair. You've been doing your grandfather an injustice all these years, Mr. Dangerfield. He was a better man than you gave him credit for. I've seen enough to know that. And I think you'll find that the Corinthian's Secret is more important than the Dangerfield Secret."

The old man winced a little at Westenhanger's words; but he refrained from comment.

"Now, to start with, would you mind letting me have the Corinthian's document and the leather disc from the safe? We may as well work with the originals, as far as possible."

Rollo stepped slowly across the room, unlocked the safe, and took out of it the two required articles which he handed over to Westenhanger in silence.

"I think we'll sit down," said the engineer. "It's going to take a little while to explain the matter."

He indicated three seats and brought a small table over, so that they could all see the document which he placed on it.

"In the first place," he began, "you once told us that your grandfather had mechanical leanings—he'd invented some kind of geared bicycle. That didn't strike me at the time, particularly; but as it came back to some purpose later on, I mention it first. On the same evening, by pure chance, I happened to notice these little holes at the corners of the squares of the Chess-board on the pavement here. These things, I mean."

He rose and pointed out one or two of them.

"When you told us that the Talisman was safe, I must confess I thought of a man-trap. The holes in the pavement suggested some kind of machinery needing lubrication; and I had some notion of a trap-door which would open when the Talisman was touched and so trap a thief. That was an entirely mistaken idea, as you told us yourself. Still, at the back of my mind I had connected these oil-holes with the presence of some machinery or other and with the mechanical tastes of your grandfather."

The distrust had passed completely away from Rollo's face. He was now listening with obvious eagerness to Westenhanger's explanation.

"The next thing was, of course, your showing us these things from the safe. They were quite meaningless to me then."

He lifted them lightly and put them back on the table.

"The next bit's hard to account for. Somehow I got a feeling that the document was the key to some problem or other, and I asked you to let me copy it. It was just an impulse. I really can't say what I expected to do with it. It certainly wasn't mere vulgar curiosity to dig out the Dangerfield Secret."

Again a flicker of distrust crossed Rollo's face. Westenhanger saw it.

"You can take it from me now, Mr. Dangerfield, that the Dangerfield Secret is of no importance whatever from to-day onwards. Least of all to you personally. Make your mind quite easy on that score."

Rollo nodded; but quite evidently he was not altogether relieved from anxiety. Eileen's face showed that she was puzzled by Westenhanger's words, but she refrained from asking any question.

"We'll take the document next," Westenhanger continued, picking it up from the table as he spoke. "You know its contents, two texts and a chess-position. The chess-position is a dud affair. There's a mate in one move staring one in the face as soon as one looks at it. Obviously the thing isn't a problem, and no one would trouble to write down an end-game so simple as this. I made nothing of it."

He looked across at the old man. Rollo's face had taken on its old mask of inscrutability. Quite evidently he could not see whither all this was leading.

"I come now to Miss Cressage's part in the affair," Westenhanger proceeded. "So far as I was concerned there was nothing confidential in the matter. You hadn't pledged me to secrecy—because you had told me nothing. Still, before speaking to Miss Cressage about it, I asked her to promise she would say nothing. We know that she can keep her promises."

Rollo's glance at the girl made it quite clear that he had full confidence in her.

"Between us," Westenhanger went on, "we hit on the key to the first text. *Nox nocti*—night unto night. Spell the word with a K, and you get Knight—the chess-piece.

Old Dangerfield sat up sharply.

"Do you know, Mr. Westenhanger, two generations of us have puzzled over that scrawl, and not one of us saw it. I· congratulate you on your acuteness, both of you. That was very clever indeed."

"Just a chance," Westenhanger had to admit. "It's a thing one could only hit upon in the course of talk, and even then it would be only by accident."

Rollo's indifference had slipped from him completely.

"And next?" he demanded.

"I think we'll set up the position on the big Chess-board before we go any further," Westenhanger suggested. "I have a reason for that, as you'll see."

He went to the case holding the chess-men and set up the pieces one by one on the pavement squares. Then he returned to his seat and took up the document again.

"You see two white knights? Knight unto knight sheweth knowledge. That means, as I read it, that one knight can do something which the other knight can't do. Very little examination shows what that thing is—it's an unaided mate in four moves. Thus."

He moved the one white knight sucessively from square to square until it reached the mating position on Queen's Seventh. Eileen watched eagerly, expecting that this time something would happen, but she could detect nothing whatever. Westenhanger had noticed her attitude. He looked across the table at her with a smile.

"That's what you saw me do yesterday. Now I'll tell you what I was looking for."

. He turned to Rollo.

"You know that each of these pieces has a long spike on its base which slides into the holes in the Chess-board? On the surface it looks as if that had been designed merely to keep the pieces from being knocked over by anyone who has to walk among them in order to shift them from square to square. But I had at the back of my mind the idea of the old Corinthian as a man with a mechanical turn, and I put that idea alongside the notion of the spikes and the sequence of four fixed moves by the white knight. And so I reached the idea of . . ."

He looked interrogatively at his hearers, but neither of them had caught his meaning.

"Of a combination lock!" he concluded, after a pause. "Your grandfather was more of a mechanic than you gave him credit for. As I understand the machine—of course, this is only guess-work—under each hole in the four squares of the knight's moves there lies the end of a lever. When you drop the knight into its place on the square, the spike depresses the lever. The whole secret of the thing is that the four levers must be depressed in that particular sequence. That guards against the lock being sprung in the course of normal play. The chances against that combination are considerable; and I expect some of the other pieces also depress lock-levers, so that it's almost impossible that the thing should be unlocked by a chance game. In fact, the whole affair is simply a clumsy forerunner of the ordinary dial lock on good safes."

"Yes, but it hasn't opened!" commented Eileen.

"It *has* unlocked something, though," Westenhanger retorted. "That was what puzzled me yesterday when apparently nothing happened after I'd played the moves. But the Corinthian was taking no chances. The Chessboard is the lock, but the thing it secures is somewhere else."

-"That sounds nonsense to me," Eileen said, decidedly.

Westenhanger smiled with a touch of friendly maliciousness.

"We've still two things which we haven't used. This is where I went wrong yesterday, Eileen," he interjected. "There's another text, and there's the leather disc. Take the text first of all. *Where your treasure is, there will your heart be also.* Remember the pun in the first case? There's another one here. I didn't spot it for a while."

He challenged Eileen's ingenuity with a look across the table and left her to puzzle the thing out for herself.

"Not see it? I'll give you a clue. 'As pants the hart for cooling streams . . .'"

He caught her eye and his glance led her gaze round the room till it came to the tapestry of Diana's hunting.

"Oh, now I see!" she cried. "You mean there's something hidden behind that stag—the hart—in the arras!"

Westenhanger assented with a nod.

Rollo Dangerfield had maintained his serenity up to this point; but evidently he now felt the strain.

"Mr. Westenhanger," he said. "You're not leading me on to a disappointment? I've guessed at something behind all this. Please do not keep me in suspense."

Westenhanger felt ashamed of the comedy he was playing. He had not thought of how it must appear to the man most concerned. At once, in response to old Rollo's rather pathetic query, he dropped the pretence that the issue was still unknown.

"I'm very sorry, Mr. Dangerfield. In trying to make it interesting I'm afraid I forgot that you might be anxious about the end of the business—afraid it was all going to peter out in an empty treasury. I've only been making believe that I'm working this out step by step as we go along. Of course I've done it all once before and found the real thing I was looking for."

Old Rollo's old-fashioned courtesy returned to him.

"I am very sorry to have interrupted you," he said. "Please go on with your story. I am quite ready to wait for the end when it comes."

He settled himself in his chair, evidently restraining all signs of impatience. Westenhanger continued:

"You'll have no cause to regret our intrusion into your affairs, Mr. Dangerfield. I can promise you that. I'll go on. With this needle I can prick through the arras and fix the exact position of the hiding-place behind the cloth. You see the stag's very small; anywhere near the centre of the body will do. I put the needle clean through and leave it sticking in the panel behind, to mark the place."

He suited the action to the word, then he lifted the tapestry and disclosed the panelled surface.

"Nothing visible in the way of a handle, you see?" he pointed out. "The panelling's quite smooth."

He dropped the tapestry into place again and came back to the table.

"Now this leather disc," he picked it up as he spoke.

"You suggested to us that it might be a child's toy. That was what eventually put me on the track. It *is* a child's toy. I've played with one like it when I was a child myself, though I haven't seen one for years now. Possibly the modern child doesn't use things of that sort. But in my young days they used to call them 'suckers.' Here's one in its normal state."

He drew from his pocket a disc of leather with a loop of twine attached, exactly like the Corinthian relic, except that Westenhanger's leather was soft and moist.

"I'll show you how it works."

He dipped it for a moment into the glass of water, then placed it flat on the table with the twine loop on the upper side.

"Now I squeeze it into contact with the table, so as to exclude all air between it and the wooden surface. The water acts as a seal. That's right. Now I pull vertically upwards on the twine. You see the centre of the disc is pulled up by the twine. That makes a vacuum between the leather and the table; and the pressure of the atmosphere pins the 'sucker' to the wood. The harder you pull, the faster it sticks. It's exactly the way a limpet sticks to a rock; and you know how tight that clings. With a thing of this size, I could lift an ordinary paving stone out of its bed. We used to pull up quite big stones with them when I was a kiddie."

By levering the "sucker" adroitly he loosened it from the table, just as a limpet is slid off its bed by a side-thrust.

"I think the rest's obvious. The Corinthian wanted some means of pulling out that particular panel without leaving any mark or attaching a handle. He used this sucker for the purpose. I'll show you."

He went over to the arras, lifted it, and attached his leather disc at the point where the needle had been. A slow, steady pull on the twine completed the work, and a large piece of the panel came forward, evidently the end of a drawer fitting back into the wall of the room.

"Your grandfather's safe deposit!" said Westenhanger.

As Rollo came forward, the engineer dipped his hand into the drawer.

"Some loose things on top. Will you take them, please? Let's see. A diamond pendant. . . . A jewelled collar, isn't it . . .? And this. . . . Here's something else. . . . There are one or two more, I think, further back in the drawer."

He stretched his arm into the cavity, felt about · for a few moments, then grasped something. His voice changed as he turned round with it in his hand.

"The *real* Talisman, Mr. Dangerfield!"

"The real Talisman, Mr. Dangerfield!"

CHAPTER XV

EILEEN CRESSAGE watched the old man eagerly stretch out his hand and take the armlet from Westenhanger's fingers.

"What do you mean, Conway?" she exclaimed. "The *real* Talisman? Why, you saw the real Talisman put into that safe over yonder not three days ago by Mr. Dangerfield himself. How do you come to have it here?"

For once, Rollo Dangerfield was so moved as to forget his courtesy.

"Is it the real thing?" he asked Westenhanger, with anxiety obvious in his tone.

The engineer reassured him.

"I don't profess to be an expert; but I can tell the difference between paste and the genuine article. These diamonds are the real thing."

Rollo carried the armlet across to the window and examined it minutely. Eileen followed him, still mystified by the turn of events, though the explanation was beginning to shape itself in her mind.

"The end of the Dangerfield Secret, isn't it?" asked Westenhanger, joining them. "I was pretty sure of my ground when I told you that the Secret had ceased to be of any importance now."

Rollo Dangerfield's lapse into unintentional brusqueness had been only a momentary one, under the stress of strong emotion. Already he had recovered his balance.

"You can perhaps understand something of what this means to me, Mr. Westenhanger, even if you don't guess the whole story. It's sometimes difficult to find words for what one has to say. I wish to thank you—and you also, Miss Cressage—for this. You can have no idea of the load which you have taken off my shoulders. You have cleared away the shams, and I can look people in the face again, unashamed. It's useless to put these things into words. I can't do it as I would like to do. But at least I can tell you, Miss Cressage, something of the Dangerfield story which will give you an idea of what this has meant to us."

He made a gesture inviting them to sit down again. Eileen seated herself, but Westenhanger paused for a moment.

"I think we'd better shut this thing up before we go any further."

He indicated the still open drawer in the panelling.

"Just wait a moment until I empty it completely."

He put his hand into the recess and withdrew several other pieces of jewellery which he added to the shining heap on the table. Then he closed the drawer, dropped the arras, and came back to the Chess-board.

"You remember you told us that after the Corinthian's death they found the pieces on this board in the positions shown on the document? It's pretty obvious what was in his mind. He knew that he might be killed in a few minutes. Probably he mistrusted his servants and was afraid to leave family jewellery at their mercy. So he opened the secret recess, tumbled the jewels into it—the Talisman was in it already—and then he closed his combination lock . . . thus."

Westenhanger walked on to the Chess-board and lifted the white knight from Queen's Seventh.

"One reverses the four moves, so, bringing the knight back to its starting-point on the knight's square."

He suited the action to the word, carrying out the four operations in the reverse order.

"Now the drawer is locked," he explained. "That's what the Corinthian did, just before he went out to his duel. And that's why they found the Chess-board in this state. Probably he hadn't time enough to put the pieces away in the cupboard, so he left them standing as they were. They gave nothing away."

He picked up the document, the wrinkled leather disc, and his own "sucker"; and handed them across the table.

"That finishes our part, Mr. Dangerfield. Now, perhaps, you'll tell us what you wish us to hear."

Rollo Dangerfield's face had regained its accustomed serenity. The tinge of suspicion had vanished completely and was replaced by a trustful expression, as he looked at his two guests. He turned first to Eileen.

"I am sorry you have been kept waiting for an answer to your question, Miss Cressage. It was my fault. You will forgive an old man's impatience when I tell you that you and Mr. Westenhanger have cleared up something which has hung over fifty years of my life. And there are other reasons, too, as you will hear."

Eileen had no need to say anything. Her face told Rollo that she had not been offended.

"You startled me not long ago, Mr. Westenhanger," their host went on, "by asking me if the Dangerfield Secret was not just three generations old. If that was a mere guess it was a very good one. Actually, what has been called the Dangerfield Secret originated in my father's day; and since it has been passed on to Eric it has lasted through three generations. And now it passes away, thanks to you young people."

He paused for a moment before speaking again.

"You must bear in mind that some of this is conjecture, and that I am trying to fit it together so as to take in the facts which have come to light this afternoon. Before I came into this room I had not the key to the problem; and I have hardly had time to fit the new links into the chain neatly. But it seems evident to me that even in my grandfather's day, there was a Talisman and a replica; and that the replica was kept under the tinted bell to conceal the fact that the stones were false. From your inferences, Mr. Westenhanger, it seems clear that he devised this particular hiding-place for the real Talisman.

"Now take the state of affairs on the morning of my grandfather's death. He knew the risk he ran—his opponent was a noted duellist; and he had no one at hand whom he could trust. Probably, as you suggested, he collected the more valuable family jewels and placed them with the real Talisman for safety's sake. We did him an injustice when we assumed that he had already sold them to pay his gambling debts.

"I don't care to speculate on his mental condition at that moment. Quite probably, after a night's carousing, he was not clear-headed. He jotted down the memory-help he used himself as a clue to the hiding-place, and very probably he failed to realise that it was no real help to anyone but himself. Then he went out—and that was the end."

With quite unconscious dramatic effect the old man paused in his narrative and sat for some instants in silence. When he spoke again it was in a light tone.

"And now I come to a fresh character. I never knew him, but I have been trying to reconstruct him in my mind from many things which were told to me about him. He was the solicitor for the Dangerfield estate at the time my Corinthian grandfather died.

"Imagine his position, Miss Cressage. He takes over the administration of the estate—you remember that my father was a mere child then—and he finds it terribly encumbered with the debts which had accumulated in my grandfather's day, a load of liabilities which even a generation failed to clear away. Credit was essential if the ship was to be kept afloat at all. And the biggest asset of the estate was the Dangerfield Talisman. So long as that remained, no one could suppose that things were seriously involved, and with care, he could just pilot us through. Without that palladium, the creditors would have come down at once and the game would have been up. Friocksheim would have come to the hammer. Everything would have gone down in the crash. And in the midst of all his anxiety he learned that the Talisman was a sham of gilded lead and spurious stones!"

Rollo broke off his narrative, leaving time for them to appreciate the position.

"I have seen the document in his own hand-writing," he continued, "which gives an account of the affair. He had taken the Talisman from under the bell and asked a jeweller what it would cost to make a replica. He thought the thing should be put in safety; and it seems that he, too, had hit on the idea of substituting a counterfeit for the real thing, the notion of a stalking-horse which I explained to you once before, Mr. Westenhanger. And you can guess his consternation when he learned from the jeweller that the thing was worth no more than a few pounds. The whole mainstay of his scheme for keeping the Dangerfield credit secure, now turned out to be worthless. There was no other easily-vended article—all the valuable jewellery had vanished, sold to pay the Corinthian's debts, as we have wrongly believed until to-day.

"He had come to a decision. Rightly or wrongly, he chose his course. He started the Dangerfield Secret as we have known it. He quieted any suspicions of the jeweller by ordering a second replica." And he embarked on a career of concealment. It was safe enough. The Corinthian had had the armlet valued out of curiosity. Everyone knew it was worth £50,000. No one had any reason to suppose that it had gone astray. And with that sham asset behind him to strengthen confidence, he pulled the estate out of its immediate difficulties. I have no right to criticise him. He worked according to his lights, with the sole purpose of handing over Friocksheim to my father when he came of age."

It was plain enough from the old man's tone that he himself might have chosen the same course had the alternatives been offered.

"We have paid dearly enough for his decision," Rollo went on. "He involved us all in his machinations, even those of us who were born long after he died. When my father came of age, the old solicitor laid the whole case before him. The estate was still in a shaky state, and an involuntary liquidation would have left us insolvent. More, in a forced sale we could not have hoped to pay our creditors in full. We'd have been defaulters and real losses would have been incurred by innocent people. On the other side, by keeping up the estate's credit, we gained time enough to pay in full, eventually—to be honest, in fact—provided that the Talisman deception could be kept in being. It was merely a choice, you see, between two forms of dishonesty; but the one alternative would hurt other people, whilst the second course laid a burden on ourselves alone. My father chose the second path. I cannot say that, in his position, I would have done otherwise myself."

His face took on a bitter cast.

"That was the beginning of the Dangerfield Secret—the trickery of the spurious Talisman. Can you wonder that I described it to you, once, as a memorial of lying and deceit? How do you suppose I felt, being driven to lie to my own guests in my own house every time I was asked to show it to anyone? The famous Dangerfield Talisman!'

He moved in his chair, almost as though he wished to free himself from some physical contamination.

"And all the time, we were in the toils which that old man had wrapped around us a century ago. How could we shake free from the web of deception? We still need the asset—at least we needed it yesterday. And to let the thing leak out would be to put a black mark on my father's name. You know what people would say about the part we have played. There was no getting clear. We had to go on as we had begun."

He glanced at his two guests as though he feared that he had wearied them by a long story; but their expressions encouraged him to continue to the end.

"People often wonder why we do not insure a thing of such immense value. How could we insure it? It would need to be valued—and the game would be up! So we have been forced into that second series of deceptions—the return of the Talisman after it has been stolen. We have to keep a series of replicas; and put out a fresh one every time there is a theft. We have to play that silly game of pretending we believe in an old legend—another lie—because we dare not call in the police if the thing vanishes, and because we dare not admit that we have lost it."

Rollo's voice became gloomier still.

"And in front of us, always, there was the risk of an inevitable exposure. We had to avoid the Government valuers in the matter of Death Duties. We could do that only by transferring the Talisman from hand to hand. My father made it over to me when I was twenty-one; I gave it to Eric when he came of age. It has never been subject to Death Duties yet. But there is always the chance of accident. If Eric died before me the whole thing would have been exposed when they came to value his estate. That possible Nemesis has been imminent for the holders of the Talisman."

He seemed to brood for a time on his retrospect. When he spoke again, both his voice and manner had altered. It was as if at last he had emerged from the shadows.

"And now, after a century of deceit, we've come out into the light again, thanks to you both! And to think that the Talisman was here all the time, within the walls of Friockskeim. Of course we had puzzled over the Corinthian's cypher; but we'd never taken it seriously, because we believed all along that he had sold the armlet and the jewellery. It never occurred to any of us that the thing was within our grasp, under our very roof. Even his own man of affairs believed that, and it never crossed our minds that anything else could have happened."

"I think it was very natural," said Eileen.

Westenhanger made no comment. He had been touched, like the girl, by the story of the Dangerfield Secret as it was now revealed. By his candid narrative old Rollo had enlisted their sympathy without having directly besought it from them; and they could understand the feelings which his position has stirred in him through fifty long years.

"No wonder he often looked as if he'd grown sick of life," was the younger man's unspoken comment.

"Well, it's all right now, isn't it?" he said aloud. "The Talisman's come back for the last time."

Eileen broke in, before the old man could reply.

"You've no idea how glad I am that we are able to help, Mr. Dangerfield. Less than a week ago, I felt that Friocksheim was a place I'd never want to visit again; it had such miserable associations in my mind, in more ways than one. But now, somehow, it's all different. We can all be happy here; there's nothing hanging over any of us any more. You understand, don't you?"

Rollo Dangerfield looked at her with something like affection showing in his eyes.

"Who could understand better than I do? It's like waking out of a nightmare to find the sun shining in through the window. And we owe our awakening to you and Mr. Westenhanger. You don't imagine I under-rate that, surely? I dare say you think you understand what this means for me; perhaps you have some faint conception. But unless you had actually gone through it yourselves you couldn't come near the real thing. It's lasted fifty years, and that's only a few years less than your two lives put together. And now—day-light! I shall be glad to have a year or two of decent life at the end of it all."

Westenhanger saw something in the old man's eyes which made him interpose with a fresh subject.

"And what about the Talisman now, Mr. Dangerfield? Will you use the Corinthian's safe deposit still? It's lain there safely enough all these years. That's why I locked the door—so that no one should blunder in and notice the hiding-place when it was open. I thought you might want it again."

"The Talisman?" repeated Rollo. "Do you know, I could almost find it in my heart to sell the Talisman— give Wraxall his desire, after all. If I had a decent excuse for doing it, I think I would. I've hated it for years. But I suppose we must keep it, now that it's come into our hands again. I want no more possible regrets, and one might regret having let it go, after these centuries. We don't need to sell it; there are other things to sell."

He bent over the table and examined the jewellery which had come from the Corinthian's hiding-place. After a careful scrutiny he picked up the diamond pendant and turned to Eileen.

"You talked about your memories of Friocksheim, Miss Cressage, and, believe me, I was touched by what you said. Now I should like you to have something which will always remind you of the old place in that aspect."

He offered her the glittering gems, and, when she made a gesture of refusal, he continued as though he had not noticed it.

"I know you don't wear jewellery, so in its present form it would hardly serve. But this central stone would set well in a ring. Get it taken out; and do as you please with the rest—sell them, if you choose. There's no sentiment in the matter; for I intend to sell the rest of the things here and use the money to clear our feet at last. So you are free to follow that good example if you please."

He saw her expression and tried a different argument.

"If you refuse, I shall feel that you think I have been trying to pay you for your help—and that you flung the payment back. Nobody could find a real payment for what you and Mr. Westenhanger have done. This isn't payment, Miss Cressage. It's a thank-offering, if you care to put it in that way. I still hope you won't refuse."

Eileen saw the pain in the old man's eyes.

"I ought to refuse," she said hesitatingly.

Then, after another look at Rollo's face, she added:

"But I can understand how you feel. I'll take your gift, though it's far too valuable. And I'll do with it just as you wish. We needn't pretend to misunderstand each other, need we? I'll sell some of the stones and clear my own feet, just as you're going to clear yours. And I'll wear the ring to remind me of Friocksheim, though I won't need it for that."

She took the pendant and examined it thoughtfully.

"It's a lovely thing . . . I feel rather tongue-tied, Mr. Dangerfield," she confessed with a smile.

"I'm glad to hear that," he smiled in response. "You'll understand better now, how I felt myself not many minutes ago."

And with that he brushed her thanks aside.

"There's one thing you can do, Miss Cressage. Come back often to Friocksheim. I shall look forward to your coming. You're one of us, now, and not merely a visitor; for you know more about our affairs than some of our family ever knew. You, too, Westenhanger. We're going to need young people about the place, since we shall be losing Helga. . . ."

Suddenly his face changed. A smile came over it, the first really care-free smile that had crossed it in fifty years. The touch of wistfulness had vanished—it was the natural Rollo coming out at last after the long suppression.

"Helga's birthday falls next week. She will be twenty-five—the age when our girls are told the Dangerfield Secret. What a disappointment for her when she learns that now there is no Secret at all!"

THE END

184

>>> If you've enjoyed this book and would like to discover more great vintage crime and thriller titles, as well as the most exciting crime and thriller authors writing today, visit: >>>

The Murder Room
Where Criminal Minds Meet

themurderroom.com

www.ingramcontent.com/pod-product-compliance
Ingram Content Group UK Ltd.
Pitfield, Milton Keynes, MK11 3LW, UK
UKHW022314280225
455674UK00004B/299

9 781471 906336